Alexander Garden

A Theatre of Scottish Worthies

And The Life, Doings and Death of William Elphinston, Bishop of Aberdeen

Alexander Garden

A Theatre of Scottish Worthies
And The Life, Doings and Death of William Elphinston, Bishop of Aberdeen

ISBN/EAN: 9783743394377

Manufactured in Europe, USA, Canada, Australia, Japa

Cover: Foto ©Andreas Hilbeck / pixelio.de

Manufactured and distributed by brebook publishing software (www.brebook.com)

Alexander Garden

A Theatre of Scottish Worthies

WILLIAM ELPHINSTON

BISHOP OF ABERDEEN

A THEATRE

OF

SCOTTISH WORTHIES:

AND

THE LYF, DOINGS, AND DEATHE

OF

WILLIAM ELPHINSTON

BISHOP OF ABERDEEN

BY

ALEXANDER GARDEN

ADVOCATE, ABERDEEN

PRIVATELY PRINTED

MDCCCLXXVIII

PRESENTED
TO THE MEMBERS
OF
THE HUNTERIAN CLUB
BY
ALEXANDER B. STEWART

TO THE MEMBERS
OF
THE HUNTERIAN CLUB
BY
ALEXANDER B. STEWART

ALEXANDER GARDEN,

POETICAL WORKS.

HE name of ALEXANDER GARDEN or GARDYNE occurs in the lifts of Scottifh Poets as the Author of two feparate works. The one publifhed during his own time is entitled, " A Garden of Grave and Godlie Flovvres: Sonets, Elegies, and Epitaphs, Planted, polifhed, and perfected by Mr. Alexander Gardyne. *Et facer & magnus Vatum labor.* Edinburgh, Printed by Thomas Finlafon. 1609. With Licence." 4to. The fecond has this title, " The Theatre of the Scotifh Kings. By Alexander Garden, Profeffor of Philofophy at Aberdeen. Done from the Original Manufcript. Edinburgh, Printed by James Watfon, and Sold at his Shop, next Door to the Red Lyon, oppofite to the Luken-booths. 1709." 4to.

Thefe two were reprinted in a handfome quarto volume, as a contribution to the Abbotsford Club, by Jofeph Walter King Eyton, Efq., in the year 1845. The Editor, his friend, William Barclay Turnbull, Efq., Advocate, having fhown me his Prefatory Remarks, I was led to point out to my impulfive friend, the Editor, that there exifted a confufion in regard to the Authorfhip, as both works were evidently by one and the fame perfon. To prove this more clearly, I addreffed a letter to Mr. Turnbull on the fubject, which he fubjoined to his "Prefatory Remarks" in that volume; and I cannot do better than give the following extract:—

"Signet Library, *2nd October*, 1845.

"My Dear Sir,—After examining with fome care the queftion regarding the authorfhip of 'The Garden of Flowres,' 1609, and of 'The Theatre of the Scotifh Kings,' I can come to no other conclufion than to attribute both works to the elder ALEXANDER GARDYNE or GARDEN, Advocate in Aberdeen. Any confufion that has arifen on this point feems to have proceeded upon a miftake of the editor of the latter work in 1709. On referring to the manufcript in the Advocates' Library from which it was publifhed, I find it affords no authority for afcribing the work to 'Alexander Garden, Profeffor of Philofophy at Aberdeen;' neither is it 'the original manufcript.' As the work itfelf was probably commenced, if not completed, previoufly to the death of Prince Henry, in 1612, but undoubtedly not later than 1625, in which year the manufcript was tranfcribed, fome pofitive evidence is furely required before we fhould afcribe fuch a laboured production to a youth who, as it appears, had not finifhed his academical ftudies till 1631.

"ALEXANDER GARDEN, who became a member of the Faculty of Advocates in Aberdeen, may have been connected with the Gardens of Banchory, and we may place his birth between the years 1585 and 1590. His defignation of "Mr." fhows that he had taken the degree of A.M. before 1609. 'The Garden of Flowres' in that year, was no doubt his earlieft performance. 'The Theatre of Scotifh Kings," completed between 1612 and 1625, was apparently followed by his 'Theatre of Scotifh Worthies.' As this work muft have contained fome interefting notices of the author's contemporaries, the hope may be expreffed that the MS. from which the quotation you have given at p. xv., from Nifbet, is ftill in exiftence. Garden's metrical verfion of Bifhop Elphinftone's Life, from the Latin of Hector Boece, bears the date of 1619."

In this letter I fupplied fuch fets of commendatory verfes as I could find written by GARDYNE or GARDEN, and prefixed to works by his friends, publifhed in the years 1615, 1622, and 1634; along with thofe addreffed to himfelf, and prefixed to the MS. of his "Theatre of Scottifh Kings," which the Editor in 1709 had omitted. In the printed title an engraving of the Royal Arms is inferted, and the Author is defcribed as "ALEXANDER GARDEN, *Profeffor of Philofophy* at Aberdeen." The MS. itfelf *furnifhes no fuch flatement*, and this has occafioned the confufion in regard to the actual Author.

Mr. Turnbull, in his Prefatory Remarks, refers to another work by GARDEN, by quoting from Nifbet's *Heraldry* the Notice and Verfes on Sir James Lawfon, extracted from GARDEN's "Scottifh Worthies." "But his 'Scottifh Worthies' (Mr. T. adds) belongs to the *Bibliotheca Abfcondita et deperdita* of our anceftors. No copy of it is known."—(p. xv.)

At this time it had completely efcaped my recollection that many years previoufly I had actually feen a manufcript copy of "The Scottifh Worthies" in the Library of the late Sir Alexander Bofwell of Auchinleck. On accidentally afcertaining this fact, and having a natural defire to examine the work, I obtained from the Honorable Richard Wogan Talbot the ufe of the volume, with liberty to have it tranfcribed or printed if defirable. Acting upon this permiffion, and having recommended the volume to the Council of THE HUNTERIAN CLUB, it was adopted as a private contribution to the Club by ALEXANDER B. STEWART, Esq., a few words of explanation regarding the work and its Author may be expected.

The information to be gleaned refpecting the Author, in addition to what is already flated, is very unimportant. The name of GARDEN occurs at an early date, and our Author, at No. 126, celebrates one whom he calls Irvine Kempt fixteen according to the following Act printed by Kennedy from Records of the Sheriff Court:—

> "At Aberdeen, the fecond day of October, 1633.—In prefence of the Right Honourable Thomas Crombie of Kemnay, fheriff principal of Aberdeen.

"The quhilk day the fheriff principal forefaid caufit call and convene before him the perfons particularlie following, quha ar the ordinar advocates and procurators of this judicatorie, and hes been in ufe to procuir in all caufes.—They are to fay, Mr. Alex. Irving, Mr. William Barclay, Mr. William Lumfden, Mr. James Irving, Mr. Alex. Davidfon, Mr. George Anderfon, Mr. Alex. Reid, Mr. Alex. Paip, Mr. Robert Reid, Alex. Thomfon, Mr. Alex. Gardyn, George Middleton, William Cordoner, John Hunter, Mr. Andrew Clerk, and George Merfer. Quhilks perfones being all perfonallie prefent, and the fheriff underftanding of their abilities, honeftie, and judgement, to continue as members and ordinar advocates and procurators of this feat; the faid fheriff, be vertue of his office and authoritie, Refavit and admittit them, and everie ane of them, to that place and priviledge, and caufit them all to be folemlie fworne for yair dew obedience and reverence to the feat, and for faithfull and trew ufeing and difcharging of thair place and charge, and for obferving of fick guid and laudabill lawes, actis, ftatutes, and ordinances, as fould be fett down and prefcrybit; and, farder, the faid fheriff declairit and ordainit, and expreflie difchargit all uther perfones quhatfumevir of all libertie or priviledge to compeir or procuir before the fheriff or his deputtis, at any time hereafter, in quhatfumever caus, or to tak upon them to be advocates or procurators, except they be firft lawfullie admittit be the fheriff, and his licence and libertie purcheflit, gevin, and grantit, to that effect."[1]

The name of Mr. ALEXANDER GARDYN, Advocate, occurs in the Fafti Aberdonenfes, laft April, 1638, p. 409, as the firft

[1] Kennedy's Annals of Aberdeen (1818, vol. ii., p. 166).

of a Committee of four appointed to choofe "ane Sub-
Principal in place of Mr. David Leiche, who had been tranfported to the Kirk of Ellon; in virtue of which they elected
and prefented to ane Reverend Father my Lord Chancellor,
Mr. Robert Ogilvie to be Sub-Principal; quhome the said
reverend father chancellor inftantlie admittet and tuik his
oathe folemplie fworne," &c. Upon the fame occafion,
"Convenit Mr. Robert Ogilvie fubprincipal, Mr. Johne
Lundie grammarian, Mr. James Sandilandes canonift, Mr.
Alexander Middletoun and Mr. Alexander Gardyne regentis,
quha all in ane voyce nominatt and prefentit to the principall Mr. Alexander Scrogie younger student of theology, to
be tryit iff he be fand worthie, to be Regent in place of Mr.
Robert Ogilvie."

Mr. Turnbull, in his Abbotsford Club volume, refers to
the MS. Life of Bifhop Elphinfton, then in my poffeffion,
and fays:—

"'This manufcript is in quarto, beautifully written, at Aberdeen,
in the year 1619. It was formerly in the collection of old Robert
Myln, and is apparently the original. A copy in a fimilar hand
was purchafed by Principal Lee, at the fale of Dr. Jamiefon's
Library in 1838.

"From the refemblance which the autograph of this MS. bears
to that of the 'Theatre of Scottifh Kings' in the Faculty Library
—as well as the fingular coincidence of ftyle in the two com-
pofitions, it would appear that both proceeded from the fame pen.
I fhould therefore have availed myfelf of Mr. Laing's friendly permiffion to print it in the prefent volume, had not Mr. Innes
intended to do fo in the Appendix to the third volume of the
Chartulary of Aberdeen; of which important publication two
volumes have juft appeared."

Unfortunately, no third volume of the Chartulary ever
appeared.

GARDEN's work is little elfe than a metrical verfion of the earlieft biography of the Bifhop by Hector Boyfe or Boethius, in a volume in which the biography of his patron forms the chief portion. It is entitled, "Epifcoporum Murthlacenfe et Aberdonenfe. Per Hectorem Boetium Vitæ." A facfimile of this engraved ornamented title of the "Prelum Afcenfianum" is given on the oppofite page, as printed at Paris, 1522, and republifhed for the Bannatyne Club in 1825.

At a more recent date, having obtained the manufcript at Principal Lee's fale already mentioned, the other was tranf-ferred to the Library of the Univerfity of Edinburgh. A facfimile page of each MS. is given. The one now in my poffeffion is evidently the original, in the old parchment cover, with thefe initials ftamped on the fide.

L.

A.   E.

This clearly fhows it had been the dedication copy to Alexander, Lord Elphinfton. There were four Alexanders in fucceffion, Lords Elphinfton. Robert, third Lord Elphinfton, died in May, 1602, when Alexander fucceeded to the title. He held various offices, and furvived till July, 1648. His eldeft fon, Alexander, who took the fecond title of Killdrumie, to whom GARDEN alfo infcribed his work, enjoyed the title of Lord Elphinfton for only twelve months, as he died in 1649.

In the prefent volume the text is given from a collation of both manufcripts, as it was not thought neceffary to ad-here flavifhly to the pedantic orthography of the original. Prefixed to this portion of the volume, a brief notice of Bifhop Elphinfton's life, along with his Portrait, will be given.

Profeffor ALEXANDER GARDEN, we may fuppofe, was the fon of the elder Garden.

EPISCOPO
rum Murthlacen. & Aberdonen. Per Hectorem Boetium Vitæ.
Prelũ Ascensianũ

As a ſtudent at King's College, he was the ſecond on the Liſt who matriculated under David Leochæus, Anno 1628. and is the firſt of "Duodecim Univerſitatis Aberdonenſis Alumni Philoſophiæ Studioſi," whoſe names are ſubjoined at the end of "Oratio Euchariſtica et Encomiaſtica in benevolos Univerſitatis Aberdonenſis Benefactores, Fautores, et Patronos; a Joanne Lundæo, Humaniorum Literarum Profeſſore, Habita xxvij, Iul. 1631. Aberdoniis, excudebat Edwardus Rabanus, 1631. 4to.

GARDEN was admitted one of the Regents of King's College, 17th September, 1635, and his name occurs on later occaſions, namely, 12th April, 1638, to 23rd November, 1643.

From Dr. Hew Scott's "Faſti Eccleſiæ Scoticanæ," vol. iii., p. 655, we obtain the following particulars:—

"Alex. Garden, while Regent, was appointed Miniſter of Forgue, in the Preſbytery of Turiff, and was admitted before Auguſt, 1645. In March, 1647, he was named by Parliament as one of the Viſitors of the Univerſity. He ſubſcribed in 1658 towards the erection of new buildings within the College, and was appointed, in 1661, one of the Viſitors for viſiting the Univerſity. He continued Miniſter in March, 1666, and probably for ſome years later, his ſucceſſor having been appointed in 1677."

It muſt be admitted that GARDEN's claims to be ranked among the old Scottiſh poets are but ſlender. He has no originality or invention, no fancy, nor eaſe or grace of verſification, which are but poorly compenſated for by pedantic words and extreme careleſſneſs or poverty of rhymes. In his two chief works, "The Theatre of Scottiſh Kings," and "The Scottiſh Worthies," he followed very cloſely the footſteps and imitated the ſtyle of two ſimilar productions in Latin verſe by John Johnſton of Aberdeen, Profeſſor of Theology in the Univerſity of St. Andrews.

The titles of thefe works may be given—

"Infcriptiones Hiftoricae Regum Scotorum, continuata annorum ferie a Fergufio primo Regni Conditore ad noftra tempora: Joh. Jonftono, Abredonenfe, Scoto, Authore. Amfteldami, excudebat Cornelius Claeffonius Andreæ Hartio. bibliopolæ Edemburgenfi, Anno 1602." (With engraved portraits of the Kings.) 4to.

"Heroes ex omni Hiftoria Scotica lectiffimi.   Auctore Johan. Jonftono Abredonenfe Scoto.   Lugduni Batavorum, excudebat Chriftophorus Guyotius, fumtibus Andreæ Hartii Bibliopolæ Edinburgenfis. 1603." 4to.

It has not been afcertained how long ALEXANDER GARDEN furvived, as no traces of him have been found later than about 1642.

In the MS. of "The Scottifh Worthies" there is fome confufion in the numbers.   In the printed text they run on confecutively; and the two correfpond from Nos. 1 to 66.   In the MS. Nos. 67 and 68 are paffed over, the paging being continued without interruption.   In like manner 127 and 128 are alfo omitted; and thus No. 150 (Forbes) in the MS. is No. 154.   After this the Nos. 151, &c., are numbered 155 on to 159 in the original MS., correfponding with 151 on to 175, have been corrected by Robert Miln 155 to 179. It is not unlikely that fome leaves of the original MS. may have been tranfpofed.

The feries of Worthies appropriately terminates with John Garden of that Ilk, who was flain at Pinkie in the year 1547, and who may have been an anceftor of the Author.

DAVID LAING.

EDINBURGH, 7th r, 1878.

A

THEATRE

OF

SCOTTISH WORTHIES

BY

ALEXANDER GARDEN

ABERDEEN, *circa* M.DC.XXVI.

TO

THE JUDICIOUS READER.

Moſt certanlie I know, doe what I can,
Thir Poeſies ere publiſhed ſhall not pleaſe
Th' hum'rous heads and mynds of everie man,
Such Antipathies ever are in theſe:
    Then ſurely (ſince nought all) it ſhall ſuffice
    If they bot pleaſe ane gratfull, good, or wiſe.

Yet I imploy to pleaſure all my paines,
Yea oft to'increaſs there kyndneſs took I caire,
And craues nought bot goodwill for all my gaines,
Which everie ane but prejudice may ſpaire:
    Bot giff they carp att all, and all diſpleaſe theme,
    I mynd nought then to move me much to ineaſe them.

AL: GARDEN.

A THEATRE OF
SCOTTISH WORTHIES.

1. ꝼerchard.

Captane of Lorne, vanquiſhed and ſlew in battell Dovall,
  Captane of the brigants, ane Vſurper of the Croun, in which
  battell himſelfe was ſlaine, in the dayes of King Reuther,
  the yeare before Chriſt 213.

Boetius in his
Scott.Chronicle,
2 book, cap. 2,
pag. 15.

Give pleading for the place occaſione brings
Our countrie Worthies valorous and wyſe,
Grave Councellors, great Captanes to our Kings,
Imployed in many perrellous interpryſe:
  Thow firſt muſt enter the triumphant arch,
  And Signifer move in ther martiall march.

For why? thow firſt, when young King Reuther rang,
His realme and reigne by Dovallus deſtreſt,
Whence great wproars and perturbations ſprang,
By Dovalls death reduced the realme to reſt;
  And all the bands that threattened bondage brake,
  So fred thy countrie by that famous faͨt.

Scot. Chron.
Holinſhed
in the 1 book,
fol. 97, in
the lyfe of
K. Rewther.

Therfore all theſe, both great and gallants grand,
For ciwick crouns or martiall ſtate that ſtryves,
Whoſe wonderous witt & hardineſs of hand
Illuſtrat hes and lawriat ther lives:
  They have ſubſcryb'd and does conſent thow ſhall,
  (Becaus moſt old) be Antient to them all.

Heroes
Io. Ionſt.,
pa. 1.

2. 𝕮𝖆𝖉𝖆𝖑𝖑.

Captane of the brigands, was Governor chofen when Gillus
wfurped the Croun, ended ane perrillous warr, flew Gillus
in Irland, reftored the Kingdom to Ewine, the juft inheritor,
who leived before Chrift 77 yeares.

Boece, 2 book, pag. 21.

Who ofter with a better fortoun fought,
Who virtuous was, or who adventerous more,
Who honor throughe mor harder hazards fought,
And found perforce enjoyed it fo before:
     Nought brave Cadall for his countries caufe,
     Before the debt more bold nor bloodie blaws.

Altho the winds thy virtews they invy'd,
And would wpon thy valour be reveng'd;
Thy ftomach yet in that extream it try'd,
Into thy cariaige conftant and wnchang'd:
     Thy victories nor (by fea wracks) thy woe
     Blew thé nought wpe nor beare thé doun too loe.

Boece, 2 book, pa. 22-23.

Thow in the heat, high furie, and the pryme
Of dangerous and moft diftempered days,
(Contemning terrors of that troubled tyme)
Our worfhipfull and worthie writters fays:
     All foes defeat, th' Ufurper fought & flaine,
     Reftor'd the kingdom to King Ewine againe.

Io. Ionf., pag. 2.

3. **Argadus.**

For his worthinefs & egregius deeds made governor when
King Conar for his wicked lyfe was depofed & impriffoned.
He ruled happilie to the reigne of Ethodem the I., &
flourifhed after the birth of Chrift 163.

Thy verill valor, worthinefs, and witt,
Ay for the peace and republict prone,
Affum'd thé in thy foveraignes feat to fitt,
When's tirranic hade throun him from his throne;
 Which faultlefs long thow govern'd & defended,
 And when thow fell (admonifh'd) thow amended.

Bold Argadus, when thow that ball did beare,
Wnfcheath'd thy fword, and bravly thow thé boore,
Whill th'outmoft Iles, forc'd throw thy force & feare,
Obey'd and thy directions did indure:
 Thy countrie thow her captane fhe decoir'd
 With lands, & laud, & thow fell fighting for't.

Then happie thryce that foe thy fprit did fpend,
And in defending of thy countrie fell;
Thy notable renoun & noble end
All after tymes fhall to extoll thé tell,
 And fhow in forceing of thy countries foe
 Thy felfe was flaine & facrifcifed foe.

Boece, 5 book.
pag. 58, 59, 60.
61.

Iob. Leflie,
Bip. of Rofs, in
his Chron., pag.
109.

Holin., in the
lyfe of King
Conar, pag. 63.

Io. Ionft., p. 2.

4. Graeme.

Was governor after the death of Fergus the 2d., his fone in
law, for Eugenius his nevoy, and in a moft troublfome tyme,
with exceeding manhood, govern'd the eftate; from him
Severus Wall is yet caled Græmes Dyke.   He gave 'the
begining to that noble name & famous houfs of Græme,
Montrofs, & Montdiew.   He florifhed after Chrift 420 yeares.

Iff this great Græm a Scott, a Brittane borne,
A Roman was, or Pight, put yow the cafe,
That did the houfs of Montidew adoarn,
And was the root to that renouned race:
   Whofe facts alfe fare as Fame cane flee hes floune,
   And gotten a greatnefs by plaine ftrength, not ftoune.

It is a wonder, and no wonted thing,
To fee a leige give to his Lords his lands;
Yet he a countrie conquifht to his King,
And wane his houfs firft honor with his hands:
   When he deforc'd thofe famous forts which Fame
   Since to this day hes baptcif'd with his name.

What multituds could but performe att length,
He hes alone demolifh't & o'rethroun;
He was withftander of the Roman ftrength,
Controling others ever was his oune:
   Without all change, ftill lyke himfelfe the fame,
   The heire of Honor & the chyld of Fame.

5. Guillame.

King Achaius brother, a princly Captane, went to France
with 4000 men of Warr, after the League made with Charles
the Great to confirme it, who did excellent fervice therwith
againft the Infidealls, reftored Poppius the 3 to his Papacie,
& the Citie of Florence to her libertie. Laftlie, he
erected diverfe Monaftries in Germanie, & ther, & in
France, is yet famous. Flourifhed the yeare of Chrift 800.

Boece, cro., 10 book, chap. 3 & 4, p. 134. 135.

Io. Major. pag. 35.

The floorifhing fame of King Achaius facts
Great Brittane could not in her bounds imbarr;
Noe, bot it throw the boundlefs Ocean breaks,
And flyes o're Ewrope to the Afian warr:
    Thence from the Eaft wnto the Weft againe
    O're the Alps it flew to France to Charlemane.

Who both enamord & admyring it,
Long to be federat with fuch a frynd,
For non befand to forder France fo fitt;
Wherfore to fute & feik the fame he fend:
    Which laughfull league (who knows not) yet ftill ftands,
    Since thefe great Kings both joyfull joyn'd ther hands.

Then, mightie William! thow was made the mene,
And firft to France with power fupporting paft,
Both to eftablifh and to intertaine
A Treatie that eternally fhould laft;
    Wherewith thow did fuch dreadlefs deads of fame,
    That Dutchland, France, & Florence fil'd with them.

Io. Iohnft.. pag.

B

6. Hay.

Boece, 11 book, cap. 8, fol. 160.

With his two fones, armed with 3 plough yoks, in a ftrait
paffage ftopt the flight of our fleeing forces, and repulfed
the power of the Daines; whereby they conquifht to them-
felvs & there pofteritie advancment, honor, and immortall
glorie in that memorable battell of Loncartie, 2 yeare of
Kenneth 3, the yeare of Chrift 942.

Io. Leflie, in
the lyfe of
Kenneth 3.
pag. 196.

When Danifh fortoun forft our fathers flee,
And hade in flight our phallanx near defeat,
Then happie Hay, thy two ftout fones with thé,
There timorus troups conftrained in a ftrait
    The furious foe to reafront to face,
    And conquer them that conquering came to chace.

Holin., in the
Scots. hift., p.
55.

Into that famous feild att Loncartie,
When on hard tearmes our countrie ftanding ftood,
Thy dreadfull dints made many Dain to die,
And att thy feet lay bubling in there blood:
    Great gallant there, thow with thy youths & yoke,
    Moft nottablie nobilitat thy ftock.

Io. Ionft.,
pag. 3.

Thow as a battall ftrong ftood in that ftoure,
Winged with the valour of thy ventrous fones,
Whofe Herculian hands in halfe ane hour,
With windrous valour & great virtew, winns
    From foes the feild, & from thy freinds the fame,
    That hes and fhall fore're renoun thy name.

7. 𝕾𝖎𝖗 𝕽𝖔𝖇𝖊𝖗𝖙 𝕶𝖊𝖎𝖙𝖍.

A young man, the ennobler of his famous name and familie,
whoſe ſingular manhood and valour att that battell in Barrie
defeated the Danes, ſlew there Captane Camus, and pur-
chaſed therfore to himſelfe and his ſucceſſors great ſeagnories
and that honorable charge to be Great Marſhall of Scotland.
He flooriſhed wnder King Malcolme the 2, the yeare of
Chriſt 1006.

Boece, in his
11 book, cap.
17, fol. 169.

Io. Leſlie. 5
book, p. 203.

Thow little Lothee, languiſhing & ſtill
For wanting water, bot thy ſtirring ſtood
Whill that this knightlie Keith thy flainks did fill
With Daniſh bouks and billoes of ther blood:
    Thow that anon but ſtreams all emptie ſtands,
    Now crimſon collor'd ſwels o're ſchore & ſands.

Raph. Holin.,
in the Scott.
hiſt., pag.
166.

Brave Martialiſt! thy glorie ſince does ſhyne
For killing Camus, bringer of ther bands;
Thyſelfe made Marſhall, & thy ſones ſenſyne
Inculpat in that calling yet commands:
    No pettie praiſe, nor little laude to thé,
    So to be ſirſt of ſuch a familie.

Io. Ionſt.,
p. 4.

High honors therfore to thy heires & houſe,
And dignities from thy deſairts redounds:
Thy deads that day, gallant, egregious,
Done for thy countrie, into Barrie bounds,
    The conſummatione of the world ſhall come
    Before they ſleep and ceaſs unſong be ſome.

8. Makduf.

Leslie, in the
lyfe of Mak-
beeth, p. 207.

Hol., Sco. Cro.,
p. 170.

Thane of Fyfe, a wyfe and valiant Captane, fled from the
tirranie of Makbeath to England, and from thence reduced
the laughfull King Malcolm the 3, flew the tirrane Makbeeth
with his own hands, wherfore he was made Earle of Fyfe.
From him are defcended the honorable houfs of Weems of
that Ilk.   He floorifhed the yeare of Chrift 1079.

I was the objeƈt of a tirrans ire,
And aime wherat his bloodie bolts was bent;
My fpoufe difpatch'd, my fortrefs fet in fire,
My felfe exiled, my fones flaine innocent:
    And yet this wrong, great & exceffive ill,
    It kendl'd more then did my courage kill.

For I triumph'd and took the tirrans lyfe,
A pofthumus fhorne from my mothers fyde:
My curteleax ftay'd much inteftine ftryfe,
And did the doubtfull defteneis decyde,
    Whairin with nane but graclefs witches guyded,
    The faithlefs King too much before confided.

Boece, 12
book, p. 7.
fol. 176.

My banifhment the trew King Malcolme brings,
And he with him fecuritie to all,
So from m'exile and my expeling fprings
My countries freedom by the tyrrans fall;
    Wherfore my felfe with gifts and glorie gat
    My houfs with honor privilegiat.

Io. Ionft.,
pag. 5.

9. Sir Alexander Carroun.

Hade his name changed, and was called Scrimgeour (a hardie feighter) for his magnanimitie manifasted att Spey with King Malcolm the 3; therfore rewarded with the hereditarie office to be principall Vexillifer to his Prince, which yet his heires the L. of Dudop, Conftables of Duntay, poffeft. He floorifhed the yeare of Chrift 1057 yeares.

Hol., pag. 178, in the Scot. hift.

Lellie, pag. 212.

When bafs and fervile feare his fprit poffeft,
That then King Malcolms royall banner boore,
Thy couraige by his cowardice increft,
And caught the collours fhaking and wnfure:
    Rebooking him thus that aftonifht ftood,
    For feare of foes or furie of the flood.

Hol., in the Scot. hift., pag. 178.

Boece, lib. 12, fol. 267.

What daftard dreeds or doubts thow for to die,
Or fants thow for this flood or for thefe foes;
Come, couard, come, & fordward follow me,
Dreed not this deep, nor doubt the dint of thofe:
    Behold ws beat ther bands, ignoble, bafe,
    And o're this Spey bot any perrill pafs.

Les., Scot. hift., p. 212.

This thow couragious to that fpritlefs fpake,
And fearlefs on the foe the collors caries,
Wherat thy Prince there did occafione take,
And the brave Carroun to his collors marries:
    Which yet the Deudopean houfs inherits,
    Thy laughfull lyne to manifaft thy merits.

Io. Ionft., p. 9.

10. 𝕾𝖎𝖗 𝖂𝖆𝖑𝖙𝖊𝖗 𝕾𝖙𝖊𝖜𝖆𝖗𝖙.

The fone of Fleannce, & the noble nepot of Banquho, for his
courage & activitie wfed in dantoning the rebells in Galloway, was made be Malcolm 3 Queftor, or great Steuart of
Scotland, from whom are defcended the illuftruous, floorifhing,
& royall familie of the Stewarts, which fo long, with great
felicitie, hes impyred & rung above ws.   He floorifhed
the yeare of Chrift 1062 yeares.

Loud thundring Ioue, great god omnipotent!
In jeopardees, and in the lions jaws,
Fenc'd thé the father & the foundament
Of his great houfs, whom now three kingdoms knawes:
     And ferv's fincearlie for there foveraigne Lord,
     With more great gifts then fkill can count decor'd.

Th' unbridl'd barrons bravlie thow debel'd,
Whofe fwords forfuorn there foveraigne Lord did fchore;
Thow caus'd them fmart that of fedition fmel'd,
And this thy Prince repay'd thy paines therfore:
     Thow was high Steward of the State inftal'd,
     From whom fo manie Kings are come & cal'd.

They firft from thé there firft high honor have,
Since firft thy facts ennobled firft ther name,
And firft begining to ther greatnefs gave,
Now fhyning feene fo eminent in theme:
     What thow began there cariaige hes increaft
     Above all midds matche to the mightieft.

11. **Gilchrift.**

For manie famous and heroick facts was highlie honored in King Malcolm the 4 his dayes, yet his fortoun changing wnder King William, was reduced to great miferie, ftoutlie fuftained it, and happilie overcame in the end. From him the noble houffes of Angous and Ogilvie are fupponed to be difcended. He floorifhed the yeare of Chrift 1165.

Hol., Scot. hift., pag. 185.

Les., pag. 224.

Boece, lib. 13. fol. 267, 289, 278, 281, 283, 284.

What fubject leiv'd & greater honor hade,
Who was nor I efteam'd more ftout & wife;
The royall blood it beutifi'd my bed,
And I went victor from the battells thrice:
   I was advanc'd, depreft, belov'd, invy'd,
   And the effects of both the fortouns try'd.

Sufpitious, fals, Janonick-jealoufies
With informatione fond made me defile,
And blot my honor with ane infamie,
And therfore juftlie judged to exile:
   Where, e're reftor'd, to recompence my fpight,
   I paffed all that any mortall might.

Io. Ionft., pag. 7.

I was the roote and the originall
Both of the houfs of Ogilvie & Angous,
From whence fo many men fo martiall
Wee know are come, & yet remaine among-ws:
   As few are found fuch families before,
   That may and will accept or want of more.

12. 𝕯𝖆𝖛𝖎𝖉.

<table>
<tr><td>

Leſlie, pag.
224.

Hol., pag. 191.
Scot.hiſt., &195.

Boece, lib. 13.
fol. 285, 286.
292.

Io. Ionſt..
p. 7.

</td><td>

Earle of Huntingtoune, brother to King William, and nepot
to King David 1; went with Philip and Ritchard, Kings off
France and England, to the Sacred Warrs, where, after great
renoun and worſhipe, woun innumerable perrills with great
patience, manheid, and magnanimitie overpaſt, returned home,
founded Lundoirs, and flooriſhed the yeare of Chriſt 1219.

</td></tr>
</table>

A Generall nought be my chance bot choſe,
In Paleſtine wnto the warrs I went,
To conqueis fame wpon the faithleſs foes:
Where firſt to my renoun my regiment
  Took Achon, in a citie fenc'd with forts,
  And plac'd the Lion pinſell on her ports.

Out through a thowſand perrills I have paſt,
And with no mene miſfortouns I have met;
Marr'd on the maine & on the waters waſt,
On that with bloes, on this with billoes bet:
  Yet both thoſe ſtormes ſtill ſtoutlie I ſuſtain'd
  With valour that with wiſdome this preivein'd.

Without adventuring I noe worſhip wanne,
Nor did but perrell purchaſs any praiſe;
A conq'ror now, o'recame & captive than,
No ſmall diſtreſs indur'd I in my dayes:
  Where danger dwelt, yea from the dures of death,
  I pul'd perforce, & oft reported ſpreathe.

13. Sir Alexander Steuard.

Grandfather to King Robert the 2, att the Larges vanquished
the Danes, & flew 24M of thair men, chaifed ther King and
Captanes Acho to his fhipps, & delivered his countrie from
there tirranie and oppreffion. He florifhed the yeare of
Chrift 1268.

Hol.,Scot.hift.,
pag. 192, 200.

Boetius, lib.
13, fol. 289.

Wat tho thow northeaft ryfe into thy raige,
And ftuff our ftations with thy tours of trie,
This hand and fword thy fweling fhall affuage,
And chace thé from our fchores wnto the fea:
    My boldnefs bot & nought my bands fhall beat thé,
    My fortitude & nought my force defeat thé.

Io. Ionft.,
pa. 8.

Thy awfull Acho, that vfurper I
Gave att the Largs a foull yet famous foile,
Where numbers of thy Norces left yet ly
A fpectacle to fpecifie there fpoile;
    And yet I have the fortitude & whips
    In nead to beat thé bleiding to thy fhips.

Bot think not for my felfe, as thow & thyne
Wnjuftly thus my panes a croun prepares,
Albeit it may be I indeed devine
The fame fometyme fhall hapine to my heires:
    And of my blood fhall come more crouned Kings
    Nor now beneath the airie region reigns.

C

14. Thomas Earle of Carrick.

Earle of Atholl, John Stewart, brother to Alexander of Dun-
donald, Alexander Cuming, Robert Keith, George Durvard,
John Quincie, & William Gordon, honorable commanders,
worthie captanes, and couragious knights, att the command
of Alexander the 3d, conducting with the 1600 fouldiers
went to Africk with Sanct Lewes, the French King, who
defyred aide att the faid Alexander, which honorable &
worthie men all dyed there, aither wpon the enemeis fword,
or be the intemperait aire & heat of the countrie, the yeare
of Chrift 1270.

The wondrous, willing, and the worthie zeall
That yow, our faithfull fathers, did inflame,
To fence and free the Chriftian Commonweell,
More nor to fpread & fet afloat ther fame,
    From tirranie and from the Turkifh thrall,
    Wpbraids our aige, & it the cold does call.

The perrill of your perfons, nor your paines,
Heat, hunger, hoftile ftrengthe, nor all extreams
Impafht yow not to pafs the partched plaines,
And dryed wp defarts brunt with Phebus beams;
    But worthie yow went by your warlick works
    From Salcins ftrengthes for to extrude the Turks.

As thefe attempts yow now immortall makes,
And bolded hes aboue both the globs your glorie,
So they this foile of flouth doth taint, doeth tax,
And fhoues it fhould be both afham'd & forie;
    Since it containes fo manie knights, God knows,
    Yet all fo cairlefs of the Chriftian caufe.

15. John Stewart.

Lord of Boote, Bunele, Ranfrew, Rothfay, and Stewardtoune, Holin., Scot. hift., 210 & 173 Leflie, pag. 235
left be the Governour Wallas, and be the flight of the
Cuming, fuftained the charge of all the Englifh armie, and
valiantlie feighting with 10,000 of his freinds & followers,
was flaine att Falkirk the yeare of Chrift 1300.

When Wallafs honor, which his valor wan,   Boetius.
The craftie Cumine fo to fpred efpy'd,   lib. 14.
Firft att his greatnefs he to grudge began,   fol. 307.
Then wrongouflie his worthinefs envied;
    But, wanting valor to exprefs his fpight,
    Cauf'd me wnkyndlie quarrell with that knight.

Which counfalls contraire to the Common-weell   Io. Maior.
No little bale wnto the countrie bred,   fo. 71.
And made my felfe for his offence to feell,
That onlie faultie was and feeblie fled:
    When flilie he hade fet ws by the eares
    To give our foes advantage in the weares.

Yet tho o'rewhelm'd with ane o'rematch of men,
Deferted to, bot nought therby difgrac'd,
I neither quench'd nor cam'd my courage then,
Bot att Falkirk of all left to the laft;
    I'll follow'd feightand for my countrie ftood,
    Backt by my brandans to my knees in blood.

16. $\mathfrak{Sir\ John\ Grahame.}$

Ane couragious knight, companion, and fellow in armes to
the valliant Wallace in all his enterpryfes, was flaine in the
defence of his countrie att Falkirk, the yeare of Chrift 1300.

My provefs paft my pedegree does prove,
And my defairts deduces my defcent;
Wnto my countrie and this land my love,
While that the laft fpunk of my fprit was fpent,
    Makes me the emull of his facts & fame,
    That firft gave honor & renouned our name.

I was his fellow & his faithfull frynd,
Into his age the ornament of armes,
And alwayes in his actions to my end,
A partner both of his good haps & harmes;
    And by himfelfe (albeit I was the worft)
    Account'd of his followers the firft.

Att Falkirk feild, wherin a fox bot faeth
Seids of feditione & diffention few,
Which made that day prove difmall by the death
Of notable and noblemen anew:
    My felfe there ane, it was too clearlie knoun,
    Was flaying flaine, not vanquifh'd nor o'rethroune.

Holin., Scot.
hift., pag. 210.

Boet., lib.
14, fol. 307.

Io. Ionft..
pa. 10.

17. Sir William Wallace.

Made Governor after the death of Alexander 3 for his glorie in
armes, comparable to the moſt excellent, nottable, & moſt
antient captanes, ane man both for his ſtrength & ſtoutneſs
matchleſs & admir'd, moſt conſtant he defended his countrie,
delivered her from thraldome thrice; a knight couragious &
moſt memorable, betrayed to his enemeis by a too much
betruſted frynd, the yeare of Chriſt 1305.

Holin., Scot.
hiſt., pag. 209,
210.

Leſlie, pag. 236.

Boctius, lib.
14, fo. 305, 306,
307, 308, 310.

Who e're more famous and more full of force,
Into that aige was any where brought furth,
Ne're put in warre with valour to the wors,
But always equall for his wondrous worth
  To Hector, Haniball, to Hercules,
  Or to th'Athenian Themiſtocles.

Io. Maior,
lib. 4, fo. 69,
70. 71, 72. 73.

When all our Barrons were in bondage bound,
Allone a libertine (this brave) abode;
No worth nor wiſdome could his valour wound,
Nor oft attempted on his treuth could trode:
  His greateſt foes, forc'd on there faith, affirms
  He was the glorie of his age in armes.

Io. Ionſl.,
pa. 8, 9.

This famous, yet ne're forced by his foe,
His freind profeſt tho falſe did ſnare wee ſee,
If treaſon can trew fortitude o'rethrow,
When with all hardineſs & honor he
  Intruded tirranes hade outthruſted thrife;
  Betraied in torments he triumphs & dies.

18. Sir John Cumin.

And Sir Simon Frazer, two hardie and honorable knights,
famous for defaiting with 8000 men in one day three feverall
tymes three diverfe armies of Englifhmen, everie one confifting of 10,000 ftrong, att Rofling, the 24 day of Februar,
the yeare of Chrift 1302.

If force with lyke and equall force defeat,
The victors valour, paines, and praifes prove,
Then with difvantage victrie win I wait,
Should more nor praife & admiration move:
    Advance the virtue, & the manhead mount
    Paft credit of the conqu'rors in account.

Whofe provefs thane depoftulats more praife,
Or who (moft martiall) admiratione more,
Since that your deids condignlie in your dayes
Made yow to match, if not in fame before,
    Thefe Romans bold that Haniball debel'd,
    And from all pairts of there Empyre expel'd.

Att Rofling, with eight thowfand men att moft,
Ye in one day fought & defeated thrife
Three tymes ten thowfand in ane Englifh hoft;
A happilie perfected interpryfe,
    Which to yow both, tho dead, diffolv'd, & rotten,
    Perpetuall praife & glorie hes begotten.

19. Sir Robert Fleeming.

A honorable and valeant gentleman, ane of the firſt that
joyned with King Robert Bruce before the ſlaughter of the
Cuming, and conſtantlie followed him in all his fortouns, and
was rewarded therfore with the Lordſhip of Combernald,
pertaining to the ſaid Cuming. He flooriſhed in the yeare
of Chriſt 1305.

That conquering King, & ne're conquer'd Knight,
Carnarvans ſcourge, he that the Cumine kill'd,
When famous faɕts, when fame & force in fight,
The regions moſt remote & fareſt field,
    He the couragious, kind, and conſtant knew
    Firſt att Dumfries, when he his feller flew.

Then in his ſturrs and tempeſts inteſtine,
Tho bot with rebells and his bondmen borne,
Whom he brought to obey that ſhould have been
By law his ſervants & his ſubjeɕts ſworne;
    So thow did ſerve, & did ſupport that Prince,
    That mak's thyſelfe and feed ſo cel'brat ſince.

Thy faith in both his fortouns firme he fand,
Sincere ſtill foore and moſt inteire he try'd,
It but a ſtot or any ſtumbling ſtand,
Wntainted trew wnto the day thou dy'd;
    Which worthie verteus thus reward he wald,
    By giving thé the countie Cumbernald.

Boet., lib.
14. fo. 210.

20. 𝕾𝖎𝖗 𝕾𝖎𝖒𝖔𝖓 𝕱𝖗𝖆𝖟𝖊𝖗.

And Sir Walter Logane, moſt valiant Knights, greatlie favouring there countrie, were betrayed, & taken by the faction of the Cumins, ſent to London, & there execut the yeare of Chriſt 1306.

Holin., Scot. hiſt., pag 215.

For being loyal to our native land,
And love to it that wee was bound to beare,
The Cumine, att the Engliſh Kings command,
Betray'd and led ws wnto London, wheare
    Wee fuffer'd for no other found offence,
    But difapproving that wſurping Prince.

Io. Ionſt., heroes Scot., pag. 11.

If't be a break where wee was bound to bide,
Or treaſone to our countrie to be trew;
If ſubjects ſlip t'aſſiſt there foveraignes fide,
Againſt a King that all the world knew,
    Sought to ſubject ws by the fword, then wee
    Confefs wee fail'd & by defarte did die.

Io. Major, lib. 4, fo. 80.

But when great Scevol, with a wondrous will,
Encourag'd only by his countries love,
Did mint tho miſt th'Etrufcan King to kill,
That Pagan Prince more pitifull did prove:
    He praiſ'd his fprit, & did affect his faith,
    And then preferv'd him from a prefent deith.

21. 𝕰𝖉𝖜𝖆𝖗𝖉 𝕭𝖗𝖚𝖈𝖊.

Ane moſt adventrus Prince, brother to King Robert 1., for the
fame of his valor by the Eſtates of Ireland was choſen &
crouned ther King, in a battell there againeſt the Engliſh,
overmatched with a multitude of men, nought abyding the
coming of his brother King Robert, but haiſtening to fight,
was ſlaine, att Dundack, the yeare of Chriſt 1316.

Holin., Scot. hiſt., pag. 221.

Leſlie, pag. 247.

Boet., 14 book, cap. 11, fol. 214.

Altho the merits of this martiall man
Envie would wrong, tyme & occaſion ſmother,
Or preas for to ſupprefs his praiſe, what thane?
It ſhall ſuffice he was the Bruces brother,
 Whom Fame hes for a Neo-Mars renoun'd,
 And Scotland for her Knight & Conqu'ror croun'd.

O! but his ventrus valour in the warrs,
And great groun glorie of his fa{ts & fame,
So was diſperſt and pearſt the Iriſh ears,
Who nearlie noting his renoun & name,
 As ane weell-worthie in there inter-regne,
 Prince Edward they appoynt & crouns ther King.

Io. Io., pa. 11 & 12.

Who oft there foes defaiting there he fought,
And tam'd them too that wndertook to tort-him,
Whill once too fordward for to fight would nought
Stay on his brother poſting to ſupport him;
 Yet not ſo much by force as Fortouns ſpight,
 Thair fell the Iriſh King, the Scottiſh Knight.

Io. Major, fo. 87, lib. 5.

D

22. **Sir James Dowglafs.**

The heroick adherent, faithfull follower of King Robert Bruce,
    and partner of all his adventures and victories; after his death,
    to performe his Princes vow, went to the Holy Grave with his
    Princes hart to be intered there, who, after 57 tymes victorie
    againeſt the Engliſhmen, and 13 tymes againſt the Infidells,
    in his returne throw Spaine, incloſed with ane ambuſh, was
    ſlaine with his followers, the 26 of Auguſt, the yeare of
    Chriſt 1330.

What Keſare, King, or what conqueſtor knew
A ſubject then wnto this cheeff a choſe?
Ane match for Mars, whoſe doeing did ſubdue,
And ſeaventie tymes in fight defeat his foes:
    O valor worthie of Apollos ſpirit!
    More nor to mount t'immortaleize his merit.

No mortall man durſt doe or doubt indure,
But (Pirrhus peer) he ſuffered & perform'd,
And att the bondage that his countrie boore
His high gainſtanding ſtomach ever ſtorm'd;
    While that his bled the thunder bolting braſe
    Her to her former freedome did reduce.

But heir when matter for his martiall might,
Nor for unforc't his ſtrengthe was to withſtand,
Then paſt this Captane & this conquring Knight,
T'entomb his Princes hart in the Holy Land,
    Wher, after forcing oft the Infidell,
    While then ay fortunat this famous fell.

23. Sir Walter Leflie.

Earle of Rofs, caled, for his magnitude of mynd and ftrength
of bodie, the Wight, wha in diverfe warrs againft the Infidells
with Charles the 4 Emperor, by his wifdome & great valour
obtained great honor & renoun; of whom are defcended the
Earles of Rothes and diverfe others barrons, wha received
from King Malcolm the Firft, then from his fuceffor, large
lands in Fyfe, Angous, Gowrie, & Garioch.　He floorifhed
the yeare of Chrift 1329.

Leflie,
pag. 211.

Worthie Sir Walter, whom the world cal'd Wight,
And for thy love & to thy honor wf'd,
To note thé with the name of noble Knight,
And in our dayes wee by Tradition doef't:
　　Welcome from Buda here, or Belgrade rather,
　　To Brittanie came thy foir-famous father.

Whofe forefight, faith, & force infatigable,
That ftout King Malcolme oft & treulie tri'd,
In purchafing a place inexpugnable,
(Then feiming fo) which hade his force defi'd:
　　That fteep ftrong rock, that high o're Edin ftands,
　　And lyke a lord o'relooks all Lauthean lands.

He here att hame, thow in the Sarc'n warres,
With Second Lues, and with Charles the Fourt,
Moft eminent fhew lyke two ftreaming ftarres,
Both heir & there into the camp & court;
　　Wherby yow both into the books of Fame,
　　For Knights compleet have eterniz'd your name.

24. **Sir William Sincler.**

And Sir Walter Logan, two honorable and hardie Knights,
famous for there fortitude in the warrs of King Robert Bruce,
and then for the going to the Holy Land with his hart, and
for many knightlie deeds in the Sacred Warrs, where they
were slaine, the yeare of Christ 1330.

Boete, 15 book, cap. 1, pag. 218.

The constant courage & the loiall love,
The hardie hearts, the reddines of hands,
Whill that the strong King stiff & stoutlie strove
By force & feight to free (halfe lost) his lands;
    That in thir two, tried in his worthie warrs,
    Makes them now glister lyke two golden starrs.

Io. Ionst., pa. 11.

The oppositions & alterations oft,
That to impead thair Prince his peace appear'd,
Made nought ther gallants leave him while aloaft
On honors rock his roiall serge was reir'd:
    No, nor when dead; but both, lo! after death
    Thir Knights well kith'd to leave ther Lord were leath.

Io. Major, lib. 5, fo. 98.

For with that hardie Counte that hade his harte,
To be inhumed att the Holy Grave,
This pare therewith to pass prepair'd depairt
To do't the honor last that it should have;
    Which deulie done, as the deceast deserv'd,
    Gainst Saracens whill they were slaine they serv'd.

25. Thomas Randolphe.

Earle of Murray, nephew to King Robert Bruce, for his wifdome & valour fecond to non of his qualitie in his dayes, & therfore choifen be his wncle (in regaird of his infirmitie) in his oun time to governe the Kingdome; ficklyke governed happilie for his coufing, King David 2, in his minoritie; died, poyfioned att the defire of his enemeis by a monk, a counterfite phifitiane, the yeare of Chrift 1331.

Holin., Scot. hift., pag. 228 & 229, et 225.

Leflie, pag. 251.

Boece, 15 book, cap. 1, fol. 118.

Egregious Earle! thow by thy mightie minde
Declares thé nepot to the noble King,
And reconfirms this knowledge of thy kinde,
By deeds of hand & hardie hazarding;
    Att Bannockburn thow gallantlie begane
    That wondros victorie that thy wncle wane.

Io. Ionft., pa. 13.

The heart of Hector, & Achilles hand,
With th' eloquent & wife Vliffes witt,
Into thy bofome with the brafen band
Of pregnant & politique knowledge knitt,
    Made thé to meritt the mageftick mace,
    T'impire (he leiving) in thy Prince his place,

Which Roume thow reul'd with witt & valor fo,
As ay the end was regular & right,
Defending frinds, affronting ftill thy foe,
That could nocht flay bot fhift thé by a flight;
    Yet in the giving wpe thy ghoft thow gain'd
    (He forft) triumph & victorie obtain'd.

26. Sir N. Hammiltone.

Holin., Scot.
hift., pag. 224.
Leflie. 7 book,
pag. 248.
Bocce, 14 book,
pag. 15. fol. 226.

Author of his name in Scotland, fled from King Edward Car-
narvon to King Robert Bruce, after the flaughter of one
Spencer, that hade detracted the victorious King Robert,
who gladelie received knighthood, and gave him the lands
of Cadzow to mantaine his ftate, of whom are defcended the
name & noble houfs of Hamiltone, fo floorifhing att this
day.   He leived the yeare of Chrift 1314.

Io. Ionft.,
pa. 13.

Cleer kithing valor in a vertuous Prince
Forc't thé againft thy countrie, faith, and freind,
(Appeal'd be Spencer) feight in his defence,
Whofe iffue made more eminent in end:
    His valour wrong'd, and this by weaknefs ftrong,
    To ftill by ftrength th' untrew detractors tongue.

Wherfore thow loft thy countrie, kin, and king,
And fled enforc'd a fugitive from thence
To Scotland, to a bountefull benigne,
And then of all the moft accomplifht Prince,
    Who treplie thé thy interefts reftor'd,
    And with thé ftill to be his knight decor'd.

Thair was no wrong to make a worthie change,
To lofs thy king and countrie gods ingrate,
Who for advancing virtue wold revenge,
And Ham'toune thé for helping honor hate;
    Bot couards, non bafs borne or fimple feed,
    Darr thé detract or difcommend thy deed.

27. Sir Andrew Murray.

Regent in the minoritie of David Bruce, did nottable and much good fervice to his countrie, ftrook & wan the battell of Panmure, defeated the Cumins, followers of the Balioll, chafed the Englifh att Roxburgh, and took manie ftrongholds to his Majeflies vfe, and fome wnprofitable demolifhed. He floorifhed the yeare of Chrift 1332.

Holin., Scot. hift., pag. 235, 6 & 7.

Leflie, 7, pag. 254.

Boece, 15 book, cap. 7, fo. 224, & cap. 9, fo. 226.

Thy fortitude, fidelitie, & facts
Wnto thy fame affords a fairer face,
Since for a Murrays mifs amends thow makes.
To exulat that former great difgrace,
    And gaine once loft renoune unto thy name,
    By him that pitch'd the ftaike into the ftreame.

Io. Ionft., pa. 14.

Into th' wnjuft and bloodie Baliolls warrs,
A troubl'd tyme & full of dangerous daies,
Through ftrength of fteall wpon the points of fpears,
The vigor of thy valour made thy waies,
    And fhortlie did performe & interpryfe
    So much as might a captanes aige fuffife.

For by thy might and manhood neir amated,
The ftrongeft ftrengths was feafed on & fhaken,
And in the feild the foes in fight defeated,
So thow triumph'd the tyme that thow was taken:
    Nought in thy flight bot following too faft,
    Thow in thair wards unwares & powers paft.

Io. Major, fol. 99, 101, 102, 103.

28. Alexander Lindsay.

Lord of Gleneſk, cheif of his name, a honorable and hardie
Knight; with fourſcore of his name, were ſlaine in armes for
defence of thair King, David Bruce, in that wnfortunat
conflict att Dupline, the yeare of Chriſt 1332.

Who will not, Dupline, bot diſdaine thy day,
Or rather raige to name thy noyſome nights,
Since miſregaird with treaſone did betray
To couards too. ſo many counts & knights;
　　And yet a boutcherlie committed murther,
　　But all activitie in armes or order.

Tho Fortune keith'd a frynd wnto thy foe,
Thow with the boldeſt barrons of thy blood,
In that foull conflict fighting failed noe,
But ſtoutlie whill ye were deſtroy'd ye ſtood;
　　To let theſe theeves & cut-throats couards knaw,
　　But Fortoun nought ther force did yow o'rethraw.

Bot heir behold your fourſcore famous freinds,
Into the verie loſſing of there life,
With thé ther captane and there cheif contends
(A glolious moſt ſtout & ſtaitlie ſtryfe);
　　For this ther countrie that ther nonaige nurſt,
　　Who ſhall doe beſt and doing who die firſt.

29. William Hay.

Earle of Erroll, flaine with his haill name, & if nought be
the Divyne Providence, he hade left his wyfe with chyld.
who boare him a fone after his death, his name and race
hade bein extinguifhed att Dupline, the yeare of Chrift 1332.

Holin., Scot.
hift., pag. 231.
Bocce, 15
book, cap. 2,
pag. 221.

Was it our fate, misfortoune, or our foes?
Wes it our fond affiance in our force?
Or was't our pride & plaine contempt of thofe
That murder'd ws but mercie or remorce?
    Yea all concur'd was caufes & o'recame-ws,
    And therfore all this day they doe condem-ws.

Io. Major,
pag. 98.

Io. Confl.,
pag. 15.

Yet creuell all, why did there wraiths devoure?
And was more mercilefs to me & myne,
Then to the reft in ane wnhappie houre,
To leave no living man in all my lyne;
    And fo my race have rooted out & rais'd,
    In paffed times fo for there provefs prais'd.

If not a ftronger nor the ftrength of man,
That Faits & Fortoune does difdaine & fcorne,
Hade fowne the feed, and fend in a fone, that thane
Was in his mothers bellie & wnborne,
    Wnto th'eftate my race for to reftore,
    To fight for it, as was my forme before.

E

30. 𝕾𝖎𝖗 𝕽𝖔𝖇𝖊𝖗𝖙 𝕶𝖊𝖎𝖙𝖍.

Sone to Robert, Earle Marſhall, with manie of his name, ſlaine at Dupline, couragiouſlie reveng'd there death, took by aſſault Perth, fortified by the Baleoll, diſmantled it, ſlew theſe therin that hade bein att the ſeild of Dupline, and execute Andrew Murray for his treaſone att Earnſoord, the yeare of Chriſt 1332.

Holin., Scot. hiſt., pag. 231.

Boece, 15 book, pag. 221. cap. 3.

Io. Major, fo. 98.

Thy lands, mens loſs, thy freinds, & fathers fall,
That on that doolfull day att Dupline dy'd,
Thow to revenge, bold mynded Martiall,
Thy valorous vindictive ſprit apply'd,
    And to releive what all the land thought loſt,
    Wherby the countrie or the King was croſt.

Io. Ionſt.. pa. 15.

Thy interpryſes into everie pairt,
They were feconded with a good fuccefs,
Concording with thy hautinefs of heart,
Thy virtue, valour & thy worthinefs:
    There was noe foe nor ſtrength that could withſtand,
    But thow dang doun, o'recame, & did command.

Perth, ſtronglie ſtuff'd with the Baleolls bands,
And packed with his peers & principalls,
Thoſe thow hemm'd in with hardinefs of hands.
And ventrouſlie wan & went o're the walls:
    The ſtifborne then thow ſtikked that withſtoode,
    Or hade att Dupline ſhed the Barrons bloode.

31. Sir Alexander Setone.

Cheefe & Lord of his name, a faithfull Knight to his countrie, greatlie incouraiged by his manlie-minded wife, choos'd rather to fuffer his two fones die by the tirranie of King Edward, then to deliver Berwick (committed to his cuftodie) to that perfidious King, the yeare of Chrift 1333.

Holin., Scot. hift., pag. 232.

Leflie, pag. 252.

Boece, 15 book, cap. 4. fo. 22 .

Give no attendance to that tirrans threats,
Nor yet obey that boutcher for his boaft,
Suppofe our fones he now with ftrangling ftraits,
Yet wee are young, altho they both be loft;
    Bot once our honor with a treafone tainted
    Can never be repeated thought repented.

Io. Major, fo. 99.

Our children knowes them for there countrie borne,
And for this Toune they take it & efteam them;
Therfore the gallants they difdaine & fcorne,
That fo yow fhould or ranfone or redeem them:
    No, no, deir Lord! or thow this toune betray,
    They both fhall die a glorious death this day.

Io. Ionft., pa. 16.

O faithfull father (& bot feconds) fones,
But matchlefs mother for thy manlie minde,
And of true honor the triumphant twinns!
And but compare wnto your countrie kinde,
    Where fhall fuch famous faithfull four be found,
    So (for lyke courage) worthie to be croun'd.

32. 𝕬𝖗𝖈𝖍𝖇𝖆𝖑𝖉 𝕯𝖔𝖜𝖌𝖑𝖆𝖋𝖘.

Hol., Scot. hiſt.,
pag. 232 & 233.

Leſlie, pag. 253.
7 book.

Boece, 15 book,
cap. 5, fol. 223.

Earle of Dowglaſs, Regent; with the greateſt pairt of the nobilitie,
earneſt to revenge the wrongs done by King Edward to his
countrie, & that infamous and perfidious faſt done to the
ſones of Sir Alexander Seaton, inconſideratly fought att
Halidoun-hill, and was ſlaine with the cheiffe of the nobilitie
about him, the yeare of Chriſt 1333.

That feeble faſt againes the law of armes,
And furor of that proud perfidious Prence.
Inſincit hurts, hoſtilitie, & harmes,
With daylie domage, wrong & violence

Io. Major.
fol. 99.

     Done to my countrie & that conſtant Knight,
     Could nought bot force a fazarde for to fight.

Io. Ionſt..
pag. 16.

Wherfore my ſprit, o'reloathing to delay,
Deferr revenge, or wink att ſuch a wrong,
To Haledoun on Magdalens day
I came & coaped with that tirrane ſtrong,
     Wherein the choak, hade not my fortoun chang'd,
     I hade reverted victor & reveng'd.

O bot the frounde! and there my chance did cheake,
And gave my luck, bot not my manhead, mate;
A fainzed flight my bands beleiving breake,
Wherby ſuch were the furie of our fate
     They both & I was in the danger drawne,
     So fell I fearelie following with my awne.

33. John Randolph.

Earle of Murray, sone to Earle Thomas, Regent, also was Governor himselfe for King David; with great honor discharged that office, and in a most turbulent tyme did great & good service to his King & countrie.   He florished the yeare of Christ 1336.

Hol., Scot. hist., pag. 231 & 235.
Boece, 13 book, cap. 7 & 8. fo. 235, & cap. 3, fo. 231.

Thy faith & facts with forwardnefs, but feare,
In foulest storms for standing of the State,
Does foorelie show thow was his fone & heire,
That for it stood in many stoure and straite,
    And ever where most perrell was appearing
    Was there found first & with the last reteering.

Io. Major, fo. 51.

The precious pairts plac'd in thy parents spreit,
Into thy courage kith'd & doeth decore thé,
Match'd with thy minde there to remaine thy meit,
Which whill he was, wes found in him before-the:
    To make thé perfect, if noght fo, yet fuch
    As from thy countrie does demerite much.

Io. Ionft., pag. 17.

With handfulls bot of men thow match'd & met
Flocks of thy foes & with good fortoune fought them;
Thofe too that durst rebell thow bravelie bet,
And in time cuming to be trew thow taught them:
    Who did fuch facts performe, nor could conclude,
    Except a branche borne of the Bruces bloode.

34. **Patrick Dumbar.**

Holin., Scot.
hiſt., pag. 230,
231.

Leſlie. 7 book,
pag. 251.

Boece, 15 book,
cap. 3, fo. 221.

Earle of March, Governor with Andro Murray (nough he
caled Corſpatrick), famous for manie facts & his conſtancie
in the defence of his countrie. He floorished under King
David 2, the yeare of Chriſt 1336.

Io. Major.
fo. 101.

What Cæſar ſomtymes wnto Tullie told
His foe may fitlie be affirm'd of thé;
He ſaw him flow & he did know him cold
In that which did concerne himſelfe, ſaid he;
  Bot what the Senat or did touch the Toune,
  In that implacable & importoune.

Io. Ionſt.,
p. 18.

So for thy countrie thy continuall care,
Reſpecting nought thy perſone nor thy paines,
Moſt manlie March, moſt clearlie does declare,
That Marcus meaning in thy mynd remains;
  For by thy force thow did in her defence
  No leſs nor he by arte & eloquence.

Into thy tyme, ane ill & angrie aige,
When all this ill was weded wnto warr,
(Pure peace expel'd) and nothing rang bot rage,
Ay with the Bruce then was thow, bold Dumbarr:
  To foes and freinds, when't was thy chance to charge,
  To theſe a terror & to the other a targe.

35. **Sir Alexander Gordone.**

Ane valeant and worthie Knight, led the rereguarde in the batell of Halidoun-hill, who couragiouſlie (tho with croſs fortoune) fought, yet returned faife, & att Kildrimmie kiled David Cumen, Earle of Atholl, ane enemie to his countrie. He flooriſhed in the yeare of Chriſt 1336.

Boece, 15 book, fol. 331, line 70.

BoeceEngliſhed, cap. 8, fo. 225, 15 book.

Thy manie marks, and on thy fcalp the fkarrs,
And val'rous wounds, that yet thy breaſt does bear,
Got in our wrackfull & invafive warrs,
Were they reveiwed would witnefs thow was there:
  One both that gote and gave oft overthrowes,
  Freind to the Bruce, but fatall to his foes.

Io. Ionſt., pa.

When that perfidious & difloyall Lord,
Wnto his King and countrie tryed wntrue,
For Englands fake oft hade wnfheath'd his fuord,
And to King David diverfe fubjects flew,
  Thow kil'd him, to thy honor, with thy hands,
  Among the bold and braveſt of his bands.

At Halidoun yet nought thought Fortoune froun'd,
Thy heart nor hand into the feighting fail'd,
That victorie did nought thy valour wound,
Nor tho they wan that vantage & prevail'd,
  Was hurt thy honor, nor the fame of thofe,
  That fell thereby the fortoune of there foes.

36. 𝕾𝖎𝖗 𝖂𝖎𝖑𝖑𝖎𝖆𝖒 𝕶𝖊𝖎𝖙𝖍.

Holin., Scot.
hift., pag. 237.

Sir Robert Gordone, and Sir Lawrence Preftone, three couragious
Captanes, overthrew and defeated two Englifh Armies con-
ducted by William Talbot & Ritchard Montfort; the faid
Talbot was taken by William Keith after the difcomfiture
of his people, and the other, Montfort, flaine be the faid
Robert & Lawrance, with the maift pairt of his companeis,
the yeare of Chrift 1337.

Boece, lib.
15. p. 333.!

Your mother countrie, with incurfions croft,
With forrane force, and with onfrends infefted,
Togedder with inteftine tumults toft,
And multituds of miferies molefted,
  Your fprits with pittie her concuffion kills,
  And caus'd yow fpare to obviat her ills.

Io. Major.
fol. 103.

When on the feilds ye th' Englifh forces fand,
Ranping in raige & lyke the Furies fairing,
Diftroying all and with a hungrie hand,
No, not fo much as facred places fpairing,
  Nor anie fex, but where there forces flitted,
  A hudge & cruell carnage they committed.

Then juftlie was your angers fet on raige,
And your bold breifts with bloodie famine fill'd,
Whofe fweling could noucht fettle nor affuage,
While that your courage hade there cohorts kill'd,
  And Talbot tane that boafted the fubjecting,
  Of Croun & King, tho fail'd in the effecting.

37. **Sir Alexander Ramsay.**

Of Dalhoufie, one of the moft valiant Captanes that was knowen
  in his dais; after manie imployments & victories over the
  enemeis of his countrie, his advancment by his adverfare,
  William Dowglafs, of Liddisdale, invied was by a pollicie,
  by him apprehended, imprifoned, and inhumanlie forced to
  die by famen, the yeare of Chrift 1342.

Ho., Scot.
hift., pag. 239.

Boece, lib. 15.
pa. 330, 334.

O hade my fortoune favored me fo farre,
And made me bleft by being one of thofe,
That in the countries caufe & common warre,
With glorie fell in fight amongft her foes!
  I hade not now one creweltie exclam'd,
  Nor hade my foe bein for his fact defam'd.

Io. Major,
fol. 104. 103,
134, 107.

Io. Iohnft.,
pa. 18, 19.

Or hade I there then perifh'd, I proteft it,
(Att the Englifh doors when I defait thair hoft,
And after that took Roxburgh or I reftit),
My death hade given no greiff wnto my Ghoft,
  That griev'd now groans, becaus I was referv'd
  In Hermitage, for to be hunger-ftarv'd.

Yet want of fpreit, nor power to repell
Effronts, nor force brought me wnto this bay,
Since non was knowen that could my courage quell,
Nor with his valor wrong me anie way:
  Altho with pollicie fuppryfed, yet I,
  Maugre my foe, difdaining death did die.

F

38. William E. Douglafs.

Holin., Scot.
hift., pag. 238.

Boece, lib. 15.
fo. 326.

Io. Ionft..
fol. 19.

Lord of Liddifdale, a Knight & Captane (if he hade not mightilie hurt his honor by the ftarving to death of Sir Alexander Ramfay in Caftell Hermitage), for many high interpryfes hardilie performed, manie victories valorouflie obtained, and much good fervice done to his countrie, nottable, famous, & renouned. Floorifhed the yeare of Chrift 1342.

Thaife glorious gifts that make a gallant great,
Witt, valor, will, a breaft robuft and bold,
With freinds and Fortoune to performe each feat,
From thy elders thow in heretadge did hold;
  And what more Mars could grant, his freinds profeft,
  By Nature thow as proper thine poffeft.

Nought given in vane nor granted was thefe graces,
Bot nottable moft when thy natione needs,
A thowfand prooffs into a thowfand places
Thow gave of thefe, brave Dowglafs, by thy deeds;
  And if nought with Dalhoufies death diftain'd,
  Thow hade the glorie of thy grandfirs gain'd.

Bot that wnworthie and fo vile revenge,
Still Treuth & Tyme as moft ignoble notted,
Whilk now noe collor nor excufe can clenge,
So palpablie thy reputatione fpotted,
  That one treffpafs thy praifes all hes fpoil'd,
  And all thy weell done former facts hes foiled.

39. **Sir John Gordone.**

A memorable and worthie Knight, encountering with the Englifh, oftentymes victoriouflie, took Sir John Lilborne there Captane, after the faid Sir John Gordone hade renewed the fight fix tymes in ane day; therafter took Thomas Mufgrave, Captane of Berwick, and with fome Knights, his complifhes. affaulted the Toune and tooke it, the yeare of Chrift 1378. *Holin., Scot. hift., pag. 246.*

When March & Murray privilic furpryfed,
And Roxburgh reft out of the Englifh hands,
They to revenge, into there wraith devis'd,
To burne our holdings and lay waift our lands;
    Who with thair armie entring and begane,
    And what was thyn they robbers firft o'reran.

Whofe raige for to refift and to requyte,
What they to thé in ther difpite hade done,
Thaire fpoile with fpoile and pryde with plaine difpyte,
Thy freinds and force thow did affemble foone;
    But what effects thy fouror there afforded,
    Raph Holinfhed thair Cronicler recorded.

Six tymes thow faught, & five tymes in that day
(Freind to thy foes) on thé thy fortoune froun'd,
Yet ever thow wrg'd and reenforc'd the fray,
Whill thow was victor & with conqueft croun'd;
    Lilburn, Mufgrave, thair captanes to decore thé,
    (Bervick debel'd) paft priffoners before thé.

40. James, Earle of Douglass.

Holin., Scot.
hist., pag. 248
& 240.

For his hardinefs called the Bellicofs, famous for wonderfull
victories atcheived over his enemeis, & fpecillie being
challenged be the Lord Perfie to the combat for difmunting
him before Newcaftell, and his notable victorie obtained att
Otterburne, where, thrice ftricken throw the bodie, he died
after the wining of the feild, in the reigne of Robert 2d,
the   day of   the yeare of Chrift 1388.

Io. Major,
fo. 116,
117, 118.

What for his Rome did Mark Marcellus more,
Nor for thy countrie thow gave overthrows,
Or thofe Horatii got they greater glore,
Nor thow combating for thy countries caufe,
   Or who amongft the antique for ther acts,
    Was found nor thow more famous for ther facts?

Boece, lib.
18, fo. 344
et 345.

Moft inclite Earle, kene & couragious Knight!
Who dow thy deeds, thy praife & provefs pen?
Who can fet furth thy fame into that fight
(Sought to the fame) before Newcaftell, when
   Thy ftrong fteel'd ftaff, with fervor of thy force,
    Hees'd hot-fpur'd Percies heels above his horfe?

Io. Ionft.,
pa. 19.

Lyke Hercules cled with his club or clave,
Where moft repair'd thow in the preas did pafs,
And knightlie there, bold, bellicos & brave,
Thow multituds did maw doun with thy mace:
   Neir Otterburne, att one tyme victore twyfe,
    Thow thaire the Campioun of thy countrie dies.

41. Patrick Hepburne.

And Patrick Hepburne, his fone, Lords of Hailles; John Lord Keith, Marfhall of Scotland; & the Lord Montgomrie, 4 worthie Nobles & valorous Knights, gave moft memorable marks of there martiall mynds, and notes of there trew nobilitie, in the battell of Otterburne, where the firft two are faid to have reftored the battell, almoft loft, and the Lord Montgomrie took priffoner Henrie Percie, generall of the Englifh armie, & the faid Lord Marfhall took his brother, Rodolph Percie, and brought them both priffoners home. They floorifhed the yeare of Chrift 1388.

Lellie in his
Scot. Cron.,
pag. 238.

Boece, lib. 16,
pa. 345.

Moft honorable both Hepburne of the Haills,
Montgomrie thow, & thow courageous Keths,
Att Otterburne your valour all availls;
And there your deeds deferves now after death,
    Yea, pithelie prows, demonftrations ftrong,
    From whence your ne're expyring praife hes fprung.

Io. Major,
fo. 117.

For in that bloodie, feirce & famous feight,
Where aufull Angous, that egregious Earle,
A Mars for magnitoode of mynd & might,
And for his princlie pairts & fpreit a pearll,
    Alace! for pittie was tranfperfed thrice.
    And yet triumphing & a victor dies.

The virtue of your valors fo prevail'd,
That it reduced that declyning day,
And victorie to ws and honor hail'd
From thefe proud Percies with plaine worth away:
    Where thow, Count Marfhall, & Montgomrie thow,
    Thaire feighting took thofe captanes captive too.

42. 𝕯𝖆𝖛𝖎𝖉 𝕷𝖎𝖓𝖉𝖘𝖆𝖞.

Holin., Scot.
hift., pag. 252.

Leflie, 7 book.
pag. 203

Earle of Crawfoord, nottablie celebrat & renoun'd in our hiftoric
for difmounting and wanquifhing the Lord Wailles, ane
Englifh nobleman, on London Bridge, in a monomachie
offered to all our countric Knights by the faid Lord Wailes,
& accepted by the faid Earle for reproachfull fpeeches
againft the Knighthood of our countriemen into the reigne
of Robert the Thrid, the yeare of Chrift 1396.

Boece, lib. 16.
fo. 348.

No fkaith to Scotts, nor there renoun'd name,
Can come be thefe thy windie wants vnwife,
Nor praife to thé, nor noe reproach to thame,
Sall by this thy wnreverent railing ryfe,
Io. Ionft.,
pa. 20.
  Whofe valore is ingroffed to thair glorie
  Ten thowfand tymes in Times eternall ftorie.

Myfelfe, altho the outwalle & the worft,
On Londons Bridge my countries Knight fall be.
Wpon Sanct George Day, harnifhed & horft,
To trache thé thare a courfe of Cavelrie,
  And force thé by thy fall in th' Englifh fight
  To talke more calmlie of my countric Knights.

My hight I hold, thow and thy countrie knows,
In prefence of thy Prince, his peers & all
The Englifh eyes, I bet thé with my blows,
And fairlie there I foil'd thé by thy fall;
  Thought falflie thine in murmuring maner mocked,
  As I hade bein faft to my fadle locked.

43. **Sir Alexander Ogilbie.**

Of Otherhouſs, Shereff of Angous; William Abernethie, Lord
  Saltone; Sir Alexander Irwine of Drum; Sir James Scrimgeor of Deudop; Sir Thomas Murray; Alexander Stratone,
  of Lawrenſtoune; Robert Davidſon, Proveſt of Aberdein;
  Robert Maule, of Panmoore; with the chiefeſt of the
  citizens of Aberdeen, all ſlaine in that bloodie battell of
  Harlaw, the yeare of Chriſt 1411.

Whoſe have thoſe been thow curiouſlie that craves,
Thir Tyme-torne tombes concumulat do knaw?
They be of great & gallant men the graves,
That feight and fell with honor in Harlaw;
    Whom comone caire & to there countrie love
    Did ſtimulat & heir to matche did move.

The Donaldens, a ſavage ſort & ſeirce,
Cume from the Out Iles (thair quarrell ſkarſelie knoun)
The countries ſprit and inwarde pairts to pierce,
Or by the doome of Deſtanie doun drowne,
    To die, dung be the barrons in that warr,
    Conducted by the inclite Earle of Marr.

Where, whill they both with ſuch a furie fought,
The ground did groane, the aire for ſorrow ſhouted,
To ſie how they to wrack each vther wrought,
That if alive or more there di'd it's douted;
    So ſeirce the feight, ſo ſtrove they ſtoutlie ſtill,
    That vigor wanted, or they wanted will.

44. Sir Hugh Kennedie.

Holin., Scot. hift., pag. 258 & 259.

Of Bargenie, a valiant gentleman; for his valour in France and his good fervice in ftoping att a bridge the paffage of the Englifh armie before the joyning of the battell of Baugee, was highlie honored be Charles the 6th, and hade his fheild decor'd with a treffure of the Royall flours of France, which yet, to thair honor, his pofteritie bears. He floorifhed the yeare of Chrift 1420.

Io. lonft., p. 21.

Brave Captane, with thy crewe of Archers keen,
Whofe promptnefs with the Parthiane might compare,
What fervice did thy winged fhefts, was feene
At Baugee-brigge before the battell, whare
    With feaven fcore thow conftrain'd 10,000 ftay,
    And ere they paft fand all that powar play.

The vertuous Cocles worthelie commended,
And for preferving of a paffage prais'd,
That bridge with noe more fortitude defended,
Nor th' enemeis with manhead more amais'd;
    Nor went t' imped the paffage of thy foes,
    Thow with a few thy perfone did oppofe.

Nor was that day thy valour wair'd in vaine,
Nor fought thow for a King that nothing caird-it;
No, thus he gifts and graced thé againe,
Thy crofs and barrs he with a gairland gairdit:
    The Royall fimboll that the French King wears,
    Of golden flours, which yet thy branches beares.

45. Sir Robert Lumifden.

Of Pettillok, a Captane in France with a Scottifh regiment; gave   Holin., Scot.
  nottable teftimoneis of his manhood in recoverie of that   hift., pag. 261.
  Realme out of the Englifh hands, cheiflie in the reducing
  Gafconzie to the French obedience; wherfore he was ever
  after called be the inhabitants therof, Le Petit Roy de   Boece, lib. 16,
  Gafcoigne.   He floorifhed the yeare of Chrift 1424.   fol. 358.

What greater more advancement would thow wifh,
What fortoun fairer hape or higher chance
Could thow expect to happin thé then this?
That be thy chivalrie and facts in France,
      Thow fould wnto that hight of honor fpring
      To be (and bot a Captane) called a King.

The countrie Gafcoigne, to the Galls difgrace,
By th' Englifh warrs wer wafted & devoir'd,
Expert Pittillak, in a little fpace,
Thow did regaine & conquefs with thy fword:
      The foe defore'd, in peace thow left thofe lands,
      To thy high honor, in the Frenchmens hands.

Perpetuall praife there purchafed thy panes,
Eternall favour & infineit fame;
And for thy manie mereits yet remaines
Notor, renown'd, & notable thy name;
      For ftill the ftile thow juftlie does enjoy,
      Wnto thy glorie, of the Gafcoigne Roy.
                    G

46. John Stewart.

Earle of Buchane, Conſtable of France, and Maiſter of the men
of armes there; & Archbald Dowglafs, Earle of Wigtoune
and Duke of Turren; both honored be Charles the 7 with
thoſe places of honor and preferment for ther brave carriaige
& high valeance att the battell of Beugee, where Earle John
killed, with his oun hands, the Engliſh Generall, the Duke
of Clarence, brother to Henrie the 5th, King of England,
and be ther valor wan the victorie to the French; and after
both the ſaid Earles was ſlaine att the battell of Vernoll,
with Lindſay and John Swintone, a valorous Knight, the
yeare of Chriſt 1424.

Io. Major,
lib. 5. fo. 127.

Thaire name mercits hes there name renoun'd,
And ſo there virtcus ſingularlie ſhyn'd,
Whill that Great Brittane would nought be the bound,
Nor could our Firth keep in there fames confyn'd:
  For Fates a feild avou'd them to advance,
  And for the place they hade appoynted France.

Io. Ionſt.,
pa. 22.

To Baugee-burg them and there bands they brought,
In France her cauſe to make her knighthood knawn;
Where with there fearce old countrie foes there fought,
There pride repreſt there armies all o'rethrawn;
  And with there troups, twyſe there triumphant try'd,
  When be Count John the Duke of Clarence dy'd.

France therfore him there Conſtable declar'd,
And th'other with a Dutchie ſhe decor'd;
They grate againe thus wold theſe gifts reguaird
With triumphs her & ſtaitlie trophes ſtor'd:
  And, laſtlie, left there blood & bones to beare,
  Att Vernoll witneſs of there valor there.

47. Sir Alexander Lebingftoun.

Knight of Calander, for his knowen valour and wifdome, after
the murther of King James the 1, in the minoritie of King
James 2, with confent of the Nobilitie & Eftates, was chofen
Governour; which calling he with honor wiflie difcharged.
and florifhed the yeare of Chrift 1436.

Leflies book, pag. 290.

When Greeks to Troy went to revenge that wrong
Th'adulter did, in Lacedemon Land,
There Senate fage fatt and confulted long,
Who fhould as cheeff with all confents command:
    And when itt hade long on that matter mufed,
    For worth and witt it Agamemnon choos'd.

So when in deeps of deeds difloyal droun'd,
And perifht was our Prince & Palinure,
Thow then accounted competent was croun'd,
And creat (as wee call it) Governour:
    And lyke ftrong Atlas thow fuftain'd the State,
    A cairfull caling, glorious and great.

A fteerfman ftout and as a gallant guide,
Thow bravelie did that galley great governe,
That (tho in tyme of many thortring tide)
Thy labours then makes now thy land eterne;
    And Fame, outfleing Brittane bounds, did beare it.
    Far, far above the airie rounds to rear it.

48. 𝕾ir 𝖂illiam Creichtoune.

Lellies book.
pag. 291.

Holin., Scot.
hift., pag. 268.
209, 270.

Ane difcreet fage and politique Knight; judged in his daies the wifeſt and moſt prudent gentlman in this kingdome, and thairfore was chofen Chancellour, both in the reigne of James 1 and 2, and hade the perfone of James 2, with the Caſtell of Edinburgh, committed to his cuſtodie.   He floriſhed the yeare of Chriſt 1436.

That Florentine, far famous and profound
In pollicie, be precepts as appear'd,
For quicknefs, knowledge, & rare cuning croun'd,
The onlie matchlefs-Matchavell admeer'd:
    If tranfmigratione be of onie fperits,
    Thow, as his heire, then onlie his inherits.

For the events of thy inventions tri'd,
As valorous, pollitique fo, & wyfe,
Mars to Minerva properlie apply'd,
Made thy renoun & that with reafone rife;
    To fcall above the fcope of others, fince
    That ſtat'fmans tyme of all politiqus Prince.

Nor did that Dutchie, where he wfe'd his witt,
And precepts of his pollicie expream'd,
More magnific nor make of him, nor it,
Nor our Eftates of thyn (oft try'd) efteam'd;
    Since certane knowledge clearlie did declare,
    Thy practeices heire furpaſt his precepts there.

49. **Alexander Gordone.**

Earle of Huntlie, a noble & couragious Earle, encountrered
   with Alexander, Earle of Crawfoord. one of the confederat
   Lords againſt King James 2d, att Breichen, whom he fought,
   defeated, & chaiſed his forces to Phinhaven; whairfore he
   was honored highlie, & rewarded with the lands of Badzenoch & Lochwaber, the yeare of Chriſt 1452.

Holin., Scot.
hiſt., pag. 274.

Lellie, pages 86,
303 & 304.

While raige difrain'd (ſtill Stats diſturbing) ſteers,
And Lords difloyall with defectione fir'd,
Theſe proud Potentats & difpleaſed Peers,
Againſt ther King, as Caſſius, confpir'd;
    And full of wraith to wrong & wrake him wild,
    Since one occaſions he a Count hade kil'd.

There freindſhipe feare, there power & ſtrength was ſtrong,
And they, too bold with threats to be throun doun,
Stood as contendants with the Lyon long,
And cumber'd both the Countrie & the Croun;
    While thow, brave Earle, at Breichen did abate
    There pryd, preferving Countrie, King, and State.

Into thy hands his Highneſs honor hang,
And prefervation of his perfone pended,
Which, as god Mars, thy martiall men among,
Thow fearclie fighting manfullie defended;
    From whence ſhall fpring a praife to thyn & thé,
    Pafing all tearms of Tyme eternallie.

50. Thomas Boyd.

Holin., Scot
hift., pag. 280 &
281.

Leflie, 8 book,
pag. 315

Earle of Arrane; for his valour & virtues nottable; maried James the 3 his fifter; fell in his Prince difgrace; was forfited; went into England, from thence to Denmark, and, as fome hold, from that to Flanders, and there dyed. And other fome alleadge that he paft to Ittalie, & there was murthered, the yeare of Chrift 1470.

Look in my lyfe and fortoun thow fhall fynd
Moft ftrange mutations in the ftate of man,
Refembling right the weathercoak in wynd,
And lyke the waltering of the waters wan;
    Now in there courfes quiet, calme, & ftill,
    And are anon rais'd roaring loud & fhrill.

So Fortoun faun'd and favoring me awhile,
She lovly lul'd me in her lape of late,
King, Cuntrie, Court, & freinds did fmoothlie fmile,
And honor huis'd me to the ftaige of State;
    But fo this lucke (to ftait of man noucht ftrainge),
    And quyet calme incontinent did change.

Holin., Scot.
hift., pag. 292

My court decay'd, my freinds and Fortoun froun'd;
I loft my lands, my wealth, & princlie wyfe;
My Prince difpleas'd, in his difdaine I droun'd,
Was forc't to flie for my releife & lyfe;
    Thus alter'd, all my ftate fomtyme efteem'd,
    And I misfortoun'd fell, confyn'd, & fleem'd.

51. Lord Bernard Steuard.

The grand, famous, & renouned captane of Charles the 8th, & Ludovick the 12, Kings of France, in there warrs in Italie; for his virtue, experience, & approved provefs, was made Viceroy of Naples, and was called the Pitie of Naples, for his moderatione in government. After manie victories & valiant acts atcheived, this Lord of Aubigney, called be King James 4 the Father of Warr, ended his lyfe in his own countrie, in the yeare of Chrift 1508.

> *Holin.. out of Joveus in our Scot. hift.; and Leflie, pag. 324, 347. 348.*
>
> *Holin.. Scot. hift., pag. 292 & 284, 286.*

Two noble Nations for renoun and name,
Faire, fertile, France & Italie weell know'n;
As thefe feaven cities did conteft & clame,
With arguments all armed of there oun;
    That high thought thirling Homer thers to be,
    So doe thofe countries now contend for thé.

France does alleadge fhe did alloat the lands,
And therfore hers which yet thy blood doe brooke;
But th' other fay's thow bravelie with thy bands,
Bold Bernard there, threatten ftand battell's ftrooke,
    And therfore hers, for thow was rais'd to reigne,
    Viceroy & Gerent for the Gallick King.

But, lo! thy mother countrie Scotland nurft
This controverfie & contentione ceafe,
And by all equitie & judgment juft,
Before thofe pleading pairties have the place;
    Since thow & thyne was in her bowells borne,
    Whofe deeds fo oft thofe kingdomes did adorne.

52. Sir Andrew Wood.

The firſt Laird of Largo; for his fidelitie to his Prince, tryed
manhood, brave victories, & nottable ſkill in ſea-feights, a
Captane famous; rewarded & honored for good ſervice to
his countrie, in the reigns of James the 3 & 4.   He
flooriſhed in the yeare of Chriſt 1490.

The admirale, admir'd, & doubted Doric,
Moſt famous for his fate & navall fights,
Renoun'd and named in that noble ſtoric
Of Jovious illuſtrious Kings & Knights;
     To ſee thé muſt not grudge as if diſgrac't,
     In honors galley on the proove be plac't.

Thy lawtie ſworn vnto thy ſacred Lord,
Thy magnanimitie & noble mynd
Eternall Tyme ſhall reakon & record,
And count thé for a conſtant Knight & kynd;
     Since noe faire means, nor could menaſſings move
     From thy ill loſt, and Lord, tho deed, thy love.

Thy venturing valour & thy victories
Depoſtulats alſe digne deſerv'd a praiſe,
For ſcouring of our Scottiſh coaſts & ſeas;
As that old Argo in the antiques dayes,
     That got ſo great a glorie vnto Greece,
     For gaining gallantlie the Golden Fleece.

Io. Iohnſt.,
pag. 23.

53. 𝕵𝖆𝖒𝖊𝖘 𝕷𝖔𝖗𝖉 𝕳𝖆𝖒𝖎𝖑𝖙𝖔𝖚𝖓𝖊.

A noble and valeant Knight (when Anthonie Darcei, or De-la-
  Bauté, came throw England from France to Scotland to
  feek feats of arms) fought with him right valeantlie, fo as
  neither of them loſt anie poynt of honor. the yeare of
  Chriſt 1507.

A gallant Frenchman of more worth then worde,
A famous Knight on foote, a fair on horfe,
Cal'd to the combate, with the fingle fword.
Our countrie Knights f'affi'd he in his force,
  Concepting hereby to renoun his name,
  And fcorne the countrie in o'recoming them.

Holin., in our hiſt., pag. 291.

If anie durſt (as he did daftlie dreame),
None perrill wold to prove his pith appeare;
But many gallants, Gordon, Gray, and Græme.
Yea hunders more, all men of honor heare,
  Requeiſts the combate, & thefe Knights they crave.
  Each of them that, that honor they might have.

Bot aither by allowance, lote, or love,
Thow then, Lord James, that hap & honor hade,
To be the man that did his provefs prove,
Into which fport fo paffing weell thow fped;
  And there fo ſtoutlie to thy takling ſtood,
  That he that prooff paſt with expence of blood.

Leſlie, pag. 344.

H

54. 𝖂𝖎𝖑𝖑𝖎𝖆𝖒 𝖍𝖆𝖞.

Holin.. Scot.
hift., p.

Called the good Earle of Erroll, High and Great Conſtable off
Scotland; a noble, valorous, & worthie Earle, ſlaine in the
battell of Floddon.   Flooriſhed the yeare of Chriſt 1512.

Thy couraige to thy countrie and thy King,
In perrells proov'd a ſaifgairde & a ſheild;
And from thy preſence ſuch ſupport did ſpring,
That made thy freinds fly ſearleſs to the ſeild;
 And with the hope that in thy hands they hade
 To doe what thow directed never dred.

Thy worthie deeds in manie dangerus day,
Such victories & ſuch advancement wan,
As neither malice, nor a Momus may
In future tyme dedecorat thy clan;
 But ſall be forc'd, tho otherwayes they wold,
 Wnto thy praiſe what thow perform'd t' unfold.

Boldlie thy blood may but all braging boaſt,
From works of valor thay ther honor hade,
And knightlie courage keith'd wnto the coaſt
Of foes defait, that oft before them fled;
 Which ventrous worth ſo ſtrengthen'd hes ther ſtorie,
 As that noe tyme ſhall terminat there glorie.

55. **Captaine Androw Bartan.**

A man formidable to mightie Kings and great Eftates, enemeis to his countrie, & for his invincible couraige, both in his lyfe & att his death, weell worthie to be remembered among the moft famous Captanes of his tyme; intercepted on the feas be the Admirall of England and the Earle of Surrie valeantlie fightand, was flaine the yeare of Chrift 1512.

Leflie, 8 book, pag. 355.

Holin., Scot. hift., pag. 292, 294.

The Spanifh Pirats firft my parent fpoil'd,
And fank his fhipe when they himfelfe hade flaine,
Wheratt my blood within my breaft is boil'd,
And raig'd whill I reveng'd thefe greefs againe;
    And fent a fhoire for there difaftrous deeds,
    In puncheons packed hunders of there heeds.

My practeifes too perrillous appear'd,
And my attemp's, the boldeft thought too bold;
My fortoune, facts, and fame Weft Flanders fear'd,
Yea made her tremble when fhe heard them told;
    And my few forces on the fleeting froth,
    Abazed the Brutans & Iberians both.

No Pirrat paft, but punifhment or pay,
Nor whill I rang went robbers wnreveng'd,
And from Dunkirkers to my dying day,
My countrie coafts (as of cut-throats) I cleng'd;
    And on the liquid lyke a King commanded,
    Whill two ftrong States to overbeare me banded.

56. Confecrat.

To the Ghofts of the egregious and heroick Earles, noble Lords,
    honorable Knights, gallant, valerous, & all worthie gentle-
    men, flaine feighting in Floddon, the 9 day of September,
    the yeare 1513, viz., the Earles of Lennox, Erroll, Craw-
    foord, Catnes, Orkney, Sinclare, Montrofs, & Caffills; Lords
    Innermeith (Stuart), Erfkine, Hume, & Vefter.

Holin.. Scot.
hift., pag. 301.

Lellie. 8 book,
pag. 364.

Lo, happie thrife! what honor to your herfs
True vertew for your valour facrad fall;
Wreitts, volums, works, & wordlefs full of verfs,
Deputed to your praifes fpeciall;
    The pearlls of pryce, that moft the mightie minde
    Toills to obtaine, and never faints to finde.

Your tombs are trophes of your deeds & death,
And monuments of your eternall fame,
Or rather fruits of your wnfainzied faith,
That of her Knights your countrie kinde could clame;
    And teftimonies of your valour try'd,
    That for her docing dochtilie have died.

Altho your fates was in that Feild to fall,
Your hands preferv'd your honor from all harm's;
Nought halfe your happinefs hade Hanniball,
To end amongft his enemeis in armes;
    Amidft there throngs and thickeft livelefs lying,
    As if entrinfhed with there doux-peers dying.

57. Sir Walter Scott.

Of Baccleugh, nottablie famous for his enterpryſe to deliver his Prince, King James 5, att his oun command, out of the Earle of Angous hands, at the Brig of Melros; who more ſtraightlie attended & overlook't, as his Grace thought, his perſone and affaires, nor ſtood with the deutie of ane ſubject. He flooriſhed the yeare of Chriſt 1526. *Holin., Scot. hiſt., pag. 313. Leſlie, 9 book, pag. 420.*

Give ſtout attemps ſhould be of high deſairt,
And in the rotulls of remembrance roll'd,
If't ſeem in ſubjects a praiſe-worthie pairt,
T'affect the freedome of there Prince control'd;
    Or from too ſtraight attendance for to take him,
    And of a thral'd a Monarch free to make him.

Then, hold Baccleugh! ne're ſhall what thow attempted
T'enlarge thy Lord, cheer'd by his cloſs command,
From that eternall trumpet be exempted,
Whilk Fame ſhall found ſet into honors hand,
    To blaze thy brave mynd, dutie, deeds, & zeall,
    Wnto thy Countrie, King, and Common-well.

Although that tyme the iſſue anſuear'd No,
Nor did ſucceid to thy deſir'd deſigne,
Fate onlie fail'd, and Fortoun was the foe
That croſt thé, in the conques of thy King;
    Yet ſince thow delt againſt the Douglaſs than,
    Whate're thow loſt, thy ventring vauntage wann.

58. John Stewart.

Holin., Scot.
hift., p. 314.

Leilie. 9 book.
pag. 421.

Earle of Lennox, a nobleman of a mightie minde; grandfather to our Soveraigne Lord, on the father fide; fought the battell of Linlithgow, for deliverie of King James the 5; alfo, where this magnifick Earle was flaine, moft highlie commended, prais'd, & lamented by his verie enemeis, the yeare of Chrift 1520.

If noble birth, with manie princlie pairts,
Imprinted in a prone & prudent fpreit
Augments, or yet perfectione more impairts,
To make the ouner alway exquifite;
  Then both thy birth, great gifts, & graces manie,
  Perfected thé, if perfect here be anie.

High lauded Lennox, for thy Lords releif,
Which tuife before in the perfecting fail'd;
Thy coufing King thé as his chiftane cheef,
The thrid tyme yet for to adventure vail'd;
  Thow boldl' obey'd, & hade perforce him fred,
  Hade nought thy forces fals or fearfull fled.

Yet there infamous flight, nor yet the foe,
Could force thé fant, nor from thy ftandart ftirr;
But lyke that brave Burgandean Count, they knoc
Thow fought alone, difdaining them & thir;
  While thow was flaine, & yet not vnrepented,
  And by thy foes both lauded & lamented.

59. **Gilbert Kennedie.**

Earle of Caſſills, a man of a great & a heroick ſpreit, by ane ambuſh intraped by his enemeis, about the tyme that the Earle of Lennox was ſlaine, the yeare of Chriſt 1526.

Holin., Scot. hiſt., pag. 314.

Leſlie, 9 book, pag. 422.

What ſhall, brave Count! as well thy virtues clam'd,
Thy countries kynd commend & doe decoir-thé?
Or for her lofs of ſuch a Lord now leam'd,
Shall ſhe thy praiſes overpaſt deploir-thé?
    No, no; thy worthe deſerveth ſo that ſhe
    Commend, decore, deplore, & praiſe thé too.

Thy valour, witneſs to the world, was
Demonſtrating thy magnitood of mynd,
Which, gallant Gilbert, to thy honor hes,
E're ſince decor'd thy Carrick & thy kinde;
    And tho the wicked they thy worth envi'd,
    Thy honor leiv's, tho by deceat thow di'd.

Audacious Earle, great & egregious youth!
Mavors his minion & the Muſes man;
Rememberance call with ane immortall mouth,
Doe what envy wnto thé contraire cane;
    Proclame thy praiſe, bevaile thy want & wrongs,
    Wnto thy honor in heroick ſongs.

60. ffrafcris.

Holin., Sco-
hift., pag. 335.

Leflie, 10 book.,
pag. 474.

A populus name, oft-tymes weill mereiting for there fervice in
the Common-wealth; ombefet with a multitude of the
Highland Clanns, the Lord Lovat, there cheeff, there
prefent, with three hundered of his name, flaine all in one
day, att one tyme, the yeare of Chrift 1544.

Much fortunate more famous was your falls,
Bold Fabians! that for your cities fake,
And in the veine of her environ'd walls
Your felvis a facred facrifice did make;
 And the three hundereth of a name, yet O!
 Great was your glore & praife to perifh fo.

And alfo was our number and our name,
And wills alfe willing for our countrie weell;
Bot Fates our fortoune did misfortoun'd frame,
And by the facill flitting of her weell;
 Nought wnto men, but leopards a prey,
 Wee fell three hunder Frazers in a day.

With forrane fors or ftrangers hade we ftrevin,
And loft our lives for this our lands releife,
The fatall fall that fure feirce Fates hes given,
Hade bein more to our glorie more our greiff;
 But to be flaine by fuch a favage fort,
 We fpight that after fpeeches fhould report.

61. John Stewart.

Called the doughtie Duke of Albanie, fone to Alexander Duke of Albanie, brother german to King James 2d, was Governour to King James 5; ane heroick Captane; a Prince, wife, circumfpect, and verie politique in all his proceedings; efter　　yeares government went to France, in the yeare of Chrift 1524.

Holin., Scot. hift., in the life of Ja. 5 pag.

Leflie, 9 book of our Scot. hift.

Well may thow, Worthie, for thy worth advance,
And but fufpicious of all pride prefume,
To march in front with ftout Rinald of France,
Or Regulus that race renoun'd in Rome;
　　Since that thy doeings did defigne, thow durft
　　Fight for thy force this famous or that furft.

The fierie face of Mars, the forcefull fift,
Nor yet of warr the wavering event,
Ne're could they make thé terrifi'd nor trift,
Nor carie thé as croft or difcontent;
　　Bot cheerfull ay, how things e're chang'd or chanc'd,
　　Thow paft them prudentlie, onpain'd, onpanc't.

For glorious dreds furnam'd thé doughtie Dook,
For th' executione, counfall, & fuccefs
Of all the exploits that to attempt thow took,
Condignlie thow collowded are no lefs;
　　So that the earth & th'aers all bordring bounds,
　　The fhoare & feas thy praifes fings & founds.

I

62. 𝕵𝖆𝖒𝖊𝖘 𝕾𝖙𝖊𝖜𝖆𝖗𝖙.

Holin., Scot.
hift., pag. 315.

Leflie, 9 book,
pag. 424, 425.

Commonlie caled the little Earle of Murray; was honorable,
wife, & famous amongſt manie Princes, for his manie virtues,
& many ambaſſages moſt happilie perform'd amongſt them.
Died in his caſtell Tarnaway, and floriſh'd the yeare of
Chriſt 1546.

When th' wſe of armes the raige of warr requir'd,
And per'lous plotts in practeis wee to put,
Thy martiall mynd ne're to attempt them tir'd,
And with the formoſt therto flew thy foot;
    Yet ever ſtill, fo reafon thé directed,
    That all thy facts but furrie thow effected.

And when for th' oake the olive branch did bude,
Or happie peace Bellonas place poſſeſt,
Thy councill quick, wyfe, godlie, grave & good,
Was thane defir'd, brave Barron, with the beſt;
    And as in warr thy prompt fprit was approv'd,
    So was in peace thy witt & learning lov'd.

Thy knowledge kith'd & courage kene concur'd,
When ather Mars or yet Minerva ment,
With counfall fhe, he with the facking fword,
To go to gall or grace the government,
    And witnes'd weell that valour, virtue, witt,
    Was all into a microcofmo knit.

63. **Sir John Borthwick.**

A Captane, for his vertue & valour, deerlie loved of his Prince, King James 5; and for his finceritie in profeffion of the gofpell, alfe mutch haited of the Roman Clergie, who, to exprefs there fpight, condemned him as ane heretick, and burnt his picture in Sanct Androis, himfelfe being then in France, the yeare of Chrift 1540.

Holin., Scot. hift., p. 322.

Leflie, 9 book, pag. 452.

Give that thy couraige, Captane, or thy caires,
Addvance the worfhipe of the Word divyne,
Ane ampler praife or pithier prepaires
For thé it is deficult to define;
 Since thow for that be merit was admir'd,
 And then to this a paffing zeall appear'd.

Th'effected facts and fortouns into France,
In ftraits with ftomach ftout, with ftrength extream,
And all atcheiv'd by chevalric, not chance,
Enucleats, & fo renouns thy name,
 That nought Columna, that accomplifht Knight.
 His honor hail'd hade to a greater hight.

And for thy pietie expreft before,
And woundrous zeall, it's doubtfull to decide,
Give honor'd with the good or hated more,
For thy difpyfing of the Popifh pryde;
 Who by decrees did thé to death condemne,
 And yet but burnt thy figour in a flame.

64. 𝕾𝔦𝔯 𝕯𝔞𝔟𝔦𝔡 𝕷𝔦𝔫𝔡𝔰𝔞𝔶.

Holin., Scot.
hift., in the
Cattalogue of our
Scotts Writters,
pag. 462.

Knight, of the Mount, Lord Lyon King of Armes; a worthie man, nottable and famous for his calling, & for his great felicitie in writting, and dexteritie in Scottifh Poefie, and foundrie of his works yet extant teftifie.   He florifhed the yeare of Chrift 1546.

Come, come, weill worthie, famous, & moft fit
To march among thir mightie men of fprits,
Thy Royall roume of right requyreth it,
And for thy worth thofe Worthies thé inveits,
  That of thy vene divyne, & virtues that
  Thy fpreit poffeft, they may participat.

When for ther King, ther countrie, freinds, or fame,
They meant to march & vadge a worthie warr,
Knight, King of Armes, thy pairts was to proclame,
Denunce, & dreedlefs to the duell darr
  The proudeft Princes and the Staits moft ftrong,
  That offer'd once to doe there countrie wrong.

High was thy honor with thy Prince & place,
And therfore rightlie thy renoun was rung;
But greater is thy glorie & thy grace,
For manie facred fong fo fweitlie fung;
  And worthie works, whofe lyck few fince or fine,
  To witnefs fuch a witt and vene divyne.

65. Pinkiefield.

Infortunatlie foughten & loost after the vauntguard, led by
 Archbald Dowglafs, Earle of Angous, hade defeat the first
 battell of the enemeis, the yeare of Christ, September 1547.

Holin., Scot.
hist., pag. 343.

Leslie, 10 book,
pag. 486.

Who could difcryve that doolfull deedlie day,
Or who that fatall and misfortoun'd feight
Wold as it was in veritie bewray,
And as no partie fpeak of it but fpight,
 Should fee it was nought valour that prevail'd,
 Nor our freinds force but fortoun then that fail'd.

For lyke a butt of brafs for to be broken
Impoffible, embattel'd ftood our bands,
Whill wrath divyne our wrongs on ws to wroken,
The victric wrang & honor from our hands;
 When aufull Angous hade the vauntguard winn,
 And for our force a glorious game begun.

O! but from thence what foull misfortoun fell,
And to what hight that maffacre did mount?
Whofe witt can writt, whofe tongue but tears can tell,
Or carlefs can that Cannas curts recount,
 Where fpent lay fpoil'd, more by fupernall pow'rs
 Then feight of foes, of all our force the flour's.

66. Archbald Douglass.

Holin., Scot.
hift., pag. 343.

Leflie in the
lyfe of King
James 5.

Earle of Angous, a couragious and noble Earle, in whom the nobilitie, martiall magnitude of mynd, hardinefs of harte & readinefs of hand of his generous anceftors, in defence of his countrie & invafione of the enemeis therof, cleirlie keithed, and was moft eminent in his dayes; & flooriſhed the yeare of Chrift 1547.

That worth wherat the worthieft did wonder,
Succeffively that his anceftors ſhew,
In voiting wife, in battell bolts of thunder,
The world receiv'd that valor it did view;
    Sic and behold in him hereditarie
    The honor of the Dowglafs houfs & heare.

There ever-wondrous valour to invade
There foes, & fervore fearlefs to defend,
The Countrie, Croun, & Prince there praifes fpred,
And there triumphs & trophes did extend;
    So from defert and like great martiall mynd,
    He now noe lefs from Fame does favour fynd.

For conftant courage in his countries caufe,
And fortitude in her defence to feight,
Alleadgance to his Lord & to his Lawes,
With hardinefs into his honors right,
    Affords him now alfe flooriſhing a fame,
    As anie one renouned of his name.

67. Gilbert Kennedie.

Earle of Caffills; a worthie Nobleman, ambaffador to France. With others of the nobilitie, died in Deip. the 15 day of September, nought but vehement fufpitione of poyfione, the yeare off Chrift 1558.

Holin., Scot. hift., pag. 362-364.

Leflie, 10 book, pag. 539.

In thé that old high honor of thine hous,
And all thy predicefsors paft appeare,
That gained the name of great & glorious,
By there heroick hands whill they were here;
    Since what in them fhew fingular does fhine
    Allone in thé, left Lord of all thy line.

A ritch ripe witt, a right refolved will,
And weell rul'd boldnefs in thy breaft was borne
To keith thy courage with thy martiall fkill,
And all thy other docings to adorne;
    Which for there wondrous worth & valor were
    Seconded feldome fince fo fingulare.

O! bot fuch worth did yet ne're want envie,
For fpightfull fpreits fuch perfect pairts difpife,
As thow in France did find & trewlie trie,
Difpatch'd with poifion, where, great Lord, thow lies
    Inter'd, and yet twyfe nottable renoun'd
    For worth & wrong gottne in the Gallick ground.

68. James Montgomerie.

Earle of Montgomerie, fone of that James, caled Montfieur De
    Lorge, a knight excellent, famous in the Civill Warrs of
    France; wrged to Juft by Henric the 2, King of France,
    kiled him with the fplinter of his fpear, and therafter (tho by
    the Prince himfelfe pardoned) againft promeis, by Queen
    Katharin de Medeces, att the feige of Donfron in Nor-
    mandie, was taken, & beheaded in Pareis, the yeare of
    Chrift 1574.

France on thy father did beftow her ftiles,
From fuch a root to raife to her a race,
With manors faire in meafure manie miles,
To entertaine his prefent port and place;
    Bot fatall for her found againes thy will,
    (Conjour'd to juft) when thow her King did kill.

And tho her Atlas by thy force did fall,
Who of the French did favour more his France?
Who gave more prooff of manhood mongft them all,
And with more valor did there warrs advance?
    Or which of them, in there religious warrs
    For Chrift, did carrie in his fkin more fkarrs?

Yet for thy fact, fo much again'ft thy mynd,
Quyt pardoned by the tranfperfed Prince,
France by her faith, both crwell & wnkynd,
Smot of thy head bot nought thy honor fince;
    And for noe fault thine in effect bot fain'd,
    Thow that reward for thy good fervice gain'd.

69. Sir James Sandelands.

Lord of Sanct John and of Calder, Knight; for his valor, his
virtues, religione & faith, famous.   Floorifhed the yeare of
Chrift 1560.

Thy fpreit and prudence made thy Prince imploy
Thy perfone, prompt to punifh & reprefs
Enormities of thofe that did annoy,
And cruciat the countries quietnefs;
　　Imploiment fitt bot for a paffing fpreit,
　　And thow the man to manadge it moft meit.

Experience prov'd th' opinion of the Prence,
Tane of thy virtues wanifht noucht in vaine;
For great deeds done and done with dilligence,
What could b' expected they expreft it plaine,
　　And did declare, for Countrie, Croun, & King,
　　Non hade more hape nor heart in hazarding.

Vn-conquer'd countrie for thy croun oft croft,
Minerv-like mother of fuch martiall men,
As none may of more bold nor better boft,
Or of more wife & worthie warriors then,
　　Account thy Calder, for his famous fights,
　　One of thy Captanes & couragious Knights.

K

70. **Andrew Stewart.**

Lord of Ocheltrie, a nobleman as virtuous, fo valorous; one
trew profeffor of the Evangell, & of a good, godlie, &
charitable life.   Floorifhed the yeare of Chrift 1561.

To come of Kings & doe from Dooks difcend,
Be thefe the trew nots of nobilitie;
Who will before thé for a place pretend,
Or princli'r prove him by his pedegree,
    Since thy defcent thow deulie dow deduce
    From that thrice great fucceffor of the Bruce?

But to be noble born and be of blood,
Wnto the ritcheft that great reg'ouns raigne,
And yet to be but gifts & graces good,
Such are wnto there ftocks & ftates a ftaigne;
    But noble birth, vernifht with virtuous warks,
    Are onlie of trew noblemen the marks.

Bot thy good lyfe, but all ambition blind,
Which in high born oft vertues eyes out blots,
Which one moft meek, yet one magnanime mind,
Was of thy trew nobilitie the nots;
    For vertue does wndoubtedlie adorne,
    The bafe birth much, but more the nobler borne.

71. James Stewart.

Earle of Murray and Pryor of Sanct Andrews; Regent in the
minoritie of our Soveraigne Lord, King James of Great
Brittane; a nobleman of a judicious, quick, and wirking
witt; was flaine in Linlithgow, the 12 January, the yeare of
Chrift 1570.

Thy Soveraigne fifter, and thy gracious Queen,
Did daylie double on thé dignities,
And nought in fhow, bot foorlie, made befeen
To thé her bountie & benignities;
    And for thy pairts, experience was plane,
    How for her goodnefs thow was great againe.

Thy nature, name, & thy nobilitie,
Cleen knaleg'd by thy courfes made them knowne,
And in thy purpofe for the pollicie,
What thow hes been abrod thy broot is blaune;
    And what thy aimes & etlings be the end,
    Who knows not now, wherto they then did tend.

Thy fortone, fate, & by th' effects, thy faith,
Did fho thy charitie into thy charge;
Thy deep defignes, thy doeings & thy death,
Thy laud and life are left ws foe att large;
    And by fuch penns profound fet furth before,
    That few will mint to fay fo much, non more.

72. Walter Lundie.

Laird of Lundie in Fife, be one vninterrupted fucceffion reckoned, and fuppofed to be the tenth from King William; therfore, and for his oun worthinefs & honorable fucceffion from himfelfe, a knight memorable and renoun'd. He flooriſhed the yeare of Chriſt 1567.

The qualities that could decore a King,
A Counfallor, a Captane, or a Knight,
Egregious old man, were efpy'd to fpring,
And lent a luſtre in thy lyfe & light;
    To bring from bywayes featlie to reforme,
    And waene from vice the ill ones & enorme.

Such qualities commendable became,
Kinde Knight, thy kinde deriv'd from noble race;
Since thow are faid defcended of the fame,
(No little to thy glorie and thy grace)
    And by deduction lineall & difcent,
    From that ſtout King the Lyon, tearm'd the Tent.

Religious Lundie, whill this lyfe thow leiv'd,
So prudentlie thow ponder'd it & paiz'd,
That in't were all the anceſtors wife reviv'd,
A fpeciall point to make the (paſt) be praiz'd;
    As thow alive beloved wes alone,
    No lefs than they (tho altogether) gone.

73. Mathew Stewart.

Earle of Lennox, Governor, & Goodfir on the father-fide, to our
Soveraigne Lord now reignand; and a Prince endued with
all the noble, heroick, & princlie pairts pertinent to a
perfone of his qualitie; traiterouflie flaine in Stirling, 4 September, the yeare of Chrift 1571.

Great Mathew, if my mufe (as minde) hade means
To pen thy good pairts & t'exprefs thy praife,
As to thy perfone, place, & fprite pertanies,
Moft worthie, wife, and valorous alwaife,
  She fhould portraie, in polifht poems thane,
  A maiklefs modell of a matchlefs man.

Whofe princlic fprcit all vulgar witts o'rewent,
Whofe judgment found, fure fatl'd, fharpe, & fage,
And whofe great actions alway excellent
Thy tyme outftript, ant'occupi'd thy age,
  And of thy fprcit paft prooffs before thy prime,
  That few attain'd wnto, into there tyme.

Whofe lyfe among the leiving bred fuch love,
Whofe graces was foe with the good agreing,
Whofe murder did s'immoderat murning move,
And fuch a during dollor att thy deing,
  And whofe great gifts was fingular & fuch,
  That non can cleer them, nor commend too much.

74. Arthour Forbes.

Brother to William, Lord Forbes; a man of fingular witt, ftout-
nefs of heart, & reddinefs of hand fufficientlie famous.
Was flaine by one of the name of Gordoune att Tilliangous,
the yeare of Chrift 1571.

Why doe the Brittons brave it out & boaft
Of Mordreds deeds, or of King Arthours acts,
Which non for current credits, and almoft
The credence from there trueft ftories takes?
  So of there force they fabl'd have, & faine
  Prodig'ous deeds, works wonderful & vaine.

Bot mark yow me, & Arthour heir behold,
His match in ftrength, bot not his mate in ftate,
His feer in fight and to abide als bold,
In everie battell, bargane, & debeat;
  Yea, for to hazard hardie, and als able
  As Lancelot or Triftram, of his Table.

Yet Arthours ftate nor his ftupendious ftrength,
His knighthood nor his courage keept wncroft;
Bot by bad luck and fatall lot att length
Born doun in battell, there his lyfe he loft;
  So I, with nev'r wrong'd valor e're invy'd,
  Fell in the feild, among my foes, & dy'd.

75. John Erskin.

Earle of Marr, a wyfe and worthie nobleman; for his fufficiencie,
witt, & worthinefs, chofen Governor in the lefs aige of the
moft excellent, high, & mightie Prince James, King of Great
Brittane.   He floorifh'd the yeare of Chrift 1572.

My mufe waike wings & too too fklender fkill,
Durft they prefume to park, or preafs to pitch,
Wpon the hight & head of Honors hill?
Or fuch a tafk onterminable tuche,
    As thy great valor, virtue, witt, & worth,
    Into fo bafe a forme for to fett forth?

The world in warr fhould then thy valour view,
And thy furpaffing pictie in peace,
In this inteer, in that tri'd ftout tri'd trew,
And knightlie conftant into everie cace,
    Which gallant gifts and goodlie graces great,
    Got thé the fteer of this monarchik ftate.

That honor yet heis'd nought too high thy heart,
Nor did promotion puff thé wpe with pride;
But as a Peer, a Prince (praife-worthie pairt)
Juft ballanc'd thy behaviour did abyde;
    So both a leige & lator of the Law,
    Moft moderat thé Calidon did knaw.

76. Sir William Kirkaldie.

Lord of Grange; a Knight in the conſtitutione of his bodie
ſtrong, & for the magnanimitie of his minde, almoſt matchleſs.   He flooriſhed the yeare of Chriſt 1572.

Yow Latine Lords & great men of the Greeks,
Achilles, Tancred, Turnus, Telamon,
Whom of the princes of the Poets ſpeeks,
And for there provefs praiſed, I ſuppone;
   This Guillam of the Grange, als ſtout, als ſtrong,
   Your compeer, knights, yow muſt admitt among.

For here he one as braveſt, beſt, and bold,
In monomachees and for ſingle fights,
One chear of cheef in honors houſs ſhould hold,
With theſe our countrie beſt combattant knights,
   Wha for his perſone, practics, pith and ſpreit,
   As ane of theſe great martialiſts hes merit.

At home, a feild, in fight, a foot, on horſs,
His knightlie courage conqueſt him commend,
And all-where made him famous for his force,
Yet could it nought eveit a vofull end;
   For too too much eſteeming of his ſtrength,
   Onluckilie, loſt him his lyfe att length.

77. Alexander Hume.

Lord Hume, High Chamberland of Scotland; for ftrength and
perfectione of perfone, & manie excellent graces of the
minde, a nobleman moft renowned.   Died the yeare of
Chrift 1573.

Now thow in little compafs are compacted,
A worthie Captane of a ventrous clann,
That lieving nothing but the laurell lacked,
According to the minde to make the man;
 Excellent great, exceeding glorious,
 Renoun'd, eternall, & notorious.

For both great power, preheminence, & place,
Great wealth, great worth, with grave & greater wit,
Conglomerat agreed all to grace
Thy famous facts, for thy great fortouns fitt;
 Yet ftill thy fprite afpyring did prefume
 To thy great haps t' add greater hopes, great Hume.

And hade thow from a facilnes been frie,
And nought too much too noble of thy minde,
Wherto the great & better fort they be
Too oft by corrupt counfallors enclin'd.
 Non of that aige, of thy eftate or yeares,
 Hade pre-excel'd or paft thé of thy peers.

L.

78. 𝕲ilcſpick 𝕮ambell.

Earle of Argyle, Lord Campbell & Lorn, Great Juſtice of Scotland: a nobleman religious, and moſt emulus of his
prediceſſors noble valour & vertues.　Flooriſhed the yeare
of Chriſt 1573.

If from antiquitie, eſtate, or ſtile,
Reſpect or praiſe, to place or perſone ſprings,
Gilleſpick, then, to thé and thy Argyle,
 Sumtyme the ſeat & antient court of Kings)
　　Muſt needs renoun and great regaird aryſe,
　　Since that was old, theſe great, & thow was wife.

From which great witt, great zeall and pitie ſprang,
Great gifts that grac'd & did the countrie good;
With valour readie to revenge her wrang,
And ſpreit to prop her when ſhe ſtouping ſtood;
　　Soore ſoleid ſignes thy obſervance that ſhaws,
　　To God, the King, the Countrie, & the Lawes.

For in Religion thow was reverent,
And her corruptions cairfull to correct;
Vnto th' Authoretic obedient,
And to the Laws hade ſpeciall reſpect;
　　Laſt to thy Countrie honor, and behove,
　　Non leiv'd (great Lord) that hade a greater love.

79. Scotland.

Her invective complaint againft Suaden for the monftruous,
inhumane, & onmanlie murder of the Scottifh regiment,
wnder the conduct of Collonell Ruthven, att Wefenberge,
the yeare of Chrift 1574.

When that great Rufhe, whom thow calls rude, arofe,
With force t' afflict thé for his right of ree,
Then thow them in thy caftells did inclofe,
Whill that thow got fupport of men from me;
    Which favage Swaden (I muft fay) I fend,
    From barbrous foes more brutifh freinds to fend.

Livoniane volfs, tho ne're fo wood or wild,
Nor horrid tiggars of the Hircan hills,
Who of the brutifh beafts moft fterne are ftil'd,
Crofs nought there kinde nor there companions kills;
    Bot gain'ft there kinds antagonifts contends,
    And force there foes & fauns wpon there freinds.

Bot thow, more favage by a hundered fife,
More brutifh, bloodie, cruell & more curft,
Nor what the witt of wifdome could divyfe,
Or Nature yet invented for the worft;
    That in thy wolfifh woodnefs did devour,
    Thy freinds farr fetch'd for thy defence before.

80. Alexander Cuningham.

Called the good Earle of Glencairne; a nobleman vertuous,
godlie, zealous, and very forward in the tyme of the altera-
tione of the Religion.   He died the yeare of Chriſt 1574.

That thow was one of theſe, religious Lord,
Glade is thy ghoſt, and now Glencairne does glore,
Who did concurr and conſtantlie accord,
From Romiſh roots Religion to reſtore;
     And from all forms phantaſtick did refine
     Her with the warrand of the Word divyne.

No faćtions heir nor forces fetch'd from France,
Nor the pretended terror of the Laws
Made thé divert, nor werie to advance
Into thy Chriſt and thy Creators cauſs;
     Bot conſtant ſtill, couragiouſlie & keen,
     Thow ever was a ſharp aſſertor feen.

Who for there countrie or there freinds doe fight,
Bot limitat and meaſur'd glorie gains,
When thé adventures for religions right,
Eternall treaſure & triumph obtaines;
     With no leſs honor heere & hes in heavne,
     One wncorrupted croune of glorie givne.

81. George Gordone.

Earle of Huntlie, Lord Gordone & Badzenoch, &c.: A mightie,
wiſe, and moſt noble Earle.

A ſeſſion grave of all the Graces ſet,
Long cairfull did conſult & then decreed;
Prevented tho thow pay'd to death thy debt,
And att the noonday of thy doing died,
    That thow yet as a ſemi-Sune ſhould ſhine
    Into thy ſeed now leiving of thy line.

And thé from groſs forgetfulneſs to guarde,
Thay convocat rotundlie in a ring,
The ſpirite of each old poetick barde,
By courſes encomâſtick ſongs to ſing
    About thy herſs, leaſt tearing Tyme eſſay
    To weare thé, Worthie, out of mynd away.

The ſubject of there oft reitred ſong
Is ſpeciall praiſe & thé defunct thy fame,
To vindicat thy vertues from the wrong,
That future times & dayes may doe to them;
    Thay conſtantlie this kind of courſe contane,
    There where they end, there they begin againe.

82. Thomas Menyzies.

Of Petfoddells, Major of the Burgh of Aberdeen, & Comptroller
of Scotland; a man for manie good gifts verie memorable.
Floorifhed the yeare of Chrift 1576.

As manie raife to be renoun'd in Rome,
That never tried ther fortouns in the fight;
Bot in the pollicie emploi'd att home,
Paft nought the ports, nor from the cities fight;
    Yet in fupporting the Republick pain'd,
    As th' arm'd there glorie in there gouns thay gain'd.

So for thy good defignes and great defert,
Thy witt moft fharp, moft fage and folid feen,
And proof'd in th' vrbane pollicie expreft,
As manie hade of thy forbears been,
    Thow as the wife and worthieft alwaies,
    Directed the Abredeans all thy daies.

And by thy carrage, conqueft and acquyr'd
(Moft fortunat) more favorars & fame,
Nor all that in that province hade impir'd,
Of whatfo'r eftate, renoun, or name:
    So for thy hap and honors yet thy Oois
    Have right and reafone juftlie to rejoyce.

83. John Lord Lyon of Glams.

Great Chancellar of Scotland; a nobleman nottable for many
noble pairts; a lover of letters & a patron of learned men;
& one for his manie fingularities worthie of eternall memorie.
Was flaine the yeare of Chrift 1577.

Shall I the progrefs of thy proav's pen,
There renoun'd ryfing from there root & race,
Since by much mercit manifaft to men,
Peremptorlie in tyme of warr and peace,
  Or finge thofe fignes in youth that fhow in age,
  Thow fhould lyke Cato kithe in counfall fage.

Trialls of the teftificats of thame,
The tongue of treuth, Times ftories, trew hes told,
And left nought to the faeth of flowing Fame
Your names nor high renouns to be inrol'd,
  Bot there are printed with fuch precious plumes,
  That nere corrupts, nor cankers, nor confumes.

Since thow in thame and they in thé are grac'd,
Thow grave great Lion, Leader of our Laws,
For thy perpollent fprite and prudence plac'd
Cheeff Chancellour of this Kingdome, who not knaws;
  I leave your lauds, leift fum fuppone I praife
  Your ghofts (among the good) that non gainfaies.

84. William Keith.

Brother-german to George, Earle Marifhall of Scotland, now
leiving; a noble youth of fingular hope & expectatione
onhappily flaine att Geneva, the yeare of Chrift 1577.

O with what woes the world thy want bevaills,
And with what greiff the godlie for thé groans!
O what a forrow all the faige affaills,
And malcontented for thy murther moans!
  Yea, yet how cairfull thy deir countrie cry's
  Her fweit fone loft att Geneve left yet lyes.

Exceiding wife, grave, good and godlie youth,
Thy fauciat foule hurt with a holy love,
To th' only trew Teftator & the treuth
A conftant motione in thy mynd did move
  To green to goe to Geneve to be nurifh'd,
  Where then His word & faith moft freely florifh'd.

O bot great Dis! that dragon old difdain'd,
And of fuch fervent faith affraid he fret it,
Therfore he reftlefs raig'd and to reftrain'd,
Laid all his lines to take thy life and let it;
  Which devlifh purpofe, ploted & projeckted,
  A hellifh hand infamuflie effeckted.

85. William Keith.

Mafter of Marfhall; father to George, now Earle Marfhall; a
nobleman nottablie indu'd, both godlie, grave, and good.
In the flour of his aige, before his father, died the yeare of
Chrift 1580.

Scrutator! quick and curious to kno
This moft renoun'd, his nature & his name,
His godlinefs and his great graces, go
Search in the fcrolls and brazen book of Fame,
    Where thow fhall fee fign'd this fententious foume,
    Lord William Keith's (too mean) the marble tombe.

Then fhall thow find, in facound phraife fet furth,
His parents progrefs and there progenie;
With ther's his works, witt, virtues and his worth,
Mark't with the manufcript of memorie;
    A monument for to remember ay
    His houffes honor to that dreadfull day.

There hes the great Grynean Apollo
Perfeétlie pen'd his more nor mercit praife;
Then after him the maiden Mufes follo,
With laurat layes above the round's they raife,
    And with the force of never failing Fame,
    This happie heros hes renoun'd his name.

M

86. Sir Adam Gordone.

Of Auchindoun; wncle, on the father fyde, to George, Marquis of
Huntlie, that now is; a captane comparable to anie of what
qualitie foever in his tyme, as his great and good fuccefs oft
teftifi'd.   He floorifhed the yeare of Chrift 1580.

What Generall might for his martiall glorie,
Or Captane know'n could for his courage clame
A ftall or ftation in th'eternall ftorie,
That Tyme hes trufted to the faith of Fame,
    But thow, audacious Adam, Honors heire,
    Might with thame for thy knightly parts compaire?

Witt to advyfe, a reafone to refolve,
And fortitude with forwardnefs conforme,
All danger, dreed & doubts for to diffolve,
With a borne boldnefs in the ftrongeft ftorme,
    As anie Captane knoun or found before thé;
    Great Gordone, thefe does grace, croun & decore thé.

With forces few fkilfull performed feats,
Th'opinion of thy provefs did approve,
Thy ftomack fteel'd ftill ftouteft into ftraits,
Allowance large, libralitie & love;
    With favour to thy followers & freinds,
    Above thefe all (great Captane) thé commends.

87. William Keith.

Great Marſhall of Scotland; a nobleman of ſingular pietie, prudence & good lyfe; outleiving his ſone William, and his
nepote; ſlaine att Geneve, extreamlie old, moſt holelie
depairted, in the yeare 1581.

Moſt mightie Marſhall, for thy mynd & means,
Sometymes lyke Telamon in tender yeares,
A galeated gallent as perteans
Thy perſone and thy place among thy peers;
    Bot nottable lyke Neſtor now in age,
    Perander, Pittacus, or Solon ſage.

What valor, ſtrength & armes, when thow was young,
Did for to make thé famous in the fields!
Thy prudencie, from long experience ſprong,
Wnto thy aige now no leſs honor yeelds,
    And maks the wiſeſt for lyke wiſdome wiſh,
    O happie Earle! in all bot not in this.

That th' aig'd ears did heir, thy eies behold,
For e're, alace! a loſs to be lamented,
Thy hopefull heyre to end when thow was old,
And nepot be by violence prevented;
    Two greeſſs too grave for anie breaſt to bear,
    If wit divine & reaſone ruled not there.

88. James Crightoun.

Of Clunie; a gentleman for the gift of the bodie & graces of the
mynd to the moſt admir'd, Admirable; invied therfore in
Mantua by the Dooks ſone therof, by night diſhonorablie
ſlaine, to the eternall ignominie of that houſe, the yeare of
Chriſt 1581.

How exquiſite eaven wold the wiſeſt wiſh,
Or curious crave a man wnto there minde!
All that both wold was to be viewde in this,
And in the compaſs of his corps confin'd;
    Of compoſitione comlie and a cre'ture,
    As if thriſe ſyn'd & re-reform'd by Nature.

A perſonage compleit in all his pairts,
To Marſs a match, a man wnto the Muſes;
And ſo excelling others in all airts,
Which for advancment, witt, or valor wſes,
    That France her rareſt witts & ripeſt than,
    And Italie it ſelfe admir'd this man.

But jealous yet that his egregious gifts
Should all the praiſe of there beſt ſprits ſuppreſs,
Which ſo aloft th' Italians laud wplifts,
A ſpightfull Prince of Mantua, merciles,
    By treacherie (ſtill to that State a ſtaine)
    This youth, a wonder to the World, hes ſlaine.

89. James Douglaſs.

Earle of Mortoun, Regent; a nottable example of the inſtabilitie
& the changes of men and mortall things; ſuffred in the
yeare of Chriſt 1581.

What prejudice is pleaſure to the ſpreit,
That purlie is to pietie diſpos'd!
How hurtfull's honor wnto infincit,
That therin as there greateſt good rejoyc'd!
  And how pernicious & diſpleaſant proves,
  Preferments high that humane minds ſo mov's!

This honorable, wiſe and worthie Count,
Once happie thought in everie outward eie,
Whoſe wiſdome did advance & merits mount
Him to be nixt the greateſt in degree,
  Fand honor, pleaſure & preferment great
  Vndid and was deſtructione to his ſtate.

Thus there is nothing firme into the Fates,
And there events wirks wonderfull & ſtrange;
Nor is ther ſtable ſtanding in Eſtates,
But all by courſe is chaned wnto change;
  And of this all, croſt with converſions than,
  Moſt nottable this mortall maſs is man.

90. Esme or Aimes Stewart.

Duke of Lennox; fone to John Stewart, Lord of Obigney in
France, Great Marfhall there &c.; come in Scotland the
yeare 1579: fingularlie beloved & honored by his Majeftie;
firft made Earle and then Dook of Lennox, which now his
fone Lodowick, a noble Prince, enjoys.   Florifhed the
yeare of Chrift 1582.

Grand Lord, thy grace lyes in ane urne nought ample,
From thy goodfir and from thy grandfirs great,
Whofe vertues was worth for a tomb, a temple,
Of purple porphire, or of polifht jeat;
    Non bot will grant that they were great, & thow
    Non will deny, or no lefs nobl'd now.

The favors that thy Fathers fand in France,
And honors done to dignifie them there,
They clame nought to, nor came they to, by chance,
Nor were there titles toome nor idle aire,
    That fome for fhois in regifters inferts,
    No, but they got them for there great deferts.

There thair's was great, bot thine more high was heir,
Non by a Prince could be promov'd to more,
For from a Count a Dook, thy cufing deir
Created thé that thow was nought before;
    Yet thy promotione, place & ftatlie tittle,
    T' his Grace goodwill & love to thé was litle.

91. John Cockburne.

Of Ormeistoun; a honorable and religious gentleman; verie
dilligent & zealous in the work of the Reformatione. He
dyed the yeare of Chrift 1583.

Firft famous found, thy lyfe was for thy lyne,
From men of noe mean mynds deduc'd & drowen;
Then for thy witt, fenfe, fingular art thow foon
Came cleerlie, Cockburn, to thy countrie knowne:
    And lyke a citie on a mountane fhew,
    With knightlie courage, Chriftiane care in yow.

Enlightned with the light that lieds to lyfe,
And with the fervour of the faith inflam'd,
In thofe religious ftormie ftours and ftrife,
Thow keept the Congregatione whill it calm'd;
    For perrell, promeifes, expence, nor pains,
    From thy firme faith noe nought a grane weight gaines.

Thy bloodfhed footh'd & taught this true, I know,
When curtfoot Bodwell lyke a limmer lay,
(A traitour tried and a tirrane too)
And wnawarrs did wound thé on the way;
    Thy fame nor honor yet nought hurt, no, no,
    Bot growne more great and feminats more fo.

92. Robert Lord Seytoune.

Cheiff and Lord of his antient name and famelie; a worthie
nobleman naturallie endewed with manie nottable and moſt
noble pairts.   Flooriſhed the yeare of Chriſt 1584.

The reaſons ſhould ariſe from that renoun'd,
That Berricks fort ſo faithfullie defended,
Long ſince with honor and triumph entomb'd,
Wherewith thow could condignlie be commended;
     If thow hade nought ſuch actione of thy oune,
     To cauſe thé be (from him thou'r come of) knowne.

His famous faith, thy facts maks thé and him,
Whill the diſloyall droun'd for ever die,
Into the ſeas of gloric faiſlie ſwim,
And for your merits there immortall be;
     Thus thy deſerts aſſiſts his ſunn to ſhine,
     And his does helpe to honor thé in thine.

Thy Father grand, that ſtout & loyall Lord,
(Altho foull warrs did to that worthie wrang)
His countrie with ſuch ſtore of Knights decor'd,
Thy parents all that from his perſone ſprang;
     That endleſs were to name or number heir,
     Yet in thy perſone praiſed all appeare.

93. Hugh Montgomerie.

Earle of Eglintowne; ane heroick nobleman; flaine att Annak,
the yeare of Chrift 1586.

How greatlie Nature thé her graces gave,
And liberallie her bleffings did beftow,
So plentifull did all mens fight perceave,
From fo good gifts lyke good effects to flow;
    And as they highlie honor'd thé that hade them,
    So pleafur'd they thy countrie where thow fpred them.

That little fpace that wrong & wraith hade fpair'd,
Brave Lord, thy lyfe difpightfullie onfpoil'd;
Works worthie of the wifeft know'n declair'd,
Invtilie thow tint no tyme bot toil'd;
    And aim'd for all or each one of thofe ends,
    For countrie, king, for honor, faith or freends.

But how all thefe were nottablie anoi'd,
(When hatefull hands hade bath'd them in thy blood)
And judg'd themfelv's injur'd, that nought enjoy'd
Thy haires when gray, whofe green began fo good;
    I pafs of purpofe to the profound pen,
    Of Mars, Mercure, or the Mufes then.

N

94. John Johnstone.

Of that Ilk; a Barron, cheef of that name, and Warden of the
Weſt Marches.   Flooriſhed the yeare of Chriſt 1587.

Cheeff born be birth and Captane of a Clann,
All from the womb ws'd & invr'd to armes;
Prompt with the ſpear to prick & plaic the man,
Amongſt the midſt and loudeſt of allarms,
       Wrongs or invaſions of the Engliſh, oft
       That reſt there reſt, repoſe & ſlumbrings ſoft.

To cooll the fervours of his hot ſpur'd freinds,
And in there furie to affront his foes,
God gave him witt that the moſt brutiſh bends,
And ſtrength to ſtrick even att the boldeſt bloes;
       O! happie he that hade concurring ſtill,
       With wiſdome worth & t'wſe them well at will.

And O! ye freinds, how fortunat to find,
And get a guide grac'd (as with graces grave);
With manhood too and to mantain'd a mind,
That bandide braggs could neither bend nor brave;
       But of more doing delt with, or if darr'd,
       Still di'mond-like, more hammered more hard.

95. Archbald Dowglas.

Earle of Angous (called the Good); ane ſingular and nottable
nobleman in his daies; indu'd with many virtues; left with
all the godlie ane veray great and eminent dolor at his
death.   Floriſhed the yeare of Chriſt 1588.

Give thow, that hade within thy breaſt imbrac't
The charities concomitat with all
Theſe gifts the good and that the greateſt grac't,
The Virtues wiſelie cal'd the Cardinall,
    May not be judg'd for happie heir, who then
    Shall ſo be ſaid amongs the ſones of men?

The firſt three ſacrad in thy ſoull ſoor ſeas'd,
Baſs thoughts, low hopes, and inward ills exill'd;
And thy cheeff perfeᴄt power thy reaſone rais'd
O're all that is eſteem'd or earthlic ſtil'd,
    T' aſcend and ſoare o're the Celeſtiall Signs,
    Diſdaining all as droſs bot divyne things.

With theſe three firſt, the four laſt by th' effeᴄts
Of all hes made thé as effeᴄted fear'd;
Which after death, as thy dew right ereᴄts
(What in thy lyfe renoun began & rear'd)
    Eternall tropheas & immortall fraims,
    Wheratt the aᴄtive honor ever aimes.

96. Sir James Halyburtoun.

Tutor of Petcur; Prepofite of Dundie; Captane of the Kings
men of arm's; ane refolved fouldier; ane cowragious and a
fkilfull Captane, as manie experiences taught in his tyme.
Floorifhed the yeare of Chrift 1588.

Whan aither glorie, praife, applaus or fame,
Thy countries Campiouns or her Knights does crave,
Come Captane, come thow & caft in thy clame,
And nought the laft nor leaft among the leave;
  For thy defarts in monie dangrous read
  Shall to prove perfect thy petitions plead.

The Frenchmens force & Englifh too att once,
That both t'incroach wpon thy countric came,
Wnder whofe burdens grave aggreev'd thé groans;
Whill that incens'd and foric for the fame
  Thow boldlie both thofe did debell, & broke
  Th' wnright'ous rackles of the Romifh yoke.

Therfore the Firth, the Forth, the Tweed, the Tay,
Our Ocean & the great Grampiane hills,
The World as witnefs of thy vertues thay,
They with thy fame & nought officious fills;
  And makes the ftouteft that does reid thy ftorie,
  T'admire thé both & emulat thy glorie.

97. **Patrick Lord Lindfay.**

And Bires; a nobleman verie religious, moft conftant, moft cowragious and wife.   He floorifh'd the yeare of Chrift 1589.

When that with fhifme rent was this foil afunder,
And with two pow'rs perponderous depreft,
That with lyke furie (as from heaven flees thunder)
The bulk of this divyded State diftreft,
    Thow kith'd alfe conftant as couragious there,
    In helping them to whom thow did adhere.

Thus, all inflam'd & in a factious fire,
Thy countrie cumbers kindl'd & increft;
Whill thefe two parties plaid for the impire,
Our mother looked out of meafure moeft,
    And when fhe counts all gone thy courage grew,
    As Leith, Longfide, Creeche & Carbarrie knew.

Yet Janus phane, faft bolted wp and clos'd,
When from the raige of warr the rulers reft,
Thow did fufpend thy fpeer to peace difpos'd,
And no few differs by difcretion dreft;
    So try'd thow ftout whill thefe wproars remain'd,
    And then in peace no lefs thy perfone pain'd.

98. Sir M. Montgomrie.

The fone of James, Monfieur De Large; in the laft Civill Warrs
of France, for his fortitude and good fervice done to Henrie
the 4, a man moft nottable; flaine att Dole, the yeare of
Chrift 1590.

This martiall and mightie man att armes,
When arm'd among his foes from foot to front;
The tyme of France religious allarms,
So warlick was, that all the wulgar wont
    He hade been Marfs, that great, grim god of warr,
    His force in feights, his acts fo awfull are.

Lyke Haniball, or Trojan Hector, he,
Difdaining death and dreidfull danger, drew
With much admiring, each cavallars eie,
His wondrous valour in thofe Warrs to wiew;
    And as tha'all wordring weived, fo tha'all advance,
    And well compaired him with the Peers of France.

For, as ftout Henric, ftomachat and ftrong,
Late Flour of France, and once Roomes errors tried
His loyaltie, his love, and labours long
Into his fervice, cre att Dole he died;
    So that great Prince himfelfe proclam'd his praife,
    And thus flaine lyes, one of his fheilds he faies.

99. John Erskine.

Of Dun; a honorable Barron; religious, wife, and in the work of
the Reformation ane moft zealous & painfull.   Floorifhed
the yeare of Chrift 1591.

Senator grave & Superintendant fage,
Refpected fo for prudence with the peers,
And honor'd for the honor of thy aige;
To fuch a greatnefs groun & grouth of yeares,
    As few fall fight or ftand with thé att ftrife,
    For fo weell led & fo long liv'd a life:

Then from which of thy gifts fall I begin,
Whilks, whill I gaized on, great and greater grow,
So that my Mufe a maine is entered in,
From whence fuch floods of thy perfections flow,
    That her conceapt chofe ftore of matter choaks,
    So worthie yet that all her pen provoaks?

Thy witt devoted to the Cuntrie well,
And conftant cleaving to the State in ftorme,
Thy holie heart, lyke Phineas, full of zeall,
In Church effaires things faultie to reforme,
    And of thy Faith thy facts perfected then,
    Well witnefs now thow was a worthie man.

100. Sir John Campbell.

Of Caddell; ane worthie and ane honorable Knight; ſhot and
ſlaine in his oun houſs by ane wnknowen enemie, the yeare
of Chriſt 1592.

This Knight deare to his Countrie, to his Clann,
And to the good and godlie gracious ay;
One both well mix'd but better mov'd, a man
(Tho full of worth) tane wickedlie away;
    While as ſecure he dream'd nought of his death,
    A pellet pearſt and did abredge his breath.

No manifaſted foe, nor man of mark,
Of note or noble minde, of pow'r or ſpreit,
Would give there word wnto ſo wile a wark,
Much leſs be att ſuch boutcherie albeit;
    There was much blood, huge fyre & harſhip ſtrange,
    But pitie ſpilt and rais'd in thé revenge.

No! bot ſome baſtard ſpreit oppon'd to thoſe,
That nought what honor was nor knighthood knew,
To currie court and credit with his foes,
Deceatfullie this Knight of Caddell ſlew;
    A feeble faɛt that ſtill reproach ſall raiſe
    To th'aɛtor, and wnto the patient praiſe.

101. James Stewart.

Earle of Murray, Lord Abernethie, Lord of Downe and Sanct
Colme. Flooriſhed in the yeare of Chriſt 1592.

If all the knighthood & the counts of France,
With all thoſe that from Rome to Carthage came,
(Whom for there worth wiſe writters does advance
And with renoun lies noted by there name),
    Were to give muſters into Mars his green,
    Nor thow non ſould more ſingular be ſeen.

Nought Abſalom, ſo for his beutie blaizde,
Nor Iſraells Saul, ſo honor'd for his hight,
Nought Peleus ſone, for pith & ſpreit ſo prais'd,
Nor Milo, for his magnitood & might,
    Nought Hector, Hercules, nor Hanniball,
    In ſtature was more ſtraight, more trime, nor tall.

And yet thy outward parts that paſt compaire
Wes bot the cadge or cace that did inclood
(The excellent and perfect figour faire
Of the moſt glorious God, moſt great, moſt good)
    Th' eſſentiall ſoul, pure, ſubteill & celeſt,
    With all the graces beutified & bleſt.

O

102. James Colvill.

Appearand of Weems; a youth for his perfpicuous prudence,
pietie, faire form & fortitude, of great expectatione; in the
flour of his aige dyed, the yeare of Chrift 1594.

Thy worthie fyr was Mars his fone it feems,
Since fo declair'd his deeds into his dayes
But with thy valour thy grave wifdome (Weems)
Does evidentlie witnefs and bewraies;
  Thow was Minerva's child, the Mufes chofe,
  The palme of prudence & of reafon rofe.

Firlt Fife gave fuck and France it fed thé fine,
Heir firft to grow thy grace and guifts begane,
There florifhed the fruits of thy ingine,
And perfect rype there plac'd & prov'd thé man;
  Sanct Valerie thy virtew wieued & wondred,
  When battring her th' Iberian bombards thundred.

But hade the Weirds that greateft worth envies,
Or fpightfull Facts with pities eyes efpy'd,
(How in thy youth thow worthie was & wife)
And gevene thé tyme for to extend & try'd,
  Thay hade feen in thé things wondrous & more,
  Nor in fyve hunder they hade found before.

103. Sir Patrick Gordone.

Of Auchindoune; wncle to George, Marquefs of Huntlie, that
now leives; a noble gentleman and a gallant knight of
a fingular & heroick fpeirit. Floorifhed the yeare of
Chrift 1594.

Of purpofe I the praife, Sir Patrick, pafs
Of all thy parantage and pedegrie,
Whofe fplendor great and glorie, in the glafs
Of thy oun worth, fuch as hes fight may fee;
    And there there acts autentick too & old,
    May reprefented happilie behold.

Integritie, treuth and trew honor held
Into thy heart the cheiff and higheft hold,
Ingenit, dewtie & difcretion duel'd,
That temperats extreams in breafts like bold,
    And therewith was vivacitie of witt,
    By courage clofs the fure confort of it.

Thefe nought in ane nought idle ornaments,
Nor perfunctorious in thy perfone plact,
As cafuall, incertane accidents,
That for the forme thé gloried and grac'd;
    No! bot ftill working virteus they th' attend
    Wnto thy glorious & gallant end.

104. John Maitland.

Lord Thirlstane; and for his letters & wisdome made Great
    Chancellor of Scotland; a wise, politique, statsman, ane
    eloquent orator, & a nottable philolog.   He dyed the yeare
    of Christ 1595.

I boldlie nought th' ambitious Beldame blind,
Whom foolls a Fortoun call, did follow first,
But with a measur'd, yet a mounting minde,
(And nought in vaine) for honors throne did thirst;
    Yet nought the Royall roumes, nor cheifest chaire,
    But nixt to that, I rais'd and rear'd myne there.

No grace decoaring could, nor gift be given,
Men subjects born but meane, to magnifie
And helpe to honor; but behold the heven,
In passing plentie, did impairt to me,
    A stomak, strength, wealth, stature, wisdome, will,
    And t'aide my freinds and skaith my foes a skill!

Yet damne me nought, deare countrie, when I could,
And nought perform'd that all that thow expected;
Th'allseing Word will witnefs that I would,
And was still to thy forderance effected;
    But when my witt works for thy well invented,
    Then troubl'd tymes turn'd them to nought intented.

105. Sir Robert Montgomerie.

Brother to Hugh, Earle of Montgomerie, flaine att Annick; a
man of great fpereit; after incredible deeds and lowrs done
and taken for revenge of his brothers flaughter, laid doun
his armes, and deteafting defire of revenge, died holilie, the
yeare of Chrift 1596.

The after tymes fall tell this & extoll,
Als long as Fame hes in her bougle breath,
And make thy praife outfpring and pafs the Poll,
For thy brave deids done for thy brothers death;
    Thy paines, th' expenfs, and all thy hazards hard,
    They will nought want (as worthie) there rewarde.

Who for a fratri-cœde was found fo fierce,
Who did fo much fo markable and ftraunge,
Or who for fuch like flaughters made fuch ferche,
And was fo reftlefs reddie to revenge?
    Few fo fraternall found are now or non,
    The caire for kinde & goodmen all is gone.

Yet when thy works of wrath thow viewed, thow wift
All that by violence thow wrought was wrong;
Thefe doings then condemned thow did defift,
And left it that did to the Lord belong,
    Remitt or vengeance for thy brothers blood,
    As it fhould feem wnto his Godhead good.

106. 𝔗𝔬

The moſt martiall and all praiſeworthie Scottiſh Gentlemen and
gallant Sojours, ſlaine att Hulſt, the yeare of Chriſt 1590.

Reſolved Worthies, and renoun'd, rejoice,
Since loſs of life your laud and glore begane,
And now is groun as great as that of thoſe
That in thoſe warrs the name of Wortheis wan;
    Death does deduce no dram for your defearts,
    No! bot more matter to your praiſe impairts.

A knightlie death infamous life before,
Heroick hearts & men of fame preſerr,
All martiall minds they eſtimat it more,
If with triumph renoun there truncks interr;
    Nor give them cities, ſegnories & ſuch,
    The love of honor ſo there ſtomaks touch.

This witneſs'd weell your actions ere yow ended,
When th' Archiduke did fulminat & forc'd
Onhappie Hulſt, therby your facts defended,
And therefrom but by death to be divorc'd;
    Your blood ſo boldlie ſpendit there & ſpilt,
    Your Tombs nor gold more gloriouſlie hes built.

107. James Lord Stewart.

Brother-german to Andrew, Lord Ochiltrie; a noble gentleman,
a famous Captane, a brave schollar, a grave statfman; Earle
of Arrane & Great Chancellor of Scotland.   Floorished &
was flaine, the yeare of Chrift 1597.

When deeds of honor high, or hazards hard,
Occur'd to be effectuat by force,
What anie martiall doer durft thow darr'd,
Yet wiflie weigh'd the advantage or the worfe:
    Thy will & vfe to actione thow inur'd,
    Through nature ftrong and dreidlefs to indur'd.

Thy fauning fortoune, nor thy frouning fate,
Thy cleare funfhine, nor yet thy cloudie day.
Thy ftanding honor, nor thy ftouping ftate,
They mov'd nought much, nor did thy minde difmaie;
    But lyke a tall fhipe in a ftormie tide,
    Thow onabafed boldlie did abyde.

And when the force of foes did moft affront thé,
There moien moft & thine was att the meaneft;
There magnitude of minde did nought furmount thé,
But thine was know'n coequall with the keeneft;
    This witnes'd was when wnawarrs invaded,
    Thy fortitude nought att thy faling faded.

108. Lachlane Makclane.

A man for his fpreit, ftrength and heroicall dignitie of perfone, to
be compair'd to the moft ancient Captanes of his Countrie;
onhoneftlie betrai'd and flaine by his fifters fone, Sir James
Mackonell, the yeare of Chrift 1598.

Who of thy Highland Peers in fpreit furpaft,
Or overmatch'd thé in a mite, Mackclane?
Yea! if I fhould all our records o'recaft,
Scarce fould I finde of infineit bot ane;
    So was thow both in partes efpied, & fpreit
    Be beft approv'd opinions compleit.

The high commend thow to thy glorie got,
(And then thy foes from gallent men & great)
Still fall it ftand to thy renoune a note;
When Time is nought and daies fhall have noe dait,
    Thy praifes fall be publifht & repeated,
    At fuch a work, with reafone, thow was rated.

Yet this thy worth that fo efteemed ftood
Wes trait'rouflie betrai'd and tane away,
And by a brench (a boutcher of thy blood)
Condignlie for his deeds condamn'd this day,
    For the rewards on treafon that attends,
    Are, dreidfull doome! difgrace and doolfull ends.

109. Sir Alexander Murray.

Collonell of the Scottiſh regiment in the Low Countries, and ane
courageous man of warr; ſlaine in Bumble with the cannon,
the yeare of Chriſt 1599.

O how farr ſall the tirranie extend,
And furie of the Spaniſh forces faire!
Sall ne're there ire, nor wrong invaſions end?
Shall nought there pride from perſecution ſpaire?
    Or ſall they ne're deſiſt from the deſire,
    Of the Wneited Provinces impire?

Shall nought but it there appeteits appeaſe?
Shall nought bot it make ſatt there meagrie minds?
Sall ne're our cies behold her holie daies,
Nor find the fruĉts of peace that France now finds?
    To mattocks turn'd the mace, the ſword, the ſithe,
    Bleſs God, & for that benefeit be blithe.

No, no, but att ane other end they aime,
And to a broader butt there bolts are bent;
Thir countries are nought but a collord clame,
It is the trew Religion they wold rent;
    And they this head for hecatombs will have,
    Which grant, good God! it may releive the leave.

P

110. James Dowglafs.

Earle of Buchane; a young nobleman amongſt the number of our
noble youths one of moſt ſingular hope and expectatione;
died in the 21 yeare of his aige, the yeare of Chriſt 1601.

Laid in the ludge of Honor heir behold
The man that Mars & that Minerve admir'd;
In yeares tho young, yet in his actions old,
And lyke a pure wnſpoted pearle appear'd;
    A Count & Knight, by kinde couragious,
    The onlie hope and honor of his Houſs.

That too ſhort tyme of life that Nature lent,
And on this proudent potentat did ſpaire,
To hav't but prejudice to honor ſpent,
He hade a circumſpect and conſtant caire;
    And nought weell done nor perfect wold approove,
    If nought in pietie perform'd & love.

Allace! ſould nought this land lament this loſs,
And for this Worthie weep a world of teares?
Who in his dauning was diſſolv'd to droſs,
And tane wntimlie in his tender yeares;
    Before was ſeen peracted be him ag'd,
    That young ſo ſoone & certane ſignes preſag'd.

III. Mark Alexander Boide.

A learned, virtuous, & weell diſpos'd gentleman; ane excellent
Poet, whereof manie records yet remaines.   After his pere-
grinatione tuiſe allmoſt through all Europe, in the vigor of
his aige, depairted the yeare of Chriſt 1601.

Brave Boyde! that by thy airt divyne lies draw'n,
And with Apolinean pen expreſt
So manie warlike Worthies of thy oune,
Out from the ſhrine of thy Hyblean breaſt,
    Thow for thy worth ſhould with theſe Worthies paſs,
    And be with them, too, rancked for thy race.

A famous Clane, a faſt and ſaithfull kinde
Beare thé a branche reſembling right the roote;
For frequentlie it falleth out, wee find,
A good tree gives againe a gracious froot;
    So ſend that noble kinde from whence thow came,
    Thé (to this ſoil) beſeeming weell the ſame.

Fraught weell with learning and the librall arts,
With tri'd intelligence into the tongs,
And other manie more approved pairts,
That to the laureat & learn'd belongs,
    Which magnifi'd, ſhall make thé & admir'd,
    And prais'd perpetuallie, ſuppoſe expir'd.

112. Alexander Irwine.

Of Drum, ane ancient, wife, and honorable, aged Barron,
died 1602.

Bold Barron! borne of noe bafe blood nor birth,
Bot from Patrician peers and parents fprong:
All men of wifdome, honor and of worth,
That by fucceffion laughfull and a long
    Have bein both good, and of there actions great,
    Into the publict and the privat ftate.

One of thy great grand-firs, a gallant Knight,
When James the Firft, a wife and worthie prince,
Was captive keept, againft all reafons right,
Or law then know'n, or yitt fancited fince,
    Was one of thefe, thofe Worthies weell efteem'd,
    That ranfon'd him, and brought him home redeem'd.

Harlaw and Brechen battells both doe beare,
(Feights famous, perremptor and perrillous)
That two of thy forbears bravlie there,
And hardilie won honor to thy Houfs;
    Which thow, with wifdome, and by hardinefs,
    To thine and thers great credit did increafs.

113. Sir John Gordon.

Of Pitlurge; a honorable, wife, and worthie Knight.

Thow grave, good Knight, fair faſhion'd, full of faith,
And wonderfullie vigillent and wife,
That nothing bot nobilitie did breath,
Heer in the limeits of a little lies;
    Whoſe placid ſpreit ſo was to peace difpos'd,
    That it eternall with the Juft enjoyſt.

Into thy tyme, thy manie travells tends
(Tranquillitie ſo all thy life thow lov'd)
To quench the countrie quarrells and of freinds,
T' amend what mal & mifcontentments mov'd:
    O worthie Knight! according to thy kind
    So wiflie weell and vertuouflie inclyn'd.

Manie be borne, ftir'd be there nature ftrong,
And confidence into ther force t' affect,
Yea fofter feids the wicked they and wrong,
And that bot for there pride and powr's refpect;
    But thow to peace was (to thy glorie) giv'n,
    A jem on earth, a jewell into heaven.

114. Sir Andrew Stewart.

Collonell; nottable & moſt famous for his militarie knowledge,
practeiſed in the Eaſt pairts, Low-Countrie warres; & att
home, for his ſingular good ſervice, renoun'd.   Flooriſh'd
the yeare off Chriſt

Two Roman rewlars and ane Epirot,
For valor all, bot warring divers waies,
Renoun'd names triumph with glorie, got
The laurall too adorne them in there daies:
      Firſt Maximus, when it ſeem'd meet he might,
      For wiſe avoiding & deferring ſight:

Marcellus ſine is celebrat and prais'd,
For valerous adventring in his warr,
And ever biding battell onabais'd,
Tho ne're ſo awfull his adverſars ar:
      And Pirrhus laſt, that Epirat renoun'd,
      Was, for the beſt encamping, Captane croun'd.

Bot of theſe gallants all theſe graces great,
And martiall mindes of theſe three mightie men,
Witt to bewar, force to effect a feat,
And how t'encampe convenientlie to ken,
      Keen Collonell, all through thy theorie,
      And practeiſes was proper wnto thé.

115. Sir Thomas Gordone.

Of Cluny; a Knight, honorable, valerous, & wife; courteouflie
inclyn'd, virtcuouflie difpofed, and affable wnto all in all
his affaires.   Flooriſhed the yeare of Chriſt

More large the lofs, and greater nor the greif,
Is that by death the Countrie-State fuſtaines;
It ſtricks the ſtanders, and cuts doun the cheeff,
Strong pedeſtalls to prop it that pertaines;
 The domage then that death does to th' Eſtate
 Exceeds the courfe and compafs of conceapte.

Each moment, month, each yeare, each day, each houre
Exempted non that mortall is among,
And in each place, experience of the pow'r
Is doolfullie taught of the Tirrane ſtrong;
 Yea, that this day, in this accompliſh't Knight,
 Wee foorlie fie with forrow in our fight.

Since when occafione did occure or crave
To marke or meafure by the minde a man,
Few was, in giving councill good or grave,
That paſt him, eln, or inch, or fpace, or fpane;
 No, non, and if to goe, to Mars his gaine,
 Who better prov'd, or feen into the fame?

116. John Marques of Hammiltoun.

Earle of Arran, Lord of Evan and Aberbrothock, &c.; a
  honorable and egregious perfonage, [in] whom the marks
  and notts of trew Nobilitie ever was moft eminent. He died
  the yeare of Chrift   .

So many reafons relevant arife,
And ftore of ftuff t' wp propt thy praife appeare,
That might make wicked wretches that invies
The Worthie moft, there eyes eclipfed cleare
     In thé the fignes of honor, to behold
     That virtew weive into the worthie wold.

No notes ignoble, nor bafe formes was found
(That could a Prince his reputatione paire)
Within thy bofome grave to get a ground;
No, nor thral'd thoughts was hid or harbr'd there,
     Thoughts that to vice and flaves to finn are feen,
     Nought noble thoughts of noble mynds I meen.

Nobilitie concording with thy minde,
With vertuous works (nought wedded to thy will)
In th' affable and mightie Marquis fhinde,
And fhew'd thow ay ftood ftaide and ftable ftill,
     One ever effaulde & religious Lord,
     Onharm'd thy honor & onwrong'd thy word.

117. John Lord Forbes.

A ſtout couragious Lord; in his youth entangled with troubles,
and in his aige in peace, both grave & godlie.   Died Anno
Chriſtie 1606.

Long with the jaw's of nightbour jarrs I juſted,
And in a warrs onkindlie wau's was volv'd,
Long of theſe greiffs that follow force, I guſted,
Yet reſolute and lyke my ſelfe reſolv'd;
    I ſtable ſtai'd and ſtood one alwayes ſtill,
    Into my fortouns faire, even odd or ill.

Nought that I took into that life delight,
Or fanc'd with freinds old to be att ods;
Nor by the profound powers of my ſpright,
And th' everlaſting gloric of the gods,
    I doe proteſt, could warrs have been prevented,
    I both did loath, miſlike them, and lamented.

But fatall caices they muſt have ther courſs,
And deeds predeſtinat they muſt be done,
Tho whills the worthie Warriors get the worſs,
And whills they ventrars in ther warrs they win;
    B' infortund fight there can come noe diſcredit
    Wnto bold breaſts, that bravlie does abyd it.

Q

118. Sir William Edmond.

Colonell to one of the Scotts regiments in the Low-Countries,
and one of the Counfaill of warr of the Wneited Provinces;
a knight that for his exceiding valour paſt all the degrees of
martiall dignities, and gave ws manie and nottable prooffs
of his ſkill, as any other of his aige.   He flooriſh'd, and was
ſlaine att Rensberge 1607.

How many mount (tho by there birth) bot baſs,
And ſcarce from good beginings great are grown.
Moſt by the means of mony that they maſs,
In ſho to Honors higheſt ſtall are ſtowne;
    Tho honor and nobilitie be noe
    Attain'd wnto, acquyred or purchaſt ſo.

Bot he, throw haunting honorable armes,
And exerceiſe, that greateſt worth, grave witt,
Accounting kingdoms but lyke countrie farms,
All other practeis does poſtpone to it.
    By means more meriting, grew by degrees
    Nixt to a great Dictators dignities.

The Low Lands warrs did ne're a ſoldar ſie,
A collonell, knight, nor commander knew,
(And with great grace one of theſe all wes he)
Whoſe fame and martiall glorie greater grew,
    Or wes, nor Edmond more renoun'd, or raiſe
    In Holland too, more honor, place & praiſe.

119. John Graham.

Earle of Montrofs, Lord Græm & Montdiew; ane aiged, wife,
& noble Earle; Great Chancellar of Scotland, and firſt High
Commiffioner for his Majeſty in Scotland.   Died the yeare
of Chriſt 1608.

That Græme, whofe greatnefs to be great began,
And in our ſtories is fo much extol'd,
From that vaſt wark, the Wall of Adrian,
Adventred, win, hurl'd doun by him, & hold,
    His fortoune firſt laid found wnto the frame
    Of thy heroick Houfs, egregious Græme.

Then that Sir John, for worth (whom Wallace ws'd)
Such wondrous knightlie courage did decore-him,
And for cheef collegue in his conflicts chus'd,
Since non he fand to be preferr'd before him;
    He on that frame of fame, that former found
    Of praifes, plac'd a mountane lyke a mound.

But thow o'regrew the greateſt in degrees,
Yea, paſt that be compairing may be prais'd;
And to be wondred of all earthlie eyes,
Ne're to be ruin'd of renoun, hes rais'd
    A monument, great Grahame, wnto thy glore,
    Nor Artemifias mole, or maufole more.

120. Sir James Lawson.

Of Humbee, Knight; he was gentleman of his Majeſties
Chamber; a gallant youth in the way of honor; infortunatlie
drown'd beſide Aberdeen, in a ſtanding laike, caled the Old
Watter-gang, ryding over-raſhlie, but without knowledge of
the ground, 1612.

Whoſe mynds ſo marbl'd & his heart ſo hard,
And who of ſteell whoſe ſtomachs are ſo ſtrong,
That would not when this hudge miſhap wes heard,
To th' outmoſt note of ſorrow ſet there ſong,
    And elevat there voice and woes alone,
    The higheſt ſtraine of any troubl'd toone.

To ſee a Gallant with ſo great a grace,
So ſuddenlie wnthought on ſo orethrow'n,
And ſo to periſh in ſo poor a place,
By too raſh ryding in a ground unknow'n,
    The flintie Fates that but all pitie proove,
    Would both to mourne, & miſeratione move.

Yitt ſhall this death the Defunƈt not diſgrace,
Nor to his praiſe prove prejudiciall,
Since men of greater rank have rune lyke race,
And loſt by lyke misfortouns fine and fall;
    For Fergus, Dowgall, and King Donald droun'd,
    And they all three Kings of this Countrie croun'd.

121. Thomas Frazer.

Of Strechin, brother-german to Lord Frazer of Lovat; a noble
Gentleman adorn'd with many honorable and worthie
qualities.   Died the yeare of Chrift 1612.

If that thy virtue, wifdome, or thy worth
Now furnifhes more fedders to thy fame,
Or (what great gifts does grace) if noble birth
Nobilitats, or more renouns thy name,
    Non is fo fure of fens, fo fharp of fight,
    Whofe reafons reach dow do determe it right.

For in thy facts found faithfull by th' effects,
And all thy labours laughfull while alive,
Thow did exprefs moft provident refpects
To make them with thy ftock and ftate to ftrive:
    In vertew alwayes cairfull to decore,
    To honor this, and to augment that more.

All thefe compacted and accomplifht pairts,
As with the good begot thé living love,
And as thy manie merits and defairts,
As full of profeit pleafant they did prove,
    So now the want of fo great worth alway
    Leaves no lefs dollor for thy death this day.

122. [James] Drummond.

Earle of Perth; ane egregious and a gallant youth, of a moſt
noble difpoſitione; in the verie flooriſhing of his aige prevented by death, the yeare of Chriſt 1612.

Greeff, groans and tears, fad figh's and forrows fo,
Crofs and cut fhort in, amaz'd & mirthlefs Mufe,
That now thé knoes (fo is fhe wrapt in woe)
Nought what inventione verfe, nor words to wfe,
     T'ingrafs the gifts & pen thy pairts, great Pearth,
     That beutified and bliſt thé from thy birth.

All excellent was th'outwards to the eie,
But th'other halfe (that was nought borne) thy beſt,
The Spirituall Powers inexplicable be,
And nought to be by th'imperitie expreſt;
     So rare thefe firſt and fo fublime the laſt,
     That th'apprehenfione of her fpreit they paſt.

To write then of thy worthinefs and witt,
Or of the fplendor of thy priors fpeek,
That mereit much my Mufe fhe muſt omitt,
For forrow for thy fake hes made her fick;
     Therfore, wnto her woes fhe giv's the way,
     Since what fhe fould they fuffer nought to fay.

123. **Sir James Stewart.**

A noble and a gallant youth, heire apparent to the Lord of Blantire; wounded in a combat in England, foughten with the
 Owe of [the Son of Lord] Whartane, one English man;
 died   .

Great courage known included in thy kinde,
From Bancho thy forbears to thy birth,
In him, in them, in thé, there blood combin'd,
Hes be th' events well witnessed your worth;
  And thine in thy last work the world view'd
  That duell where thow died, tho nought subdew'd

This magnitood of minde some much commended,
But more the quarrell and the cause condemned,
That both wnto that bealfull bargane bended,
And in a furie for to fight, inflam'd
  Thy martiall minde, for greater fortons fit,
  If nought fearce wrath hade overvail'd thy witt.

That cursed combat where thy lyfe was lost,
With all the courage that a Knight became,
Thy discontented kin and countrie crost,
And ever fall be sorie for the same;
  Yet thow there got, what I ame sure thow fought,
  Renoune and honor with thy bloodshed bought.

124. **To the Memorie of**

All the valorous & honorable Scottish Warriours flaine in the
Religious Civill Warrs in France, wnder the conduct of that
renoun'd & victorious King, Henry the 4th.

Religious fighters for the faith in France,
Thefe obelifks, thefe trophea's, and thefe tombs,
Memorialls in your rememberance,
Erect and rear'd in thefe reverend roum's,
    Wife Pallas, Mars, and Pietie did place,
    Your Countrie, Yow, and Gallia to grace.

Your valor Mars, your witt Minerva will
Have on thefe tombs t' eternitie extended,
In livelie lins that learned Ladies fkill,
Your courages and knowledge hes commended;
    And Pietie (fweet foulls) folemnlie fhall,
    With gloric evergreen, o'regroun them all.

O weell fpent paines, weell waired was your blood,
Well loft your lives, and wondrous weell deferve yow
(For fervice oft fo neceffar and good)
Such ever powerfull patrons to preferve yow
    From envies ill, from tearing Time and Fates,
    Eternallie that noe time terminats.

125. John Gordone.

Earle of Southerland; ane heroick and moſt noble Earle, worthilie
lamented; in the ſtrength of his aige depairted this life, the
yeare of Chriſt 1615.

Aſtrea ſad in ſeck and ſable ſute,
Diſcheveled about her hade her hair,
Nought murning like a maide, bot manlie mute,
Croſt and confounded for thy cauſe with caire,
    Wpon thy tomb a ſtone lyke ſtatue ſtands,
    With fixed feit, cloſs eyes, and croſſed hands.

And ſo by ſilent ſignes ſuch ſorrow ſhows,
As witt can nought invent, nor wreit, nor word,
No, nor our humane hearts compre'nds nor knows,
Nor tho yet know'n could mans concept record;
    So with diſpleaſures ſhe oppreſt appear's,
    That ther's noe place for plaints nor time for tears.

Yet by this ſolemne ſilence it wold ſeem
That this moſt mœſtfull Maid but murmur means,
More pithelie nor by high plaints, t' expream
Th' aſſaults of ſorrows that her ſoull ſuſteans,
    And for thy want, wiſe, worthie Earle, will ay
    With vult and nought with voce her woe bewray.

R

126. Irbine Kempt Garden.

A man of admirable and ſtupendious ſtrength, called the Kempt
for killing of a feirce and mightie boar in the den of Garden,
and got the ſaid lands therfore, being the firſt that boor
our name, & from whom all that boor the fame are deſcended.   He flooriſht about the reigne of King Gregorie
the Great.

When they, whom Fame for nottable renoun'd,
Are nam'd, numbred, and notorious,
And with the cape of land for lawrell croun'd,
To make them gallenter and glorious,
    Should thow, that was as excellent as old,
    Reſt onremembred, reckned, or onſcrold?

No, noe; the kiling of that cruell beaſt,
His head throw'n of and from his den furth draw'n,
As is in thy primevident expreſt,
Hes caus'd thé be Kempt Irvine cald & knawn,
    Thy ſtyle and laud thow from thy Lord for that,
    And wee from thé our name of Garden, gatt.

That Boars head, bloodie, rugged of, & rent,
(When others ſhorne or beatten of it beares)
In figne of honor for thy hardiment,
Thy recta-line yitt as thow wan it wears,
    So be that fimple onſupplied bage,
    All come of thé are knaw'n in everie aige.

127. Sir James Stewart.

Called the Black Knight, fone to the Lord of Lorne; ane noble
& a worthie Knight; maried Queen Jean Seymer after the
death of King James 1., her husband, the yeare 1439, &
begot on her John and James, Earles of Atholl and
Buchane, and Andrew, Bishope of Murray; was removed
from Court be moyen of the Earle of Dowglafs; therafter,
failing to Flanders, was by the Fleemings taken, and in
Flanders died, the yeare of Chrift 1446.

Leflie, in the
Scot. hift., pag.
192 & 298.

Thy worthie vertues, they indeid defire,
I grant, a more Homerick mufe nor mine
To furnifh food and fewell to the fyre,
That fould them to the future times define;
    And perfectlie both forme & fet them forth,
    According as they were, & thow was worth.

Illuftruous Lord! my Mufe immature yet,
Loath that the floorifh of thy fame fhould fade,
Or be pen't in Oblivions pitchie pit,
Wherin of mereits is no mentione made,
    But there, all that deferv'd, lye dead & clean
    Oblit'rat are, as they hade never bene.

Therfore fhe will, fince it fo much deferv'd,
Nurifhed with nectar and ambrofian breath,
From th'all fuppreffing priffon to preferv'd,
Wfe then the dungeon & the den of death,
    That it may vivid wax and never vane,
    Bot evermore remembered remaine.

128. **Sir Andrew Gray.**

> Ane Englifh gentleman, the firft of that name in Scotland; for
> the love he beare to the worthie King James the 1, came in
> his Graces fervice, & weell efteem'd be the faid King got in
> recompence the heretrix of Foulls, Helen Mortimer, in
> mariaige, from whom the houfs of Gray is defcended. He
> floorifhed the yeare of Chrift 1424.

When James the Firft, that wife and worthie King,
From England home there long detain'd reteir'd;
In whom there did fuch wondrous prudence fpring,
That Englifh both did mark it, and admeir'd
     That in a Royall youth, of fo few yeares,
     So manie princlie pairts fo foon appears.

Which admiratione mightilie did move,
And into diverfe there of ftate did ftirr
A firme affectione, liking, and a love
To ferve and hold of him; and thow of thir
     Was nought the laft, nor meaneft, bot a man
     Refpected moft and beft thought of thefe then.

This gracious King the leaving of your land
To thefe & the paft nought wnrecompenft,
No, but his Highnefs, with a liberall hand,
Yow all to honor and to wealth advanft;
     And ther, be th' heretrix of Fowlls, made heare
     To that old Knight, Sir Roger Mortimer.

129. James Lord Ogilvie.

Father to James Lord Ogilvie that now is; a courteous and a
noble Lord, belov'd and highlie honor'd with his Prince; sent
cheiff in a Royall ambassage to the Corronation of Christian
the 4, now King of Denmark, etc. Departed this present
life, the yeare of Christ 1597.

Most lovlie Lord, in forme and fashions faire,
In courtesies and complements compleit,
That with the best componde thow might compare
In pregnancie and powers of the spreit;
    The gifts and graces of the minde, I mean,
    That ornaments best to the best hes bein!

This thy innate and noble naturall,
Thy educatione, travells, and thy sight,
Each helping others and conjoyned all,
They have prepaired and proportion'd right
    Thé a pure polisht spreit, as good as great,
    And ripe to rule beneath a Royall State.

Weell did the pearle and paragone of Princes,
Thy soveraigne Lord, thy Prot'us pairts espie
Out of his wisdomes sharp-ride-sight & sences,
That built in his Basilik bosome ly;
    Thé therfore and thy witts be wislie ws'd,
    And once to be his cheeff Embasdore chous'd.

130. John Earle of Cassills.

A wife, renouned and noble Earle; depairted the   yeare of
his aige, the yeare of Chrift 1615.

Carrick, thy Count and weelbeloved Lord,
With all thy nigh'bring Provinces deplore;
Into whofe bofome witt and valor ftor'd,
And daily to his death augmented more;
    Into that breaft no bad, nor baftard thought,
    A habitatione hade, nor feat hes fought.

Concerning worthipe or religious rights,
But ftablic rearing on the ftedfaft rock,
His leivlie faith impoftures he difpights,
And all there mad mal-ventions he did mock,
    Accounting mercenar that humane means,
    Which to fupport Plutonean pride perteans.

Thow'r intereft the King and Countrie too,
He laiks a loiall leege, a lover it,
A learned, wife, and Lord moft loving thow,
To ferve him Lord thé and defend her fit;
    So Carrik, thow the Countrie, King & Faeth
    Are intereft all by th' Earles wntimlie death.

131. **Patrik Earle of Kingborne.**

Lord Lion, Belleville, & Glamfs; a religious, wife, folide, and
worthie Earle.   Depairted this life, the yeare of his aige
the yeer of Chrift 1615.

Who greatter graces hade of graver yeares?
Who of his place of greater fpreit hes fpir'd?
Who hes more prudent proven among the peers,
Or with more parts praife-worthie hes appear'd,
    Into that too curt courfe of life (bot lent)
    And little fpace that heir Earle Patrick fpent?

His faith faft fixt was naither fond nor fain'd,
In's courfes conftant but recalling knaw'n;
One neare for feare, nor want of ftomak ftain'd,
Nor be inducement from that deutie draw'n,
    That to ther God, ther Soveraigne Lord & Law,
    Good Chriftians and loiall fubjects aw.

No, no; non can that Count expyr'd reprove,
Nor anie point to his difpraife impute;
Bot rather will (into his lyfe fuch love
His working wifdome wan) rife & refute
    The calumneis that envie dare obtrude,
    Glammfs, gainft thy Earle, fo great, fo grave, fo good.

132. George Gordone.

Earle of Huntlie, Eangye, Lord Gordone, Loquhaber, & Badzenoch, Great Chancellar of Scotland; ane heroick and noble
  Earle, notablie famous in the Scottiſh hiſtorie.   Flooriſhed
  the yeare   .

Reſt noble Lord, firſt famous for thy kinde,
Then nottable was for thy calling knawne;
Bot markable moſt for great gifts combin'd,
Which makes thé ſo be through all Brittane blawne,
    And everie throat to be a ſhalme to found
    Theſe virtews that, Great Noble, thé renoun'd.

Thow borrow'd non, thy virtews were thine oune,
Thow filſh'd from non there feathers when thow flew,
Nor ought that now fuſteins thy ſtatue's ſtowne,
Bot all thy golden graces with thé grew;
    And what e're did adorne thé to thy death
    Began to bud when thow began to breath.

Bot how they ſpred and ſprang into thy youth,
And floriſh'd in thy tyme of tutelage,
Or how, in ſtronger ſtate or greater grouth,
They buire faire fruct to the ending of thy aige,
    Now oceans and ſpeats of praiſe diſplayes,
    When clos'd with credit is thy date of dayes.

133. **Alexander Bruce.**

Of Earlshall; ane honorable Barron, adorned with many good
& godlie graces.   Dyed in the yeare of Chrift 1600.

Thow that does from that thunderbolt, the Bruce,
(Borne both his foes to beat, debell and brave)
Thy lawfull line and thy difcent deduce,
The higheft honor that thy Houfs could have;
    Such was thy cariaige, knaw'n in everic place,
    As beft becum from fuch a Root & Race.

Firft to thy God thow hade a great regaird,
To King and Countrie then thy caire exceeded;
Thy tables, too, were princlie-lyke prepair'd,
To all and wnto non deny'd that needed;
    Yet to fuperflous formes oppon'd exprefs,
    That feem'd bot fib to ryot and excefs.

No brainfick-heads was harbour'd in thy houfs,
Nor non difpighting pietie nor peace;
Thy noble nature deligat and douce,
Could nought allow fuch laulefs fpritts a place;
    No, but it plainlie did expell the proud,
    And lou'd non bot the godlie and the good.
        S

134. Sir John Carmichaell.

Of that Ilk, Knight; a valerous Gentleman, fomtime **Warden** of
the [Middle] Marches; ryding to correct the infolencie of
fome rebellious Borderers, was flaine be
1600.

While be Commiffione and the Kings command,
Wnto the Border Lands neir England, where
The torrent Arve does ftrick wpon the ftrand
And fat the feilds and weari'd valies there,
    Thow then, Lord Warden, went to give the Law,
    For bringing rebell-ryders wnder aw.

Some perverfe fpreits, oft practeifed to fpoile,
That then difdain'd directions to indure,
Or laufullie to labour, love or toill,
Moft cruelly to cutt thy throat conjoure;
    And as they plot they practeis and performe,
    And ftroak thé with ane wnexpected ftorme.

A deed, no doubt, indigne to be declar'd,
A bold and contumelious contempt,
That thow could nought for thy great fpreit be fpaired,
Nor for thy place be from that ill exempt;
    But inhumainlie made away, God knaws,
    In fpight of heavenlie & of humane Laws.

135. Sir Thomas Lyone.

Of Baldoukie, Knight; brother-germane to John, Lord Glames,
etc., Great Chancellar of Scotland; a foleid, wife and
martiall minded gentleman; one of the Lords of Counfall &
Seffione; Treafurer of Scotland, the yeare   .

Preferment, praife, and honor high pertaines
To thofe that reftlefs nought remiffly rinne;
They that extreamitie of ftorme fuftaines,
As went'rars wife moft worthilie fhould winne,
    And they whofe virtews does there names renounc,
    Them cheiflie Honor does commend and croune.

Thow then that ftronglie fo State ftorms fuftain'd,
Nor mean nor few Republict races ran,
And manfullie in all thy matters meen'd,
Still leiving like a great and gallant man,
    In the expreffion of a fpregnant fpreit
    Hes for reward this croune of Honor merit.

Them as thy juftum thow injoy it muft,
To make thy ghoft be glaid and gloric too,
When thefe thy bones falbe diffolv'd to duft,
And turn'd to earth and afhe, as they are now;
    ·Since that the gifts of thy great fpreit procures,
    That wndefac'd ev'r thy defarts indures.

136.

Now glorious are there Ghofts that for there God,
There King, ther Countrie, Faith, or for there Freinds
Doe by the force of foes, the rack, or rod,
There vitall fpirits prodigallie fpend;
    And happie them the World accounts and calls
    Whom to like fine, like fate, or fortoun falls.

Whofe Ghofts more glade fhould be and glorious then,
And whofe renouns more rolled through this round,
Whofe deeds and death amongs ws mortall men,
For better cauffes clameth to be croun'd;
    Gif for the Churches, the Countrie, King, or Kin,
    It glorious be to doe and die therin.

Then greeflefs, glade, and glorious is thy Ghoft,
Now plac't where praife and pleafures are compleet,
That with thy Soveraigne Lord, thy life hes loft,
And fell before him fightand att his feet,
    Whaire nought few of thy freinds to him and thé
    Declair'd ther loialtie and love, did die.

137. Walter Stewart.

Lord of Blantire; ane of the Extraordinary Lords of the Session,
one of the Octavians, and one of His Majestys honorable
Privie Councill; a prudent and discreit gentleman, depairted
this lyfe the yeare 16   .

AND

Sir John Preston.

Of [Fentonbarns], Knight, Lord President of His Majestys
Session; a honorable, learned, & judicious gentleman,
departed this lyfe the yeare 16   .

Advert Viator and advance thine eyes
Wpe to those moldie monuments & tombs,
Wherin, thow worthie, worshipfull & wife,
(Too narrow straight and closs concreated rooms)
  There terrane trunks, there flitting tents, there traesh
  Heir bot a while are folded in there flesh.

There spirits pure, that from the purest sprang,
Corruption could nought keep, nor clay inclose;
From whence they come they green'd againe to gang,
And throw the durrs of Death their glaidlie goes,
  Whaire they attending (mirthfull does remaine)
  A re-unciting glorious againe.

For name, renoun, nor praise they neid nought pans,
Nor what detractione after death can doe;
They reigne in rest where is no change, nor chance,
Nor where is neid to eek, nor add wnto
  That passing all and perfect plenitood
  Of glorie into God, the greatest good.

138. Earle of Orknay.

(Or Earle of Bothwell, Duke of Orknay).

Magnanime minds, why mufe ye as amaz'd,
To fee your fellous feirce and froward fates?
Oft Tyme and Fortone ruin'd hes and rais'd
Bafs blood, high born, and altred all eftates;
       Be nought amazed then, nor think it wonder,
       Tho Kings be croft and Majeftie ly wnder.

On Neptuns back my barge feem'd fett fecure,
While with the lions love it fail'd circounded;
But few that God fo fetl'd fic, nor fure,
And I not obftant thefe am thus confounded;
       Time hes my truft, my life and ftate betray'd,
       And in my fate, my fall and wrack bewray'd.

Heroicks yet the Fortoun, Fate, and Time,
To ruine yow attempt and t'alter all;
Yow fhould be femi-dean and fubleim,
And ftoup nought for diftreffes temporall;
       But in the lofs of life, and change of States,
       Be refolute and feare not force of Feats.

139. Sir Robert Keith.

Of Benholme, brother-german to George, Great Marshall of
Scotland, now leiving; a honorable and noble mynded
gentleman, depairted the prefent lyfe, the yeare 16

All yow that valor, worth, or courage carie,
That noble birth and gallant fprcits refpects,
T'attend thefe tropheas, tomb & triumphs, tarrie,
That now renoun in honor heir erects,
    Of this moft Mars-like Marfhalls brother bold,
    Whofe worthinefs was worth a grave of gold.

And yow that rarities and wonders wold,
Or wifh to view things marvellous yow may;
Heir love and honor, hand in hand, behold
March with the Mufes all in doole this day;
    Bellona brave, and Mars the mourners cheeff,
    Gods feldome fene to figh, or groan for greeff.

Nought to this Worthie to be wanting yit,
They in a mortall manner and humane,
This high-borne-heros-herfe to honor it,
All cled with caire & cypres croun'd doe daigne;
    And with fad Anthems, blak & luri'd layes,
    Shall grave in gold this Worthies worth & praife.

140.

Whane change of Time and chance of Feat confpires,
And mens mifcariaige as a curs concurrs,
Throns they orethrow, prefs and pull doun Impires,
Great Kefars, Kings and Dukes drives out of dures;
     Chance, Change and Time, like cancre, moaths & freats,
     Yea, wndermines all men and mundane States.

What Time, what Change, what Chance and m' vnfreinds might,
Could all confederat agains me frame,
Both with difdainfull and deferved fpight,
Conbin'd t'obliterat and blot my name
     Out of the Rolls and Records of renoun,
     How foon m'offended Prince they fand to frounc.

Chance, Change and Time yit juftlie did conjoure,
And for my follies fram'd my fall and foill,
Which me from th' hight of my beft fortouns bure,
Fleim'd and defam'd wnto a forraigne foill;
     Whair I bot vext did wait on others will,
     Whill Death woutchaf'd to eas and end my ill.

141.

Moſt pregnant Worthie, worſhipfull and grave,
In worde, in vote, and in thy working wiſe;
With gifts more nor gray hairs grac'd is thy grave,
Whairin thy reliques reſts and ludg'd now lies;
    A wonder once, a world of witt and worth,
    Th' Vliſſes of this Iland ſince thy birth.

Before thé few, and ſeldome ſince are ſuch
In giving of a councill ſage and found,
In turns materiall that the State did twich,
Non faithfull forowarder nor thow was found,
    Ane as in State that in the Church advis,
    Nev'r fail'd, nev'r did difficult things refuiſe.

For in what was thy witts and ſpreit imployd,
Thy tongue, lyke Tullies, told, thy pen expreſt.
Or than thy cuning compaſs'd and convoy'd,
And what difficill was to doe, thow dreſt;
    Yea, whan awry (ſeem'd works of greateſt weight)
    And crooked kyth'd, thow cauſed them ſtand wp ſtreight.
             T

142. **Sir John Skeen.**

Of Currihill, Knight; ane eloquent Orator, learned Jurist, skil-
full Antiquarie; principall Clerk of the Registers and Rolls,
and one of the Lords of his Majestys most honorable Privie
Councill.   He died 1617.

Gif martiallie, or be what means of might,
(Amongs the noble Romans e're renoun'd)
A citizen ane other sav'd in fight,
He was with civick wreaths decor'd & croun'd;
    And therfore honor'd more & thought of thofe,
    Then he that hade triumphed and taen ten foes.

Gif then the faver of a citizen
Thefe worthie Romans grac'd & fo reguarded,
How shall the paines and practeis of thy pen
Be worthilie, as they were worth, rewarded,
    That fav'd fo many thowfands of this Isle,
    Whill thow refyn'd the stuff, refram'd the style?

Of th' Ancient Monuments, the Modern Laws,
And foundamentall Statutes of Estate,
Works of great witt and knowledge who nought knaws,
Into two volums both as good as great;
    Wherin thefe Law's are be thy labors dreft,
    And to thy praife, plain'd, pollisht & expreft.

143. **Alexander Burnet.**

Of Leyes; a honorable, wife & politique gentlman.   Died
anno 1620.

Suift filver ftreams, fmooth, flaw and foftlie flyd,
No, ftay yow ftill, rin retrograd and turne,
Re-gorge againe, dead bot a motione byde,
With cairfull Crathes to lament and mourne,
     And as my Leyes along the mourners bears,
     Deave them with din, and droun them with thy tears.

And I, I fhall re-echo everie roare,
Refound our forrows and our fhouting fhrill,
While they wnto the criftall celing foar,
And all the Earth as they wpfleing fill;
     For he our love is to be buri'd borne,
     That me fo much and Dea did thé adorne.

In cariaige comlie, in his counfaills faige,
Pollitique he was, provident and wife;
Ane ornament and honor to his aige,
Now in the phane, which he caus'd frame, he lies,
     Awaiting, as all that be mortall muft,
     (To reigne in reft) the ryfing of the Juft.

144. Sir Thomas Menzies.

Of Cults, Knight; Prepofite of the burgh of Aberdeen; ane
accomplifhed & a worthie gentlman; returning from Court
to Scotland, depairted this life, in the North pairt of
England, the yeare 1620.

S age facred Mufe! prepare thy felfe t'affift
I n fable cyphers for to fet my fong,
R efang thy flute and with a flebile fift
T urn'd to the tune moft tearfull tunes among,
H eirs a Thanatick theame, t'extend and ftraine
O ctav's in voe, ov're everie common vene.

M oft meftfull Citie, moan and murne with me,
A nd from the laweft vaile and vults of voe
S earche for the caires that yet wnknawne be;
M afk mufters then and fwarmes of forows fhoe,
E xceeding all and all exceffive more
N or hes bein told of in the times before,

G roan Tragick girle and paffionatlie plaine,
Y ell with thy voce a deed and doolfull dittie,
E vir ejulat, groan and regrate againe,
I n tearmlefs tears the forrows of this Cittie;
S ince, to her great & wondrous voe in volor,
O h! ominous to it expir'd her olor.

145. Alexander Setone.

Earle of Dumfermling, Lord Fivie, &c.; Great Chancellor of
Scotland, and High Commiffioner for his Majefty in Parliament, anno 16   : ane egregious Earle; a fingular, good
and gratious Judge; a great and grave Statfman; of a profound and prudent providence and witt; and moft worthie
of immortall memorie.   Depairted this prefent life, in the
yeare 1622.

Accomplifht Count, when broot of Fame hade blaw'n,
And doubtfullic dilated hade thy death,
Tho too too trew, as t'have bein cleerlie know'n,
The Virtues therewith wrong'd weept & were wracth,
    The Graces groan'd, the Mufes all they murn'd,
    All th' Arts there cheerfull lookes in luring turn'd.

The Princes plaind, the mightieft bemoan'd,
The learn'd lament't, and voefull was the vife;
The confcrip-fathers when they think wpon't,
Was he with there eyes the ludging where thow lyes;
    And all the Jurift's with there clients come,
    And offers tears for tribute to thy tombe.

Egregious grave, thrife highlie happie thow,
That fo rare heavenlie troups, rich earthly traines,
Deplores thy death and to advance awow
Perpetually thy praifes with there paines,
    And make thy mercits bend above and ftreatch
    O're Mundane reafon, and all mortall reatch.

146. James, John, and Allan Stewarts.

Brothers, cufings-german to King David Bruce, and brother to
Robert the Second, King of Scotland; Hugh, Earle of Rofs;
Kenneth, Earle of Sutherland; Alexander Bruce, Earle of
Carrick; Andro, James, & Simon Frazers brother; all
worthie and valerous noble perfonagis, flaine in that
wnhappie feild of Halidonehill, 1333.

Boece, lib. 15.
fo. 328.

The Romans raige in warr and fought, bot how,
All nations help did with there ftandarts ftand;
Bot valerous and worthie Worthies yow,
That bot few Clans and Cohorts did command;
    And with fupport, aide, and fupplies bot fmall,
    Made oft your foes before yow fold and fall.

Io. Major.
lib. 5, fo.
99 & 100.

They for there oun effect, now friends, then foes,
With Fortoun favring as there freind did fight,
And with or gainft there mother countrie goes,
To roborat, or robb her of her right;
    As did that Antone, Marks, & Marius,
    Great Pompey, Sill, and Caefer Julius.

Bot ever famous yee, all force defeat,
Triumph'd on all attemps and wracks of warre,
And tho to fall in fine, it was your fate,
While fearlefs (doughtie) yow defending are
    Your Countries querrell and your Kings; what then?
    Yow leave, tho dead, therby immortall men.

147. 𝕽obert 𝕾tewart.

Sone to the Earle of Lennox; a noble & worthie Captane, never
　　wearied with the voes incident to warrs; Good-ſire to that
　　noble and famous Bernard Stewart, Lord of Obegny, &c.;
　　renounced ſo in the Frenſh, Scottiſh, Engliſh, and Italian
　　hiſtories; was ſlaine, with the Earle of Buchan, John
　　Stewart, Conſtable of France, and Archbald Dowglaſs,
　　Earle of Wigtone and Duke of Turone, att the battell of
　　Wernoll 1422.

Io. Major,
lib. 6, fo. 127

Bold Worthie! yow that thy begining brings,
And reakins from that root and Royall race,
Th' illuſtrious ſtocke and ſtemme of Steward Kings,
Whoſe glorie now this earthlic glob doth grace;
　　The wnconquer'd courage thow at Vernoll ſhew,
　　Thy pedegree from Princes ſprung proves trew.

Boece, lib. 16,
fo. 358.

It were diſgrace to him that thinks him come
From famelies of ſuch a famous fame,
So long, ſo nottablie renoun'd, to whom
Might aither be imputed baiſlie blame,
　　Or that his actions did not anſwer all,
　　And in ſome ſort ſhaw meer majeſticall.

Thow wiſelie this into thy wiſdome viev'd,
And Honor held thy diameter and ſquare;
Diſhonor baiſs, as ſhamefull thow eſchew'd,
And never did approve, that did impare
　　The glorious grandour, great renoun & name,
　　Of theſe from whence for to be come ye clame.

148. 𝕮𝖔𝖗𝖉𝖔𝖓.

In the reigne of King Malcolme Cainmor, this gallant man,
whose proper name is nought exprefl amongs diverfe others
valerous & proudent gentlmen, was then veric famous for his
courage and fingular good fervice in the faid Princes warrs;
and in great honor and highlie favour'd be reafon in his
faid Prince his prefence, in the wood off Huntlie, with
magne ftrength, & much magnanimitie, he overmaftered
and flew a terrible great boare, wherfore he was created
firft Lord Gordon, and caries in teftimonic therof three
boar-heads cutit of in a golden feild, of whom are that
numberous and noble name floorifhing this day defcendit.
He floorifh'd about the yeare 1063.

Ferrerius Pede-
montanus in In-
cremento et Ori-
gine Gordoni-
arum Familiæ.

Whan that renoun'd King, Malcolm Cainmor, rang,
Which was the Third in number of his name,
Thefe eminent and men of mark amang,
That hither on noc fmall occafions came;
  And were (for manfull & there martiall deed
  In our State ftories) regiftrat, wee read.

Boece, lib. 12,
p. 264.

Non more efteam'd, nor than thought of than thow,
Ane offspring more hes fpred in fo fhort fpace,
Yea, near to numbers numberlefs, he's now
Grow'ne from the Gordon ground of thy great race;
  And to a grandour fuch efteem'd hes ftor'd,
  That as thow than this countrie fince decor'd.

Leslie, lib. 6,
fo. 209.

Hol., Scot.
Hift., pag. 176.

Thy gloric great, gain'd by that gallant deed,
(The manfull maftring of that monftrous Boare)
Illuftrat fince and fhynes fo in thy feed,
Perforce perform'd thy Princes face before,
  That clarefeis and thy couragious kinde,
  Thy mightic martiall and thy manfull minde.

149. Sir William Gordon.

A wight, valiant, and worthie Knight; nottable and famous in
the reigne of Alexander the 2ᵈ; with diverſe others of the
Nobilitie of the Scottiſh Natione, Patrick Dumbare Earle
of March, and David Lindſay of Gleneſk, went with Lodo-
vick, the 7 King of France, to Jeruſalem to the Sacred Warrs;
and there, waliantlie ſeightand, with manie other noble
Chriſtians, were ſlaine about the yeare 1232.

Ferrerius de montan, incre-mente Origine Gordoniarum familiæ.

Among the numbers of our noble Knights,
(And nought a few our ferteill countrie afforded)
That are found famous iuto forraigne fights,
As ours and other Chronicles recorded;
    Sir William, thow was noted ane of thoſe,
    That hatch'd high honors in the Heathen foes.

Boece, lib. 13, p. 294.

The firſt moſt famous honorable warr,
And onlie worthie valour to advance,
T' all force and ſeights to be preferred farr,
The loſs of life be there th'event and chance;
    For higher honor is to loſs all ſo,
    Nor conquer kingdoms from a Chriſtian foe.

Thy courage there did thy deſcent declare,
And there the pictie of thy ſpreit was ſpyed,
That ſpair'd thy proves heir and proof'd it there,
Where valiantly advancing there thow dy'd;
    The noble quarrell & the Chriſtian clame,
    To th'endleſs gloric of the Gordons name.

U

150. ffor-beſt.

Ane ancient worthie gentlman; the head & cheeff of ane great
familie, markablie remembered in the Hiſtory of Scotland,
hade his name changed from that of his forbears, called
(   ) and by the occaſione of the kiling of a
mightie bear, or rather a boare, was called "For-the-beſt,"
and by contraction Forbes, as all the families deſcended
from him are ſoe named to this day. He flooriſhed in the
reigne of Robert the Firſt, about the yeare 1317.

My father, freinds, and all my kinſmen kinde,
And what was thers, there ſtrength, there ſtates, ther ſtore,
With there wſurping fatall foes was fil'd,
And in there pow'r what they poſſeſt before;
    My pregnant Mother only ſcaps there hands,
    Wnknow'n, and force fled wnto forraigne lands.

Boece, lib. 14.
fo. 300.

Whaire whill I to a twentie yeares attain'd,
To long and large with folks wnknow'n a while,
With me my murning Mother there remain'd,
Attending better tymes then ſtill exile;
    For when the conquering Bruce here all commands,
    I come againe, and clam'd my fathers lands.

But being by that Prince deſpon'd before,
To cauſe his wiſdome with his valour ſhine,
He doth a ſtate (tho nought the fame) reſtore
To me as much as I could clame for myne;
    And if the treuth our Annalls hes expreſt,
    My name was chang'd and I was cal'd Forbeſt.

151. **Malcolm Earl of Lennox.**

And Gilbert Hay, Lord Erroll; two honorable noblemen, the
constant and faithfull followers of the victorious King,
Robert the Firſt; and two that attended and never forſook
him in all his   . They flooriſh'd in his reygne
about the yeare of Chriſt   .

Weell-worthie Worthies of a wortheis name,
And worthie all the honors to inhereit,
That faultleſs faith and conſtancie can clame,
Or magnitude of martiall minds can mereit,
　　Since through your faith now hence three hunder years,
　　Freſh floorifhing and faire your fame appeares.

Whill th' ev'r matchleſs memorable Prince,
The bold King Robert, that conducter brave,
For martiall ſpreit and practeize never ſince,
(Shall Nature boaſt that ſuch a grand ſhe gave)
　　Wiſelie gave way to Time fearce feats & foes,
　　That then t' oppreſs him all there powr's oppoſe.

Then ſtedfaſtlie to him in all his ſtraits,
While others hade noe hope, yow did adheare
In all his fortouns, when raw roots he eats,
And when he triumph'd too, both ye were there,
　　As latelie to adorne yow, Daniell
　　Into King Edward Long-leggs Life dois tell.

152. 𝕯𝖆𝖛𝖎𝖉 𝕳𝖆𝖞 𝕮𝖔𝖓𝖘𝖙𝖆𝖇𝖑𝖊.

Keith Marſhall;   Strathquhan, then Chamberlane
to the Chancellor of Scotland; John Randolph, Earle of
Morray, and Earle of Strathearne; James Lindſay of
Gleneſk; John Lyon of Bonewill; Roger Scrimgeor;
[William] Fraſer; Alexander Gordone; John Waus;
Michaell Scott; Dowgall Campbell; Maurice Murray;
Alexander Bodevall, called the Flour of chivalry; Robert
Leſlie; and John Myrtoun; with many other gentlmen and
commons, ſlaine att the battell of Durham, 17 October 1346.

Boece, lib. 15,
fo. 336.

All they for worthie deeds that glorie gain'd,
And hev'd there honors out of hote alarms,
All they in pret'red tymes that he obtained
Fame for there faɛts and aɛtions in ther armes;
      Yea all remembred into martiall ſtorie
      Deſerve no more renoun, no greater glorie.

Leſlie, lib. 7.
p. 255

Nor yow all gallants and egregious Earles
Have, att the laſt expyring of your ſperit,
About your Prince wnparaleled pearls,
That day att Durham where ye dy'd demerit;
      When as your valour to your foes a wonder,
      Or life leaſt yow laid many of them wnder.

Hol., pag. 241.

Yet tho your deſteneis decre'd that ye,
Into that famous fight among your foes
Debaiting, ſould for your King David die,
And in that bloodie campe your courſes cloſe,
      Such floods of fame ſlou'd from your purple ſtream's,
      That notifies, & nottablie, your names.

153. The Earles

Of Dowglafs (called William); Fife; Sutherland; Wigtoun; and
Monteath; honorablie, after manfull and valerous feighting
with there foveraigne Lord, King David Bruce, were taken
with him in the battell of Durham, 17 October, the yeare
1348.

What tho ye captive were, thrice worthie Counts,
Your hearts difdain'd for to defert your King,
Where through your glorie graves your mercits mounts,
And from your priffon does your praifes fpring;
    For to have fayntlie fled, and left your Prince,
    Hade been a deip defect, a foull offence.

And as thofe Princlie Peers above the poolls,
That with him there there fpireit plac't are fpent,
So with your noble names remembrance poolls,
Enritched are with gold engrav'n and grac'd;
    And are your lauds, they are no less, fince Fate,
    T' attend your captive King, prolong'd your date.

And yet nought want of ventring nor goodwill,
No, nor of ftrength nor ftomach to withftand,
Your foes that caught yow and your freinds did kill,
And a're your oft-croft Captane did command,
    No but the Fat's preordaind they fhould fall,
    And yow furveive for to revenge them all.

Boece, lib. 15,
fo. 336.

Leil., lib. 7.
pag. 255.

Hol., Scot.
Hift., p. 241.

154. John Lion.

The firſt Lord Lion of Glamms; a man adoarn'd with many
nottable and ſingular graces of the minde, advanced to the
court and favour of King Robert the 2^d; and maried
Elizabeth Stewart, daughter to the said mightic Prince, and
therby got many faire lands, high honors, and great
dignities; and was made Chancellor of Scotland; &
wnhappilie ſlaine in Forfar, be James Lindsay Lord of
Crawford, the yeare   .

By no fain'd Fate that th' Heathen hold divine,
But deſtinat and be Divine decree,
It was ordain'd, Lord Lion of thy line,
That thow the firſt ſhould riſt renoun'd to be;
    Since that thy nature, name & noble minde,
    Expreſt thow ſprang & come of Lion kinde.

Thy high attemps above baſe ſpircits ſprings,
And lot ſuccefs did ſecond thy aſſiſe,
Thow ſcorn'd to linck but with the line of Kings,
Directlie whence diſcended are theſe ſayes,
    As trew tongu'd knawledge reckoning them records
    All lawfull from thy loyns ten Lion Lords.

Egregious ſonns with thé there great-grand-ſyre,
All in your tim's amplie advanc'd & rais'd
To places of reſpect in this Impire,
And by the Princes your promovers prais'd,
    For weell imploy'd paines into your places,
    The higheſt honor of heroick races.

155. **Thomas and Nicholas Erskine.**

Alexander Lindſay, and William Cuningham of Kilmauers, 4.
heroick and noble gentlmen, defeated ane ſtrong Engliſh
Hoaſt that landed on both the ſydes of the Firth. cruelly
deſtroying, killing, and herrying all before them where they
come, and burnt St. Colmes Abay, & many touns in Fyfe;
and att laſt were by thoſe noble and valerous gentlmen
valiantly routed, put to flight, ſlaine, taine, or drouned,
attempting to re-enter ther ſhips, in the reigne of King
Robert the Second.

Ane Engliſh armie Armada all in ire,
With barbarous bloodie harts and boutcher hands,
Beyond the Forth and into Fyfe with ſyre,
Moſt mercileſs all where they came commands;
　　No Churches, no, nor th' Abbays there forbearing,
　　But Tigre-lyke all tuging doun and tearing.

There violence all wraiked and devour'd,
Th' old they rept wpe and new born babs they brain'd;
Matrons miſus'd and maidens they deſlour'd;
The Holie houſſes ſpoyled and profain'd;
　　Cities they ſack't, the farms perforce in ſlamm,
　　And each the devill play'd proudlie in the ſamme.

This rent your ſoulls, and rais'd yow to revenge
With wondrous valour thoſe wnworthie wrongs,
Which as with ſtomach ſtout, with ſtrength as ſtrange,
Ye ranklie rag'd, theſe inhumane amongs:
　　And ſo vindictive were yow and weell will'd,
　　That all that came to hand were caught or kil'd.

156. Adam Gordon.

Sir John Swinton; John Levingſtoun of Callander; [Sir Alexander]
    Ramſay of Dalhouſſie; Walter de St. Clare; Rodger
    Gordon; and Walter Scott; all honorable, valerous, &
    oft renoun'd Knights; ſlaine in a battell att Hommildoun,
    fighting againſt Harie Percie, the Duke of Northumber-
    land, & George Dumbar, Earle of March, then a rebell
    to his countrie, & Patrick Hepburne of Haills, ſlaine att
    Niſbet, with ſundrie gentlemen of his houſs; fightand, as
    ſaid is, againſt the ſaid Duke & Earle, in the reigne of
    Robert the 3d, about the yeares 1402 & 1403.

Moſt loving ſonnes wnto your Mother-ſoil,
And all moſt valiant ventrars for her weell,
Wnnat'rally when ſhe contempt and ſpoill,
Yea force from March diſloyall faꞔts did ſeill;
    And for her peace tho ſome your ſprits there ſpended,
    Yet with your lives nor ſames nor honors ended.

For ſtill poſteritie ſhall preach your praiſe,
And all that's cairfull for the publiꞔt peace;
But martiall mynds ſhall magnifie and raiſe,
And moſt of all commend yow in this caice;
    To make from all there bloodie beds your worth
    (Yitt glorious graves) your laud and ſame fly furth.

Such powerfull vertew hade your purple wounds,
Such living force hade all your dying falls,
That both ſtill your heroick honor ſounds,
And yow your Countries killed campeons calls;
    The honor that heroes highſt hold,
    Howbeit moſt dear for to be ſought & ſold.

157. **William Dowglafs.**

Earle of Angous; Alexander, Lord Elphinftone; & Adam
Hepburn of Haills; three martiall & egregious Noblemen,
defeit Henrie Perfey Duke of Northumberland, att Pyperden,
in the reigne of James the 1.; flew Harie Cliddifdale, John
Ogle, & Ritchard Perfey, knights, with 15 hundereth
gentlmen, and commons, and 40 knights therof: Alexander
Lord Elphinftoun, fo feirclie following the flying enemie, is,
with two   knights, and twa hundereth in the feight,
and there flaine about the yeare   .

When the Northumbrian Prince the Perfey arm's,
Rackt with four thowfand bold men in his bands,
And with all malice hurt and hofteill harmes,
Brack's in our Borders and the Limit-lands,
    Whill by your worthie walors they were then,
    Stai'd and conftrain'd to fight att Pipperden.

Where nought few hour's moft feirclie there ye fought,
And nought amongs yow militar omitted,
That aither fhould be done in deid or thought,
And that commanders great in feighting fitted;
    For all the captanes & attenders too,
    Did all that they in there degrees fhould doe.

With courage all yow conftantlie contend,
For life and honor, countrie, freinds & fame,
Whill your wndaunted, aufull armes in end
Quel'd all there Cohorts and confounded thame,
    Tho thow Lord Elphinftone there loft thy life,
    In that feirce conflict & that bloodie ftrife.

X

158. 𝕮𝖎𝖑𝖑𝖎𝖆𝖒 𝕯𝖔𝖜𝖌𝖑𝖆𝖘.

Sone to Archibald, Lord Galloway; wan great fame & honor, for his
     high proves & noble valiancie, etc.; wherfore King Robert 2
     thought him worthie of high advancment, and gave him his
     daughter Giles in mariaige, and with her the Lands of Nid-
     difdale. This William was a blacifh color, not overcharged
     with flefh, bot bigg of bone; a mightie perfonage; wpright
     and tall; valiant, courteous, amiable, free of liberalitie,
     merrie, faithfull and pleafant in companie; but heirwith of
     fuch ftrength that whenfoever he ftrook with mace, fword,
     or fpeare, doun he went, were he never fo weill armed;
     with 800 he fought and defeat 3000 Englifh, flew 200 &
     took 500 priffoners; in Spruffe chofen admirall; envyed by
     the Lord Clifford, was appealed to the combat, but before
     the day (being feared of his foe) was difhonorablie laid in
     wait for, and before the day of tryall, wpon the Bridge of
     Danzike; was flaine about the yeare 1394.

How much thy ftrength and ftomach was efteem'd,
And how much made thy manhood thé admeer'd;
How much thy fpreit thy pedegree expreem'd,
And proof'd thé then even with the beft that fpeer'd,
     But derogatione wnto Royall races,
     Comparable in all in other caces.

So was thy valour valoued and vented,
So was efteeme'd thy actions in the Eaft,
In Spruffe report fo made thy provefs painted,
That there th'admeir'd thé as a Mars almaift,
     And therfore choofe thé Cheeff and Admirall,
     To there Sea-forces and there navies all.

But his envy and to thy honor hate,
Did caufe the Clifford, to thofe warrs invited,
Began a braill, a bargane and debate,
That privatly thy praifes ftill defpyted;
     And ye appeal'd, bot or th'appoynt'd day
     On Danzik Bridge did to his fhame thé flay.

159. [**Robert**] **Dowglafs.**

Mafter of Mortoun, Dalkeith, &c.; and [Laurence] Oliphant,
appearand heires to [William] Dowglafs, Earle of Morton;
and [Laurence] Oliphant, Lord Oliphant, two generous and
martiall minded Noblemen, depairted from Scotland the
yeare of Chrift [1584].

Egregious gallants in your greeneft youth,
Why fhould the World nought wonder & admeir
The deep defire and the dipfaik drouth,
That did into your fpringing fpreits appeare,
 Whill as the vigour of your valours wount,
 To make your doings your defignes furmount?

The knightlie couraige of your weell know'n kinde
Could nought comport, difpence with, nor indure
To be inclos'd, coapt wp, ingadg'd, confin'd,
Nor in this waterie-walled Ifle immur'd;
 Your mounting minds, heroick hearts fo high,
 Beyond her frontiers all (tho faire) did flie;

And made the Worlds remoteft ftrands the ftage,
Wheron your virtews valour fhould be view'd;
Which worthily hes for reward and wage,
Such glorie gain'd as death fhall ne're fubdew'd,
 Whill Heav'ns conceave and ftarry coap fhall coome,
 The Earth below, your ludging tent, your tomb.

160.   **Devoted**

To the Immortall Memorie of all Collonells, Captanes, Commanders and Gentlemany Servurs of the Scottifh Nation,
flaine in the moft memorable Warrs in the Low-Countries
thefe   yeare by paft

And wnextracted yet your tropheas ftands,
And non to publifh your exploits prepaire them,
Which doe indeed deferve a hundereth hands,
And all the fkill of knawledge to declaire them;
    For Belgick by yow knaw fhe ne're o'recame,
    But authors yow or actors in the fame.

Your perfones to her perrells yow oppos'd,
And ne're for death or danger was, I dred,
Oft for her try'd tint wan triumph'd and lofs'd;
Yet ne're lyke couards from her colors fled,
    But 'gainft th' Iberian boldlie brooked bounds,
    Or gallantly glafs'd with your gore there grounds.

What honor herefore Belgick all yow aw's,
Heroicklie deferv'd, non will deny;
For the Caftilians to there coaft yet knaws,
With lauds and glory in your graues yow ly,
    And with a boldnefs brave your bloods yow bled,
    And great exploits with pettie powars exped.

161. George Keith.

Earle Marifhall, Lord Keith & Altrie; Ambaffador to Denmark
for the Mariaige of Anna with the moft mightie Monarch,
James, King of Great Brittane, France, etc., 1590; Lev-
tennant in the North of Scotland, & High Commiffioner
in Parliament, the yeare 1609; a wife, a learn'd, and a courteous noblman.   Depairted this prefent, the 5 of April,
1623, and of his aige the 70.

The glore of thy foregoing Grand-fires, great
Prœminence and fplendor of there place,
Thefe brave beginers, ftructors of there ftate,
There good guberning and there gallant grace,
    There worthie deeds and folemne fervice fince
    Imploy'd oft for the Publict weell and Prince.

Admeirablie hes magnify'd there name,
Yea ftellifi'd and ftreach't it to the ftarrs,
As proves our ftories to there praife fupream,
In times of battell and of bloodie warrs:
    A glorie great no lefs to thé then thame,
    Heire of there honors, fortons, faeth & fame.

Thy cariaige, knowledge, and thy candor cleare,
Imployments high in honorable affaires,
Ingraphs thy glore hings wpe thy honor here,
And of auld Earle the account compleit declar'd,
    To be a fubject to ane after ftorie,
    T'augment the grandor of the Marfhalls glorie.

162. George Hay.

A noble gentleman of high hope; fone to Frances, now Earle
of Erroll; Great Conftable of Scotland, etc., depairted in
France the yeare 1622; and Lawrence Gordone, fone to
George, now Marquefs of Huntlie, a noble youth of fingular
expectatione; depairted this prefent lyfe, the yeare of
Grace 1623.

Speek Argus-eyed and millé-mouthed Fame,
Why groans the Graces greived & agaft?
What ftirrs this ftrange diftemprature in thame,
And what ane wnknow'n crofs doth overcaft,
    Such clouds of caire t'eclips there cheerfull eyes,
    That wount to glade the Earth and grace the Skyes?

Why wondrous rofull weeps the Virtews all,
As fpircitlefs, depreft and drooping dyes,
Who as they are fhould keith them Cardinall,
And ftill be ftout, ftill temp'rat, juft & wife;
    And for no chance, no change, no, no for non,
    (As mutable) be mov'd to mirth or moan.

Aud why amaz'd does all the Mufes murne,
And as diftraught dois roar and rend ther haire?
What doeth there Pindus or Parnaffus burne,
Or is Appollo chaced from his chaire?
    No, bot there lowes, there lifes, there Lords here lyes,
    And murning thus all acts there Obfequeis.

163.

Thy Anceftors as eminent as old,
Ay honor'd for there honor worth refpects,
For Virteus cariaige and for courage bold,
In publict prov'd be many faire effects,
    Monts thé this monument, this finlefs frame
    Of marble nought, bot of immortall fame.

This flux of fame that from thy fathers flows,
Deriv'd and dew to thé for thy defcarts,
More greater with thy gifts and graces grows,
And higher then th'Egiptian fteeples ftarts.
    For what there goods, there gifts, there graces gain'd,
    Thy couraige nor thy cariaige never ftain'd.

Nor did thy deeds difgrace nor wrong the word,
But proudent what thow promeis'd did performe;
Ne're wndeferv'd did thow wnfheith thy fword,
Nor with thy freind in his diftrefs did ftorme;
    But like a wifeman that of Wortheis came,
    Poiz'd what thow purpos'd & expead the fame.

164.   Lindſay.

A proper name to him than whilk now is the ſurname of the
    wholl Clan; a generous, ſpireited Gentlman; in the tyme
    of Kenneth the Second, rewarded with large lands for his
    good counſall and ſoveraigne manhood in the overthrow
    and extirping of the Pights: this is drawn from the
    Oratione made be David, Earle of Crawfoord to King
    James 2d, when he craved pardon for the rebellion with
    the Earl of Douglaſs, about the yeare 1.45   .

Into his ſpring then in perfecter yeares,
His vigour will'd, his ſpireits prickt him too,
And courage his conceats calls wp & cheers,
Somewhat of worth t'attempt, t'intend & doo,
        That ſhould deſigne the deeps of his deſires,
        Ev'r from the pappe promp & diſpos'd to eſpire.

Wherfore whill Alpins ſone, King Kenneth rang,
The root wpe-renter of the Pictiſh race,
His men of mark and militants amang,
His courage conqueſt him a Captanes place,
        In which his valour, witt & virtews wan
        As much applaus as any other than.

That nev'r ynough, nor too much praiſed Prince,
A wiſe rewarder of a worthie deed,
Advanc'd him for his ſervice, ſo that ſince
In ſolemne ſort, his ſucceſſors & feed,
        To honors neireſt to the Royall race:
        But wnder heavn, no State heir ſtable ſtay's.

165. David Lindſay.

Earle of Crawfoord; Alexander Ogilvie, of Innerquharritie;
John Forbes, of Pitſligo; Alexander Barclay, of Gartuly;
James Maxwell, of Tellen; Invein Garden, of that Ilk;
Duncan Campbell, of Conſyth; William Garden, of Bur-
rowfield, barrons; & many gentlmen ſlaine att the battell
of Aberbroth, the yeare of Chriſt 1445, 9 callend of
February.

My Muſe reſolv'd to ſearch and ſeek no more
For nottable and men of noble fame,
Into our Annalls as ſhe ws'd before,
That could a croun of commendation clame;
    For valor, or for works of witt, or both,
    That graced are, and there ingraphted Goth.

The bleeding Ghoſts of thoſe about ingroſs'd,
As yet in armes and paſſion ſeem'd t'appeare,
That by Arbroth were in that battell loſt,
And ireſull aſk her and in ſplen they ſpeare
    Why ſhe did hipp them that with honor hade,
    As any there their bloods as bravely blade.

Howbeit with groans they granted that the grounds,
Of theſe there greeſſs indeed were not ſo great,
That gave ſo many deaths and deedlie wounds,
To breed ſo blood a battell and debeat;
    Yet they proteſt, there proves there expres'd,
    Requyr'd to be recoorded with the reſt.

Y

166. Alexander Lindſay.

The nixt eminent ſucceſſor to that Lindſay, the firſt which wee
find of that name, ſlaine att the bridge of Stirline, in the
quarrell of King Robert the Firſt, about the yeare 1306;
Alexander Lindſay, ſone to the precedent Alexander, was
ſlaine att that mightie maſſacre made att Dupline, the yeare
1332; after this Alexander ſucceided, both heire to his
lands & fortoune, for he was ſlaine att Halydoun Hill, the
yeare 1333; then David Lindſay, ſone to John, brother to
the former David, ſucceided, and was the firſt created Earle
of Crawfoord; fought for his Countrie with the Lord Wells on
the Bridge of London, on St. George Day, & vanquiſhed
him.   anno 1396.

Into that famous firſt King Roberts reigne,
That valerous and thunderbolt in warr,
Who bett in battell that brave Engliſh King
Neir Bannockburn, and drave him to Dumbar;
    Att Stirling Bridge, I th' Engliſh power oppos'd,
    And was in combat kill'd by them inclos'd.

My ſucceſſor be law & be my line,
In David Bruce defence att Dupline dy'd;
His heir againe lyke fortone & lyke ſyne,
Att Halidon with honor ſtoutlie try'd,
    And fell for Scotlands freedome & defence,
    Tho treaſon ther tint all, & negligence.

His nephew nixt in his default of heirs,
That commonlie was Earle Beardie call'd,
The noble notes firſt of our countie vearſe,
And was condignlie in that ſtate inſtall'd,
    When for the Land on London Bridge he fought,
    With honors charg'd & home with triumphs brought.

167. James.

Marquis of Hamiltoun, Earle of Arran and New Caftll, Lord
Evandale, etc.   A wife & gallant nobleman, depairted the
prefent, in England, the   day of the yeare 1625.

March mother Breitan all in mvrning maner,
And make thow forrow fubjeft to thy fong,
Since death and dolor with there bealfull baner
Triumphs thy Princes and thy Peers among:
    Let nought bot fable and the blake be borne,
    And noe fkye collour be nor fkarlet worne.

O Brittane! now thy beft and braveft men,
Thy nottable and non bot Nobles dies,
And thefe into there coffins cary'd then
Are ofteft objefts to thy weeping eyes;
    Murne then therfore and matchleflie be mail,
    Since dayly day's thy braveft & thy beft.

Great Lord! in England it hes bein thy lot,
Wherin thy old for-bears firft did breath,
And nought where they great lands and honor got,
In Scotland, to have pay'd thy debt to Death;
    Yet tho thow there expyr'd or th' afh & wrne,
    Scotland fhall ay for thé her Marquefs murne.

168.

Thy gallant prefence & thy grand afpect,
Thy brazen breaft and thy high beilded braine,
Did works of worth and facts of fame s' affect
With perrill practeiz'd and tho prooĕt with paine
    That never feeble feare, nor force of foes,
    Could hold thé from the hazarding for thofe.

Yet virtew, wifdome, with defire divine,
Religious love and lowlinefs of heart,
Compofe thé in thy courfes to inclyne
T' all found fitting to a prudents parte,
    And caufe thé in thy carriaige fweetlie fho
    That headftrong will thy virtews wronged no.

In all th' adoes into thy waxing dayes,
Thy prooffs were practeifes of fpreit & pith,
But worthie all, and fuch were thy affayes,
As did a Count become conforted with
    Non but thofe that were with deferts indeu'd,
    For never thow of lofs nor lend allow'd.

169. David Lindsay.

Earle of Crawfoord, Lord Lindsay; a young nobleman too much
caried with the conceats of too too young counsallors, mis-
manadged & crofs-caried the great estate of his Noble
forbears, and dyed the yeare 16   .

Altho that youth did wreist thy witt awray,
And hair-brain'd heads held thé as captive caught,
That fuck'd the cisterns of thy substance dry,
And brought thy Hous & noble name to naught;
    Yet since fans blotts scarce any be that breath,
    Oblitrat be thy o'refights after death.

The fortouns of thy Fathers famous hous,
That revrend once, now no respected race,
Crofscoming accidents and profperous,
That Clans sky scalling and declyning cace,
    Thy gloring and thy greef for both in raw,
    Charactred in thy countenance wee saw.

The sweet remembrance of there rich renoun
Incres'd thy joyes and made thy glaidness grow,
But sadd records of there farr falling doun
Did all contents and joyfull thoughts o'rethrow;
    There splendor spent and glorious grandor once
    For this yow joy'd, for that thy ghost yet groans.

170. John Earle of Mont-Rose.

Lord Graham and Mont-diew, Lord High Commiſſioner for
  that Monarch of immortall memorie James, King of Brittane,
  etc. in matters Ecclefiaftick, & Cheef Prefident of the
  honorable Privie Councill; a valerous, wife, and worthie
  Earle; depairted the   day of   the yeare 1626.

Whoſe pinſell can portray, paint, or expreeme,
And leivlie to the life out limne & lay
The bounties blooming in thy breſt fubleeme,
Out braving all that Brittane boaſt of may;
      For prudence, proves, fprit & pictie,
      Perfected hade perfectione all in thé?

The volumnes that avoutch old vereties,
From aige to aige exhibeit hes on Earth
Such perfect paterns to pofterities
Of thy for-bears bountie to thy birth
      And fince fo fhyn'd in thy oun witt and worth,
      That whither moft deferve is doubtfull yett.

So excellent in armes was each of thofe,
And fo fitt fund to governe in there gouns,
And thow for couraige great againes thy foes,
With wifdome grave hes gotten fuch renoune,
      That judgment doubts gif it in this may doe
      Give all the glore to them, or all to yow.

171. **John Lord Ramfay.**

Vifcount Hadingtoun and Earle of Huldernefs; eternally renoun'd
for manifafting in his younger yeares fo refolute and noble
valour in the releif and aide of his foveraigne Lord, James
King of Great Brittane, etc., in that trefonable attempt of
Gowry, by killing him and his brother with his hand in
Perth, the firft [fifth] day of Auguft the yeare 1600.   Departed in England 1625.

This matchlefs motto and this martiall word,
Given thé by that wnparaleled Prince,
That hand, that percied hart and crouned fword,
Whofe like nought once before nor given was fince,
    Gives both a glorie, grandor and a grace,
    To thé and thine and all the Ramfays race.

To have it by thy Soveraigne faid, that thow,
Heroick Huldernefs, with hardy hand,
Hade boldlie brought two brother bad to row,
And did in triumph on there ftomachs ftand,
    In the releeving of his life, what glore
    On earth could any fubject feek for more?

Yea multituds and millions of his men,
His loving and his loyall-fubjects, fhall
Yet wifh thy lot, and wold have ventur'd then,
Suppofe perfwaded to have perifh'd all;
    But it thy deed was by decree divine,
    Then herefore be the glorie there of thine.

172. Thomas Erskine.

Thrife fortounat and famous I confefs,
Borne to adorne this natione and thy name,
Thow noblie now deferve renoun, no lefs;
Nor thyn anceftors did, whofe ftrength extream,
 Cowrage, kene-eag'd, dreed dints and deeds of hand,
 Oppofe there pow'r that prefs'd t'opprefs this land.

There martiall minds immortallie did mereit,
And o're the fphears on penns of praife does fpring,
But honorable and happie thow inhereit
Above all goods and gold, a greater thing,
 Wnblamifh'd honor and wnbounded glore,
 Eternall and interminable ftore.

How that immortaleized Monarch now,
Thy Prince, preferving proves did approve,
And in what honor high he held thé too,
His lordly patents, large and livlie love,
 Lo! with th'immargend diton drawen wp there,
 To crown thy courage ever fhall declare.

Craig
woorthies

IN

Immortall remembrance of
that worthie reigning Roch —
Albeid change of ... raigne
...fo Britan departed 262

Thow that be rayr behold and passing hey,er
This mountanet ander altho notight made of marble
Nit thow within the womb therof thero lyjs
The urah (a wound'rd wonder for the warble)
And sundz of a Roch that sometime hang —
So sweet that y'ndois stroke a parteaf thing

This Roch, which more then any uthe Roch
It raygd in word acompt nor Caledon
As iwellisht pearls darin'd with apollo's trink
More prisd nor parian or porpher ston
Whose ... nor Zephir ... the founded ...ller
And therfore now plac'd for apollo's pillar.

Then hyred her maids pansit Ruby soft
And lay on Laurd for apollo's love
To crowin this roll that the quick range furlossd
Whose mollid measurd modulat did move
(In lyvlie stanzas and sterne stretching style
... admonas mon the mountans of this yle

173. In

Immortall rememberance of that fweitlie reigning Rock, Alexander
Craige of Rofs-Craige, Banfo-Britan.   Depairted 162 .

Thow that be hape beholds, and paffing fpyes
This mountane mean, altho nought made of marble,
Wit thow, within the womb therof there lyes
The wrak (a woundred wounder for his warble)
    And ruines of a Rock that fomtime fang
    So fweet that Pindois fhooke & Parnafs rang?

A Rock much more then any Rubie rich,
A Craige in more accompt nor Calcidon,
A pollifh'd Pearle trim'd with Apollo's tuich,
More pris'd nor Parian or Porphor fton;
    Whofe voice nor Zephir-winds hes founded fhriller,
    And therfore here plac'd for Apollo's pillar.

Then fpred her purple panfes, ruby rofes,
And lay on lawrell for Appollo's love,
To croun this coll that this quick Craige inclofes,
Whofe mellid meafurs modulat did move
    In lyvlie ftanzas and ftarrie ftreatching ftyle,
    T'admeir as men the Montans of this Yle.
          Z

174. 𝕹igell, 𝕿homas, and 𝕬lexander 𝕭ruce.

Breither to the firſt King Robert, valerous and martiall noblemen.
Nigell, betrayed with the caſtell of Kildrimmie, delivered
to the firſt King Edward, and in Berwick cruellie put
to death; and the ſaid Thomas & Alexander, traiterouſlie
taken be there countriemen, followers of King Edward,
&, in diſpight of there brother King Robert, were beheaded in Carleill the yeare 1306.

Thryſe generous, thrice grand and gallant Knights,
Yow manfull Breither of the martiall Bruce,
Whoſe awfull armes and fervour in his fights,
His diadem di-repted did reduce;
    The Fates defy'd his foes, perforce defate
    Triumph'd, re-rais'd his throne, reſtor'd his ſtate.

What ſhall I firſt, your ſtocks, your ſtrengths, your ſtates,
Your couraiges, your conſtancies commend,
Your fortouns faire, your ſtrainge, your many ſtraits,
And gallant jeſts wnto your glorious end?
    No, no, my Muſe too mean, my ſkill is ſkant,
    Such three cheeff Chiſtanes, and ſo choſe to chant.

Yit ſince your lives ye loſt, and by all laws
Kill'd in cold blood, and captives caught cutt off;
Yea, boutcher'd beaſtlie for your Brothers cauſe,
She tyes wnto your tombs this Epitaphe;
    Heir valor wrong'd lyes to the Buchers blame
    Dead, living by illimitabill Fame.

175. John Garden.

Of that Ilk, ſlaine with ſundrie of his name and freinds in the
vauntguaird with Archbald, Earle of Angous, in the Feild of
Pinkie, the yeare 1547.

Gif everie chiſtane, leader, Lord & cheef,
As did the Dowglaſs what they doth hade done,
And march'd to Timby, to have lent releeſe
To thoſe that fought, it hade bein ſene & ſone
    St. Andrew hade, and nought St. George that day,
    The glorie gaird and victor went away.

Bot ſome were ſlaw, ſome ſainit and full of ſeare,
And ſome that others valor did envy,
Swa that theſe ills together thronging there
The vauntguaird wrang'd, and then all went away;
    Where through thow fell, and many manfull more
    Did die, were ſlaine, and ſacriſeis'd therfore.

And yet altho our Camp miſcariage croſs'd,
Thy glorie was, and ours thy Ooes, that thow
Thy deareſt life for thy deare Countrie loſt,
And ly's in Honors bed and boſome now,
    As does all ſuch that panſe nought for no perrell,
    And hazarding dies in there Countries quarrell.

The Author, on the margin of a confiderable part of the Manufcript, quotes the authorities on which his verfes are founded, confifting of a few well-known works. The editions may here be fpecified:—

No. I.—HECTOR BOETHIUS.—The title of his Chronicle, as originally publifhed, is: "Scotorum Hiftoriæ a prima gentis origine, cum aliarum & rerum & gentium illuftratione non vulgari, etc., Quæ omnia impreffa quidem funt Iodoci Badii Afcenfii typis & opera: impenfis autem Nobilis & prædocti viri Hectoris Boethii Deidonani: a quo funt & condita & edita." After the preliminary leaves of Dedications, and various leaves of "Scotorum Regum Catalogus," "Index," &c., a feparate title has this Infcription, "Quæ impreffa funt Typis Iodoci Badii & impenfis Hectoris Boethii." On a fubfequent leaf a letter of Alexander Leo, Moravienfis ecclefiæ Cantor, addreffed "Scotorum Nobilitati," has the date "Ex Parrhifiorû Academia celeberrima Ad Idus Martias, M.D.XXVII., ad calculum Romanum," folio.

This hiftory was republifhed, and contained "Libri XIX. duo poftremi huius Hiftoriæ libri nunc primum enittuntur in lucem. Acceffit & huic editioni eiufdem Scotorum Hiftoriæ continuatio, per Joannem Ferrerium," &c., Parifiis, 1574. Some copies are dated 1575, but the volume itfelf was printed at Laufanne. As thefe editions are not divided into chapters, Garden may have occafionally made ufe of the old tranflation by John Bellenden, Archdeacon of Moray, entitled "Heir beginnis the Hyftory and Croniklis of Scotland:" Printed at Edinburgh by Thomas Davidfon, about 1542, fmall folio.

No. II.—JOHN MAJOR.—The original edition of his History has the following title:—" Historia Maioris Britanniæ, tam Angliæ, quam Scotiæ, per Joannem Maiorem, nomine quidem Scotum, professione autem Theologum, e veterum monumentis concinnata. (woodcut Prelum Ascensiaum). Venundatur Iodoco Badio Ascensio. (There is added on the page, Fo. CXLVI.) Ex officina Ascensiana, ad Idus Aprilis M.D.XXI." 4to.

No. III.—RALPH HOLINSHED.—The First and Second Volumes of Chronicles, &c.

> 1. The Description and Historie of England.
> 2. The Description and Historie of Ireland.
> 3. The Description and Historie of Scotland.

First collected and published by Raphaell Holinshed, William Harrison, and others. 3 vols. in 2. London. 1587, folio. The work was originally published, with woodcuts. 2 vols., at London, in 1577, small folio.

No. IV.—FRANCIS THINN.—"Ane English Writer." was one of the Continuators in the above edition of Holinshed. 1587.

No. V.—JOHN FERRERIUS.—History of the Gordons. This work, dated 1545, by the Continuator of Hector Boyce, still remains unpublished. It has this title in a copy amongst the Balfour MSS., in the Advocates' Library:—"Historiæ Compendium de Origine & Incremento Gordoniæ Familiæ, Johanne Ferrerio Pedemontano Authore, apud Kinlofs, fideliter collectum, 1545."—(See Bishop Nicolson's Scottish Historical Library. Lond., 1702, p. 242.")

No. VI.—JOHN LESLEY.—De Origine, Moribus, et Rebus Gestis Scotorum Libri Decem. . . . Authore Joanne Leslæo, Scoto, Episcopo Roffensi. Romæ, in Ædibus Populi Romani, M.D.LXXVIII. 4to.

No. VII.—JOHN JOHNSTON.—"HEROES ex omni Historia Scotica lectissimi. Auctore Johan. Jonstono Abredonense Scoto. Lugduni Batavorum, Excudebat Christophorus Guyotius sumtibus Andreæ Hartii Bibliopolæ Edinburgensis." 1603. 4to. Pp. xvi., 56.

As Garden's "Theatre of Scottifh Worthies" (like his former work, fee p. 16) is fo clearly founded upon this work of his predeceffor, in the felection of the Heroes, and in the profe notices, as well as the verfes that follow, fuch references to it will be added in thefe Notes, which are not fpecified in the margins, on to No. 139.

ALEXANDER GARDYNE.

At page 11, in referring to the courfe of Garden's education, it was fuggefted he might have been a ftudent in the Marifchal College, Aberdeen. This, however, may chance to be a wrong fuppofition. On looking over the Lifts of Students (copied many years ago), from Regifters of the Univerfity of St. Andrews, under the head " Nomina Incorporatorum qui fubfcribunt Articulis Religionis (ut fupra) Anno 1601, menfis Januarij 26, Collegii Salvatoris," Alexander Gardyne is fecond on the lift. This name and date fo coincide as to render it at leaft probable that the Poet and Advocate may have received part of his education at St. Andrews.

No. 9.—SIR ALEXANDER CARRON.—In the MS. after the Prefatory Notice, which ends: " he flourifhed the yeare of Chrift 1057 yeares," and the name Scrymgeour in the margin, there is interlined, in the handwriting of Robert Myln, the words " Enjoyed till the reigne of King Charles the 2d, when the tytle became extinct."

No. 17.—SIR WILLIAM WALLACE.—

> " But always equall for his wondrous worth
> To Hector, Haniball, to Hercules,
> Or to th' Athenian Themiftocles."

In fuch unmeaning comparifons, of which Garden was fo fond as to repeat them (fee, for inftance, Nos. 98, 101, &c.), he might with advantage have copied or tranflated from Johnfton (p. 9) the

following lines, put into the mouth of Sir William Wallace, with
the title :—

> " Ejus Oratio ad Edovardum I. Anglorum Regem, ad defectionem
> folicitantem.
>
>> " Non promiffa, minæ, terrórve avertere poffunt,
>> Patria libertas me mihi chara magis.
>> Degeneres animos tangant hæc talia, certum eft
>> Diis patriæ hanc animam reddere velle meæ."

Followed by fimilar verfes, with the title—

> " Ejufdem Oratio ad Robertum Bruffiarum ad Carronem amnem."

No. 24.—SIR WILLIAM SINCLAIR.—Father Richard Auguftin
Hay, in his "Genealogie of the Sainteclaires of Roflyn" (in his MS.
Collections dated 1700), celebrates Sir William St. Clair and Sir
Robert (not Sir Walter) Logan, who carried the heart of Robert
Bruce to the Holy City for its burial in Jerufalem.   On their return
from this pious undertaking, they were flain in the year 1330 by the
Saracens in Spain.   Father Hay further fays "A modern Poet hath
made the following verfes on Sir William Saintclaire and Sir
Robert Logan, two honourable and hardie Knights," &c. :—

> " The conftant courage, & the loyall love
> The hardie hearts, the reddines of hands,
> Whill that the ftrong King ftiff and ftoutlie ftrove
> By force & flight to free (half loft) his lands;
>> That in thir two, tried in his worthie warres,
>> Makes them now glifter lyke two golden ftarres.
>
> " The oppofition and alterations oft,
> That to imped thair Prince his piece appear'd,
> Made nought, ther gallants leave him while aloft
> On honours rock his royall ferge was reir'd :
>> No, nor when dead; but both, lo! after death
>> Thir Knights weell kithed, to leave their Lord were leath.
>
> " For with that hardie Counte that had his harte,
> To be inhumed att the Holy Grave,
> This pare, therewith to pafs prepair'd depairt
> To do't, the honor laft that it fhould have;
>> Which duely done. as the deceaft deferved,
>> Gainft Saracens, whill they were flaine, they ferv'd."

Correſponding with Garden's poem, without either mentioning his name, or in whoſe poſſeſſion the Manuſcript was.

No. 40.—JAMES, EARL OF DOUGLAS.—Johnſton ſupplies the date xxi. Julii. A.C. 1388.

No. 43.—SIR ALEXANDER OGILVIE.—Johnſton (p. 20) celebrates theſe Heroes, ſlain at Harlaw, June 24, 1411, under a general head, "ΚΕΝΟΤΑΦΙΟΝ Magnanimis Heroibus, ac civibus, qui ſe Donaldinis Inſulanis objecerunt in Memorabili ad Harlaum Pugna, Roberto Stuarto Prorege pro Jacobo Primo, ad diem 24 Junii, Anno Chriſti 1411."

No. 50.—THOMAS BOYD, EARL OF ARRAN.—Jo. Jonſt., p. 22, ſays he was interred at Antwerp, "cui Carolus Audax Burgundus affinis & amicus in exilio ſepulchrum cum honorifico ellogio poſuit, circa Annum Chriſti 1470."

No. 51.—LORD BERNARD STUART, of the houſe of D'Aubigney in France, who diſtinguiſhed himſelf in the Wars of Naples and France, in the reign of Louis XII., came as an Embaſſy to Scotland in the year 1507, and died in the houſe of Sir John Forreſter, at Corſtorphine, June, 1508.—See in Proceedings of the Society of Antiquaries (vol. xi., p. 353), account of "the Forreſter Monuments in the Church at Corſtorphine."—Alſo William Dunbar's Poems, 1834, vol. i., pp. 129-133, vol. ii., pp. 311-313.

No. 52.—SIR ANDREW WOOD OF LARGO.—His gallant exploits are commemorated by Lindſay of Pitſcottie in his Chronicle on two occaſions; firſt when Sir Andrew Wood, with two veſſels, the *Yellow Carvell* and the *Flower*, ſucceeded in capturing five large Engliſh veſſels in the year 1489. Again, his not leſs gallant exploit, when oppoſed by the Engliſh Captain, Stephen Bull, he took captive three large veſſels, and carried the priſoners to Dundee.

No. 55.—CAPTAINE ANDROW BARTON.—Jo. Jonſt., p. 34. He calls this famous naval captain, "Andreas Britannus." The exploits of this famous ſea captain are celebrated in Engliſh ſong. Biſhop Percy, in his Reliques of Ancient Engliſh Poetry, publiſhed from his MS. Collections a capital old Englifh ballad, of the Reign of Queen Elizabeth, and an explanatory note, with the title "Sir Andrew Barton," (vol. ii., pp. 179-195). It is divided into two parts, the firft containing 136 lines, the fecond 162.

No. 56.—CONSECRAT, &c.—Jo. Jonft., p. 24, who records the difaftrous refult at Floddon, under this head:—"ARA Magnanimis Heroibus qui cum Jacobo IV. Rege in funefto Praelio ad Fluidonem occubuerunt, ad diem 9. Septembris Anno Chrifti 1513."

No. 57.—SIR WALTER SCOTT OF BUCCLEUGH.—He was fignalized for his attachment to the young King James the Fifth in 1526, and furvived till October 1553.

Nos. 58, 59, and 60 occur in Jo. Jonft., pp. 25, 26.

No. 63.—SIR JOHN BORTHWICK.—Jo. Jonft., p. 27. After noticing Borthwick's condemnation and efcape, and that his Effigy only had been burned at St. Andrews as a heretic, he fays, " Multis annis poftea fuperfles, fenex placidâ morte obiit," and refers to Cardinal Beaton's Articles, &c., which were paffed againft Borthwick in 1576, contained in (the firft edition of) Foxe's Acts and Monuments, &c.—For further particulars of Borthwick, fee the note in Appendix to Knox's Works, Vol. I., No. VIII., p. 533, and the Procefs of Declarator, &c., 1540-1561, in Mifcellany of the Bannatyne Club, Vol. I., p. 257. His death took place before 1570, when, according to Calderwood, "This worthie Knight ended his aige with fulneffe of daies at St. Andrewes."

No. 64.—SIR DAVID LYNDSAY, of the Mount, Lyon King at Arms.—Jo. Jonft., p. 37. He is too well known among the Scottifh Poets to require any fpecial notice.

No. 65.—PINKIEFIELD.—Jo. Jonft., p. 28, with the title " EPITAPHIUM fortiffimorum civium qui ceciderunt in funefta clade Pinkia ad Muffelburgum, quæ incidit in diem 10 Septembris Anno Chrifti 1547."

No. 67.—GILBERT KENNEDY, EARL OF CASSILLIS.—Jo. Jonft., p. 29. In the previous page Johnfton has introduced JOHN

MELVILLE of Raith (Johannes Malvillus Rethius), 1548, who happens to have been overlooked by Garden.

No. 68.—JAMES, EARL OF MONTGOMERIE.—Jo. Jonſt., p. 29. This Count de Montgomerie, although deſcended from a family in this country, has no proper claim to be included in "A Theatre of Scottiſh Worthies." Whether his name was James or Gabriel, who accidentally was the cauſe of the death of Henry II., King of France, in June 1559, he was pardoned by the King himſelf. But, having diſtinguiſhed himſelf as a Huguenot, he made a narrow eſcape at the infamous Maſſacre of St. Bartholomew in 1572, but he never was pardoned by Catherine de Medicis. He was taken priſoner at the ſiege of the town of Domfront, and carried in triumph to Paris in June, 1574, where he was beheaded.

No. 69.—SIR JAMES SANDILANDS OF CALDER.—Jo. Jonſt., p. 30. See Note in Knox's Works, vol. i., pp. 249-301. He died about the year 1560, and has frequently been confounded with his ſecond ſon, Sir James, who, in 1543, was Preceptor of Torphichen, and thus became head of the Knights Hoſpitallers of St. John of Jeruſalem in Scotland.—(Knox, vol. i., p. 301, vol. ii., pp. 125-131, &c.)

No. 69.—With ſcarcely an exception, on to No. 105 of this ſeries of the Worthies, they are celebrated by John Johnſton among his "Heroes Scoti," pp. 30-54.

No. 70.—ANDREW STEWART, LORD OF OCHILTRIE.—Jo. Jonſt., p. 30. Known as the good Lord Ochiltree. Various notices of him will be found in Knox's Hiſtory of the Reformation.

Nos. 71, 73, 75, and 89.—REGENTS OF SCOTLAND.—During the minority of King James the Sixth, there were four Regents in ſucceſſion, three of whom met with a calamitous termination of their career:—

No. 71.—JAMES STEWART, Earl of Murray, whom Garden ſtyles "a true Profeſſor of the Evangell," was appointed Regent July 22, 1568; and murdered at Linlithgow, January 23, 1570.

No. 73.—MATHEW STEWART, Earl of Lennox, was murdered at Stirling, September 4, 1571.

No. 75.—JOHN ERSKINE, Earl of Mar, died at Stirling, October 28, 1572.

No. 89.—JAMES DOUGLAS, Earl of Mortoun. He was appointed Lord High Chancellor in 1563, and elected Regent of Scotland, 27th November, 1572. He held the Regency from 1572 to 1578, when his resignation was accepted by the general Convention of the Nobility. He was afterwards arrested, tried, and beheaded at the Crofs of Edinburgh, June 2, 1581.

No. 74.—ARTHUR FORBES.—See William Gordon's History of the Family of Gordon, vol. i., p. 381. Edin., 1726, 8vo.

No. 75.—JOHN ERSKINE, EARL OF MAR.—"Chofen governor in the lefs aige of the moft excellent, high, and mightie Prince James," &c. He was elected Regent of Scotland during the King's minority in 1571, and died in the following year, as above.

No. 76.—SIR WILLIAM KIRKALDIE OF GRANGE.—It is fcarcely neceffary to add that this diftinguifhed man was taken prifoner after his gallant defence of Edinburgh Caftle in May 1573, and executed at the Crofs of Edinburgh.—See Bannatyne Mifcellany, vol. ii., pp. 65-80.

No. 78.—GILESPICK CAMBELL (or Archibald, Earl of Argyle). —He was appointed Lord High Chancellor of Scotland in January, 1573, and died at the early age of 43, in September, 1575.

No. 79.—SCOTLAND.—Jo. Jonft., p. 36. In place of "Savage Swaden" he has fimply "Succia," Sweden, with this infcription:— "ΚΕΝΟΤΑΦΙΟΝ Scotorum militum, qui ab amicis & sociis improbâ rabie contrucidati funt in caftris, ad Wefenburgum, medio inter Revalium & Narvam itinere in Livoniâ. Anno Chrifti 1574."

No. 81.—GEORGE, FIFTH EARL OF HUNTLEY, who had for a time been Lord Chancellor of Scotland, March 30, 1566, died October 20, 1576.

Nos. 84, 85, and 87.—WILLIAM KEITH.—There is fome apparent confufion in thefe three Keiths, Earl Marifchals, &c., which I need not attempt here to unravel.—See Douglas's Peerage by Wood.

No. 88.—JAMES CRICHTOUN OF CLUNIE.—Jo. Jonfl., p. 41. Surnamed "the Admirable Crichton."—See Tytler's Life of Crichton, fecond edition, Edinburgh, 1823, 12mo.

No. 89.—JAMES, EARL OF MORTON, Regent, was beheaded at the Crofs of Edinburgh, June 2, 1581.

No. 91.—JOHN COCKBURN OF ORMISTON.—See various Notes to Knox's Hiftory of the Reformation, edition 1846-48. In giving an extract (vol. i., p. 455), from a MS. Hiftory of the Family of Cockburn, written about 1722, fome of thefe lines are quoted as derived from Garden's Scottifh Worthies, but I added, "unfortunately it cannot now be traced," fo completely had the MS. preferved at Auchinleck efcaped my recollection.

No. 92.—ROBERT, LORD SEYTON.—This moft likely was George, fifth Lord Seyton, who died 8th January, 1584. His fecond fon Robert became fixth Lord Seyton.

No. 106.—HULST.—A Town in Zealand, 16 miles W.N.W. of Antwerp. In the Wars of the Low Countries the town fuftained various Sieges.

No. 111.—MARK ALEXANDER BOYD, a younger fon of Robert Boyd of Pinkill, in Ayrfhire. He was born in 1562. In his early days he was fent abroad and diftinguifhed himfelf, partly as an author, in publifhing Latin Poems and Epiftles addreffed to James the Sixth, in 1592. He returned to his native country, where he died of a flow fever, 10th April, 1601. Sir David Dalrymple, Lord Hailes, in 1787 publifhed a biographical account of Boyd and his writings, which will be found in the Appendix to the third edition of the Annals of Scotland (vol. iii., p. 420). Edinburgh, 1819, 8vo.

No. 116.—JOHN, MARQUESS OF HAMILTON, died at London in the prime of life, March 30, 1625, aged 36.

No. 120.—Sir James Lawson of Humbie.—In the Appendix to Nisbet's Heraldry, vol. ii., p. 93, there is an account of the Lawsons of Humbie, and referring to Sir James Lawson as served heir to his father in 1607, it is added, " Alexander Garden, in his 'Scottish Worthies,' says, he was a gentleman of his Majesty's Chamber, a gallant youth in the way of honour, but was unfortunately drowned beside Aberdeen, in a standing lake, called the 'Old Watergang,' riding over rashly, not having knowledge of the ground. This happened Anno 1612, upon which accident the fore-cited Mr. Garden composed the following poem:"—

> " Whose minds so marbled and his heart so hard,
> And who of steell whose stomachs are so strong,
> That would not, when this huge mishap was heard,
> To th' outmost note of sorrow set their song:
>   And elevate their voice and woes alone,
>   The highest strain of any troubl'd tone.
>
> " To see a Gallant with so great a grace,
> So suddenly unthought on, so o'erthrown,
> And so to perish in so poor a place,
> By too rash riding in a ground unknown.
>   The flinty Fates, that but all pity prove,
>   Would both to mourn, and miseration move.
>
> " Yet shall this death the Defunct not disgrace,
> Nor to his praise prove prejudicial,
> Since men of greater rank have run like race,
> And lost by like misfortunous fate and fall:
>   For Fergus, Dowgal, and King Donald drown'd,
>   And they all three Kings of this realm crown'd.

No. 122.—James Drummond, as eldest son, succeeded his father Patrick, third Lord Drummond, in the year 1600. He was created Earl of Perth, March 4, 1605, and married Dame Isabell Seaton, daughter of Robert, Lord Seaton, and first Earl of Winton, April 19, 1608, and died at Seaton House, December 18, 1611, when only twenty-one years of age. He was buried in the Collegiate Church of Seaton, where a stately marble monument was erected to his memory, by his widow.

No. 126.—Irvine Kempt Garden.—In the MS. Robert Miln has interpolated the reference "Sie Sir Thomas Urquhart's Exquisite

Jewell, p. 151-152." The date of Urquhart's Jewell is London, 1652.

No. 133.—BRUCE OF EARLSHALL.—See a brief notice of that family in Fifeſhire in the Proceedings of the Society of Antiquaries of Scotland, Vol. XII., Part I., p. 79.

No. 134.—SIR JOHN CARMICHAEL, Warden of the Middle Marches, was ſlain by the Borderers of the name of Armſtrong, June 16, 1600.

No. 137.—WALTER STEWART was Commendator of Blantyre previous to 1580. In 1593 he appears as one of the Lords of Seſſion as Lord Blantyre, and died March 8, 1617.

No. 137.—SIR JOHN PRESTON OF FENTONBARNS was appointed a Lord of Seſſion in March, 1595, and elected Lord Preſident in June, 1609. He died June 14, 1616.

No. 138.—ORKNAY.—The reſt of the title, as given in the printed text, was ſupplied by Robert Miln.

No. 139.—SIR ROBERT KEITH, brother to George, Earl Mariſ-chall, "now living." This Earl Mariſchall, who became .the founder of Mariſchall College, Aberdeen, in 1593, had ſucceeded to the eſtates and title in 1581.—See No. 161.

No. 140.—Robert Miln, in place of the blank at the head of this number, has added, "This ſeems to be on Queen Mary." His conjecture was probably correct.

No. 144.—SIR THOMAS MENZIES.—The name is of conſiderable antiquity in the north, and from Gilbert Menzies, in the year 1426, to Paul Menzies of Kinmundie, in 1634, perſons of the name re-peatedly occur, holding the office of Provoſt of Aberdeen. The "Worthy" celebrated by Garden, Thomas Menzies of Durne or Cults, was Provoſt in the years 1615 to 1620. He was ſo much eſteemed that James the Sixth, on viſiting Scotland in 1617, con-ferred the title of Knighthood on him in the Privy Chamber in the preſence of many of the nobility of both kingdoms. Alexander

Skene (under the name of Philopoliteius), in his "Survey of the Famous City of Aberdeen," 1685, gives the following statement, which has been repeated in later works (Kennedy's Annals, vol. i., p. 137, vol. ii., p. 232, Nichols's Progreffes of King James, vol. iv., p. 616):—"This Sir Thomas Menzies of Cults having procured that famous Pearl, which was found in the brook or burne of Kellie, as it runs into the river of Ythan; which Pearle, for beauty and bignefs, was the beft that hath been at any time found in Scotland: Our faid Provoft having found, by the judgement of the jewelers in Edinburgh, that it was moft precious and of a very high value, went up to London, and gifted it to the King (this was in the year 1620), who in retribution gave him twelve or fourteen chalders of victuall about Dumfermling, and the cuftom of merchant-goods in Aberdeen during his life. But it pleafed God he dyed at Wooller, on the Border, in England, on his return home."—(Pp. 238-239).

No. 146.—Garden here departs from his ufual chronological order. As his "Theatre" was written at various times, the alteration may have been occafioned either to fupply omiffions, or merely from the leaves of the Author's MS. having been tranfpofed by the tranfcribers. But this is not a matter of any great importance.

No. 150.—FORBEST.—Matthew Lumfden, in his Genealogy of the Family of Forbes, written in 1580, commences with a fimilar reference to Hector Boyce. The Forbeffes, he fays, as they took their furname from the flaughter of a beaft, "I will refer to that moft cunning Doctor, Mr. Hector Boyce, holding him famous and authentic, as may be feen in the thretteent book of his Chronicles," &c. This Genealogy was printed at Invernefs, 1819, 8vo.

No. 152.—The battle of Durham, or Neville's Crofs, took place in 1346, when King David the Second and the Scots were defeated, and he taken prifoner.

No. 154.—SIR JOHN LYON, of Glammis, was raifed to the Peerage as Lord Glammis in 1374. He married, not Elizabeth, but Lady Jean Stewart, the fecond daughter of King Robert the

Second, who appointed him Lord High Chamberlain in 1380. He was flain at Forfar, in a duel with Sir James Lindfay, of Crawfurd, in the year 1395. In the prefatory note to the MS. Lord Glammis is erroneoufly ftyled Lord Chancellor in place of Lord Chamberlain of Scotland.

No. 156.—The battle of Homilden, a hill within a mile of Wooler, where Sir Henry Percy (the celebrated Hotfpur), with his numerous band of Englifh bowmen, gained a decifive victory over the Scottifh forces, was in the year 1402.

No. 157.—WILLIAM DOUGLAS, EARL OF ANGUS, &c.—In the year 1435 a truce, which exifted with England, being infringed by Sir Robert Ogle younger, of a powerful Yorkfhire family, who croffed the Borders, and ravaged the country in the fouth of Berwickfhire, or, according to Ridpath, the Border hiftorian, "The Earl of Northumberland, with a body of four thoufand men, advanced towards the Scottifh Marches, but was met within his own territories at a place called Pepperden on Brammifh, not far from the Mountains of Cheviot, by William Douglas, Earl of Angus, at the head of nearly the fame number of forces."— ("Border Hiftory," p. 401, 1776.) The date appears to have been in September, 1435, but Bower, in his Continuation of the Scotichronicon, fays:—Anno fequenti conflictus de Piperden, 10 die Septembris, ubi devicti funt Angli, et capti de marchianis et eorundem caftellanis ad fummum 1500, per dominos Willelmum de Douglas comitem Angufiæ, Adam Hepburn de Halez, et Alexandrum Ramfay de Dalwolfi. Occubuit ibi, ex parte Scotorum, dominus de Elphinfton, et, ex parte Anglorum, Henricus de Clenchale ejufdem, et utriufque regni interfecti non ultra numerum XL. mediocrium perfonarum."—(Vol. ii., p. 500-1).

No. 159.—ROBERT DOUGLAS, Mafter of Morton, was the fon of William Douglas of Lochleven, who fucceeded in 1581 to the eftate and title of Earl of Morton. Along with Lawrence, Mafter of Oliphant, both of whom were concerned in the Raid of Ruthven, 1582, they perifhed at fea, when efcaping to the Low Countries, in the year 1584.

No. 161.—GEORGE KEITH, Earl Marſhall, as here ſtated, died in the year 1623. According to a previous note (No. 85) he ſucceeded his grandfather, while a child, in 1581. Garden's note, "Now Earl." points to the fact that Garden's Theatre was the reſult of ſeveral years' literary labour.

No. 164.—The Oration here mentioned is preſerved in Lindeſay of Pitſcottie's Chronicle. It gives a rehearſal of the Genealogy of the houſe of Crawford, made to King James the Second in 1454. when the Earl of Crawford and his followers came and expreſſed their deep penitence in having taken part with the King's rebels. Lord Crawford, however, did not long ſurvive, as he was cut off by fever within the courſe of ſix months, in the year 1454, and was buried with his forbears in the Church of the Greyfriars, Dundee.

Nos. 164, 165, and 166.—EARLS OF CRAWFORD.—So far as Chronology is concerned, it would have been well to have tranſpoſed theſe Nos. In No. 166 we have David, Earl of Crawford, along with a notice of his predeceſſors, not forgetting the one concerned in a chivalrous combat on London Bridge in the year 1390. While No. 165 is devoted to Earl David, who was ſlain in 1445; and in No. 164, his ſon, who ſucceeded him, and who only ſurvived till the year 1454.

No. 166.—ALEXANDER LINDSAY.—In the preliminary notice the reference at the end is to the challenge and combat on London Bridge, in the year 1390.—See Tytler's Hiſtory of Scotland, vol. iii., p. 80. Tytler ſays, "Sir David Lindſay of Gleneſk, who was then reputed one of the beſt ſoldiers in Scotland, ſoon after the acceſſion of Robert the Third ſent his cartel to the Lord Wells, an Engliſh Knight of the court of Richard the Second, which having been accepted, the duel was appointed to take place in London, in preſence of the King." Sir David Lindſay of Gleneſk, who married the King's daughter, was created Earl of Crawfurd by Robert the Third, in 1398.—(Wyntoun's Chronicle, b. ix., ch. xix.)

NO. 170.—JOHN, fourth EARL OF MONTROSE.—He was appointed Prefident of the Council in Scotland in July, 1626, but died in November the fame year. This date proves that Garden continued to make additions after the death of King James; but before there was any occafion to refer to James Graham, the fifth Earl, then in his fourteenth year, who fo diflinguifhed himfelf, and was afterwards created firfl Marquefs of Montrofe. The well-known biographer and memorialifl confeffes that his future Hero's anceftors, "though of high lineage, courage, and patriotic loyalty, were not hiflorically remarkable."

NO. 171.—SIR JOHN RAMSAY, of Eaflbarnes, for the fhare he had in connexion with the murder of the Earl of Gowrie in 1600, befides grants of lands, was created Vifcount of Haddington. He accompanied the King to England, and was created Earl of Holdernefs.—See Crawfurd's Peerage of Scotland, p. 181.

NO. 172.—THOMAS ERSKINE, who alfo had a prominent fhare in the faid tragedy at Perth, 5th Auguft, 1600, was educated along with the King, and was appointed one of the Gentlemen of his Bedchamber in 1585. In 1600 he had a grant of the forfeited eftates of Dirleton, Eafl Lothian, which belonged to the Ruthven family. Having accompanied the King to England, he was created Vifcount of Fentown in 1606, and Earl of Kelly in 1619. He furvived till June 12th, 1639. The words "Thou nobly now," &c., fhow that he was alive at the time when they were written by Garden, and may explain the abfence of the ufual introductory profe notice.

NO. 173.—ALEXANDER CRAIG OF ROSECRAIG.—It is pleafing to find among "the Scottifh Worthies" our old friend Alexander Craig of Rofecraig, whofe Poetical Remains, in a collected form, were printed for the members of the Hunterian Club in 1873. Each of them complimented the other by indulging (no doubt as a piece of wit) in punning on their refpective names—Alexander Craig or Crag, from *Rupes*, a rock; and Alexander Garden, his *Garden* of Flowers. It is flrange that Garden fhould have left blank the year in which Craig died. This happened at Banff in or before the year 1627, as the fervice is recorded, in the Inquifitiones, &c., No. 1372, " December 20, 1627: Jacobus Craig, hæres Magiftri Alexandri Craig de Rofecraig, *patris*."

2 C

THE LIFE
OF
WILLIAM ELPHINSTON
BISHOP OF ABERDEEN

BY
ALEXANDER GARDEN
1619

WILLIAM ELPHINSTON.

BISHOP OF ABERDEEN.

THERE are few perfons in early times who have received fo much praife as this excellent Prelate, WILLIAM ELPHINSTON, Bifhop of Aberdeen. Yet in many points of his hiftory there is great uncertainty, as the ftatements are either contradictory or unfatisfactory; for inftance, his parentage, the date of his birth, and his early courfe of life. His firft biographer, Hector Boyce, whom he patronifed in his *Vitae Epifcoporum Aberdonenfium*, did not confider dates to be of great importance, and omits fuch nearly altogether. Yet the one or two dates which he has given are not unimportant. The date of the Bifhop's birth is not ftated. The prefent volume, which contains a rhyming verfion founded upon the chief part of that work in praife of his great patron, Garden does not profefs to fupply fuch a defect. According to the ordinary authorities, he was born at Glafgow, in the year 1437. It might be more correct to affign the date to 1431, as Hector Boyce exprefsly fays, in reference to his laft illnefs, "Sed ne ipfa quidem fenectus, communis et inevitabilis mortalium morbus, licet contuderit, effregit: ut qui, *tertium fupra octogefimum annum agens* in gravibus Reipublicae negotiis, caeteris acutius differebat," &c. Thefe words are thus rendered by Garden as to "the yeare of his age and deathe,"—

This happie Prelat, his
Departour was 't appears,

In th' aughtie three yeer of his age;
    When fullie threttie yeeres,
Belov'de and honor'd ev're,
    Heere he had Bifhope bene;
Whiche from the bliffed birthe fell fyf—
    Ten hundreth and fourtene.

His father was of the fame name, and by fome writers reckoned a younger brother of the noble family of Elphin-fton, who became a merchant-burgefs of Glafgow, and his mother was Margaret Douglas, of the Houfe of Mains in Dunbartonfhire.[1]

According to the Peerage of Scotland, Sir William de Elphinfton, Dominus ejufdem, who flourifhed at the end of the 14th century, had three fons. The third fon was William, firft of the Elphinftons of Blythfwood, in Lanarkfhire, who married Margaret Douglas, of the Houfe of Mains, in Dunbartonfhire. A younger fon of theirs was William Elphin-fton, Bifhop of Aberdeen; his father, William, after he had become a widower, having entered into Holy Orders, and became Archdeacon of Teviotdale.

Garden, in defcribing the Bifhop's family pedigree, fays:—

In Glafco Burrow he was borne :
    His pedegree and lyne
From Elphinftoune, a Houfe
    Old, opulent, and trew,
And yit a famous Famelie
    Legittimat he drew.

The words of Hector Boyce, on which thefe lines are founded, fays:—" Is in inclyta Glafguenfi civitate, et Univer-fali fchola infigni, natus, ex vetere Elphinftonorum familia habuit originem."

Thus Crawfurd ftates, "While Mr. Elphinfton was a widower, out of a principle of devotion, or fome other

----

[1] George Crawfurd's Officers of State, 1726, p. 47.

motive, he entered into Holy Orders, and was firft made
Rector of Kirkmichael, and at length Arch-deacon of
Teviotdale, in which ftation he died on the 30th of June,
1486, after he had had the comfort of feeing his fon Bifhop
of Aberdeen." [1] Bifhop Keith and others repeat this ftatement. But it is by no means probable that his father, at a
fomewhat advanced time of life, fhould have ftudied theology,
and obtained preferment in the Church "after he became a
widower." There is, however, fome confufion regarding two
perfons of the fame name, which at that time was not un-
common.

Like many of the Prelates of that period, however, who
required Letters of Legitimation, Elphinfton was not an
exception. Although the fact itfelf may be otherwife afcertained, I may here refer to a letter addreffed to myfelf
by the late John Riddell, Efq., Advocate, fo well known for
his refearches in all Peerage cafes and other collateral
fubjects, and give it in full in the Appendix No. I.

In reference alfo to the Bifhop's ftudies at the Univerfity of
Glafgow, Boyce informs us, " Confummatus in philofophia
quintum annum fupra vicefimum agens magiftratus infignia
in liberalibus, difciplinis fimul atque facerdotium eft adeptus."
Thefe words are literally rendered by Garden—

> Swa confirmat become
>   Into philofophie,
> Into his fyve and twentie yeere
>   His courfe conclooded hee;
> And manumiffed then,
>   Withe laude the Laurell wraethe,
> And at that tyme his Priefthood there
>   He got togidder baithe.

In receiving his education at the "pædagogium and
Univerfity of Glafgow," we find in the Annals of the

---

[1] Crawfurd, as above, p. 47.

Univerſity in the year 1451, in the *Nomina Incorporatorum et Congregationes Univerſitatis*, the eleventh name recorded is "WILLELMUS ELPHINSTOUNE," and in the 16th March, 1451-52, "MAGISTER WILLELMUS ELPHINSTOUNE."

There are other entries referring to the Elphinſtons in the large and valuable collections, entitled "Munimenta Alme Univerſitatis Glaſguenſis: Records of the Univerſity of Glaſgow from its foundation till 1727." Another ſimilar important contribution was printed at the expenſe of the Earl of Aberdeen, K.T., and preſented in his name as Preſident of the Spalding Club, viz.: "Faſti Aberdonenſes: Selections from the Records of the Univerſity and King's College of Aberdeen, 1494-1854," Aberdeen, 1854. Profeſſor Coſmo Innes, the Editor, in his Preface has carefully examined various matters illuſtrating the life of Biſhop Elphinſton. I may take advantage of his labours,[1] without attempting to reconcile ſome diſcrepancies of dates, and give the following extract (p. xiii.):—

"It is impoſſible (he ſays) perfectly to reconcile Boece's narrative with the dates fixed by the records of the Univerſity of Glaſgow. Some confuſion ariſes alſo from the identity of name, and ſometimes of office, in the father and ſon. But, it would ſeem, that even more than two perſons of the name muſt have held benefice in the Church, and place in the Univerſity of Glaſgow at the ſame time.

"William Elphinſtone, apparently our Biſhop's father, is ſtyled Canon of Glaſgow, from 1451 down to 1483, holding the offices of Dean of Faculty of Arts (1468), Prehendary of Ancrum (1479), Archdeacon of Teviotdale (1482). The following dates ſeem to apply to the Biſhop:—

"1457.—William Elphinſtone 'ſcolaris' matriculated.
"1459.—He took his Bachelor's degree.

[1] I may add that in a work of this kind, where ſo much reſearch and accuracy of tranſcription was eſſential, Profeſſor Innes was fortunate, as he tells us, in having ſuch competent aid in Mr. Francis Shaw as Sub-Editor.

" 1462.—He took his Mafter's degree, 'poft rigorofum examen.'

" 1462-4.—Active in Univerfity affairs.

" 1465.—W. de Elphinftone, junior, rector of Kirkmichael, was a Regent in the Univerfity.

" 1471-2.—W. Elphinftone was Official-General of the Diocefe of Glafgow, and Dean of the Faculty of Arts.

" 1473.—Mafter William de Elphinftone, Official, took the degree of Licentiate in Canon Law, and was Dean of the Faculty.

" 1474.—W. de Elphinftone, Official, a Mafter of Arts, Licentiate in Decrees, and Rector of Kirkmichael, was chofen Rector of the Univerfity."

It would be fuperfluous to fwell out this volume with any detailed account of the later incidents of Bifhop Elphin-ftone's life, which at leaft are fo acceffible in a variety of works. A few dates, however, may be added.

In 1478 he was appointed Official of Lothian. Three years later he was made Bifhop of Rofs, though fome delay took place in his Confecration, perhaps on account of his birth. He was nominated Bifhop of Aberdeen in the autumn of 1483; yet his Confecration only took place between 17th December, 1487, and April, 1488. He was employed on various Embaffies during the reign of King James the Third, and held for a brief fpace the office of Lord High Chancellor of the Kingdom until the King's death, 14th June, 1488. Among the great works in which Bifhop Elphinfton was engaged were reftoring the fervice and the fabric of his Cathedral, the foundation of King's College and Univerfity, and the erection of a Bridge over the Dee. He furvived to lament the fate of King James the Fourth and fo many of his countrymen, at the fatal field of Floddon, the 9th September, 1513. He himfelf died amidft univerfal regret on the 25th October, 1514.

David Camerarius or Chalmers, in his work entitled
"De Scotorum Fortitudine. Doctrina, et Pietate, ac de ortu
et progreffu hærefis in Regnis Scotiæ et Angliæ, Libri
Quatuor. Parifiis, 1631," 4to, at p. 157, 12 die Junij, gives
an account of "Beatus Guillelmus Elphinftonius Epifcopus Aberdonenfis," commencing with an elaborate de-
fcription of the magnificence of the Bifhop's Cathedral
Church, erected at Aberdeen, " Hæc fciens recenfere volui
ut videat lector quam magna fuerit apud Scotos gloria
domus Domini, dum apud eofdem Catholica et Romana
floreret religio;" and concluding with the account of his
death with the words, " Poft hæc nomen Jefu et Mariæ inter
mortuis vocibus identidem appellans placidiffimè efflauit
animam anno Chrifti 1514, anno fui Pontificatus 30, ætatis
verò 84." This ftatement, of courfe, as already remarked,
would fix the date of the Bifhop's birth to the year 1430
or 1431.

Bifhop Elphinfton has long enjoyed the honour of a
learned author. In particular, there are two works that
have frequently been mentioned in connexion with his name.
The firft is the Continuation of the Scotichronicon, or
Book XI., preferved amongft the MSS. in the Bodleian
Library. This later portion of the volume was printed for
the Maitland Club, under the title "The Life and Death of
King James the Firft of Scotland," edited by Jofeph
Stevenfon. Glafgow, 1837. 4to. This MS. was then
thought to be the only copy known, but others have fince
been difcovered, including one in the College Library,
Glafgow, which had belonged to William Schevez, Arch-
bifhop of St. Andrews (1478 to 1496). It was very clear,
however, from allufions in the book by the writer to the
time when he accompanied the Princefs Margaret, for her
marriage with the Dauphin of France, that Elphinfton could

not have been the author, which refers to events in France about the time that Elphinston was born. In defcribing the various MSS. of the Scotichronicon, and the authors of the Continuations, Mr. W. F. Skene clearly eftablifhed the fact that the one in queftion was known as the LIBER PLUSCARDENSIS, and that the true author was MAURITIUS or MAURICE DE BUCHANAN, who had been in France from 1429 to 1460.—See Mr. Skene's communications to the Society of Antiquaries, vol. viii., p. 239, vol. ix., p. 13, and vol. x., p. 27; alfo his Preface to vol. i. of the original text of Fordun. I may alfo refer to a fhort notice on the fubject that appeared in the Society's Proceedings, vol. xii., p. 28.

The fecond work ufually attributed to Bifhop Elphinfton contains the Lives or Legends of the Scottifh Saints.

In regard to fuch a work, it is generally confidered that the introduction of the Art of Printing into Scotland was, in a great meafure, owing to Bifhop Elphinfton in the year 1507, who obtained a grant of exclufive privileges in favour of Walter Chepman and Andro Myllar, two burgeffes of Edinburgh, in September, 1507.

According to this document, one of the chief objects contemplated was to fupply Church Service books "efter our awin Scottis Ufe, and with Legendis of Scottis Sanctis, as is now gaderit and ekit be ane Reverend father in God, and our confalour Williame Bifchope of Abirdene and utheris, be ufit generaly within al our Realme alffone as the fammyn may be imprentit and providit," &c.

The principal work of this clafs, and the one undoubtedly referred to, was the "Breviarium Aberdonenfe," a rare but well-known work in two fmall fized volume, filled with contractions, Pars Eftivalis and Pars Hyemalis (fee Bannatyne Club Catalogue, &c., p. 82, No. 96), printed at Edinburgh

in the years 1509-1510, 8vo; and fince republifhed at
London in 1854, page for page, in two handfome volumes,
4to.

In a preface, which was intended to be prefixed to the
Club copies, fome months after their circulation, I ftated
as follows:—"The work was prepared and completed
under the perfonal fuperintendence of William Elphinfton,
Bifhop of Aberdeen, a prelate who has obtained a high
character as an enlightened and liberal patron of learning.
It may be inferred from the words of his contemporary
biographer, Hector Boyce, and other writers, that feveral
of the Leffons appointed in the Proprium Sanctorum to
be read on the feftivals of the Scottifh Saints, either were
written by the Bifhop himfelf, or were the refult of refearches inftituted by his order into the ecclefiaftical annals
and traditions of the nation. That the work was the refult
of great care and labour need fcarcely be remarked. For
the purpofe of having it printed for general ufe, and under
his immediate infpection, we are fully warranted in attri-
buting to this Prelate the fcheme which fecured the eftab-
lifhment of a printing Prefs in this Country." Pp. 20, 21.

Profeffor Innes, in his Preface to the "Regiftrum Epifco-
patus Aberdonenfis," printed for the Spalding Club, 1845,
2 vols., has alfo given a fketch of the Bifhop's Life, as it was
moft requifite, he fays, "to endeavour to give fome chronological precifion from Records or authentic documents to the
events of Bifhop Elphinftone's epifcopate and his life."—
(Preface, p. xliii). Yet he affigns the ordinary date of his
birth as 1437, and concludes with fimply faying that Elphinfton lived to extreme old age. He elfewhere, in a quotation
from Spottifwood's Hiftory, mentions Elphinfton, when he
was eighty-three years old. He further repeats the palpable
miftake, in referring to Bifhop Elphinfton's Hiftorical Col-

lections, as preferved in the Bodleian Library, Oxford;
as well as the vague ftatement that "A confiderable number
of Elphinfton's MSS. are ftill in the Library of his own
Univerfity, but they feem to be entirely Law Notes and
Commentaries." Thefe, of courfe, could not have been
written by the Bifhop, but there are other volumes containing "Nic. de Tudefchis Lecturæ fuper Decretalium
Libri, &c., dated Parifiis, 1470," 5 vols. Alfo "Gloffæ Cle-
mentinæ," &c., and another volume of " Lecturæ fuper Libro
IV. Decretalium," each of them marked " LIBER MAGISTRI
WILELMI DE ELPHINSTON."

The books here referred to I examined feveral years
ago. There are a confiderable number that have this infcription, " Liber Magiftri Will. de Elphinfton;" and they
doubtlefs formed, as it were, the foundation of the Library
attached to the Univerfity. I had noted in particular—

1st. Six large volumes written on paper, partially injured
and imperfect, which belonged to Bifhop Elphinfton; they confift of " Lecturæ fuper Libros Decretalium," &c., with a colophon at the end of the laft
volume, "dated xi Maij, MCCCCLXIX."

2nd. Five volumes of a fmaller fize, and not fo well preferved (the firft volume being greatly injured
by damp), with the name of William Elphinfton
in various parts, and confift of treatifes on the
Decretals, Canon Law, &c.

According, however, to the more precife titles given in
the lift of MSS. fubjoined to the " Catalogue of the General
Library of the Univerfity of Aberdeen," (vol. ii., 1874, p. 793),
I find I had overlooked the fact that the earlier volumes were
actually written by the elder Elphinfton, and thus ferve to

throw fome light upon his hiftory. For inftance, three volumes are thus defcribed:—

"Juftinianus: Lecturae Grofbeli, Reteri, Ricardi de Turnaco, et aliorum in Titulos felectos Codicis, Inftitutionum, Digeftorum, et Feudorum, fcriptae per Will. Elfynfton, in Artibus Magiftrum, et Lovanii Studentem, MCCCCXXXIII."

Alfo two volumes of "Reterus (Hen.): Relata fuper Libri XXIV. Digeftorum Titulo de Soluto Matrimonio, fcripta per Will. Elfynfton in Artibus Magiftrum et in Legibus Studentem Lovanii." "Relata fuper Libri XLV. Digeftorum Titulo de Verborum Obligationibus, fcripta a Willelmo Elfynfton Lovanii, MCCCCXXXIII."

In examining the Regifters of the Univerfity of St. Andrews, under this head,

"Licentiati Anno Dom. M.CCCC^{mo} triceffimo,"
the name, as I imagine, occurs of the Bifhop's father,

"DNS. WILL^{s} DE ELFYNSTON."
This date at leaft harmonizes with his receiving, in due courfe, the degree of A.M. before proceeding to profecute the ftudy of Canon Law at the Univerfity of Louvain in 1433.—(See p. 20).

Keith, in his Catalogue of Bifhops, fays:—"William Elphinfton, Archdeacon of Argyle, is 'Electus et confirmatus Roffen,' in the Rolls of Parliament, 2nd December, 1482, and on the 21ft of February, 1482-3, 'Electo et confirmato Roffen,' and is Bifhop here the fame year." On the 17th of May, 1485, the Parliament of Scotland, in an embaffy fent to the Pope, ftating, amongft the other articles, the following:—"And attour to mak Supplicacioun to oure Haly Fader that, fen he has promovit Reverend Faders Robert Blacater to the bifchopric of Glafgow, William Elphinftoune to the bifchopric of Aberdeen, and Johnne of Hepburne to the priorie of Sanctandrew, quhilk ar thankfull perfonis to our Souveran Lord and of his fpeciale counfale, and reffavit and admittit be his Hienes to the temporaliteis: That therfor his Halynes wil defend thaim therein gif ony perfonis walde tende to mak thaim truble or more pley again thame." The refult of this Supplication probably ferved only for a time.—(See Appendix No. I.)

The Portrait of Bifhop Elphinfton is on pannel, and may have been painted abroad: it has appeared in more than one publication; and was firft engraved for Pinkerton's "Iconographia Scotica," 1797. Pinkerton fays it is taken from a painting, apparently contemporary, in the Univerfity of Aberdeen. There is alfo an excellent old copy of it in the Univerfity Library there. The moft fatisfactory likenefs was given as the frontifpiece to the important volume already quoted, " Fafti Aberdonenfes. Selections from the Records of the Univerfity and King's College of Aberdeen, 1494-1854. Aberdeen: Printed for the Spalding Club, 1854." In the large paper copies of the volume the portrait is given in colours. The prefent portrait is not inferior to any of thefe, with the advantage of having been taken direct from the original Painting.

—

No. I.

LETTER FROM JOHN RIDDELL, ESQ., ADVOCATE.

Edinburgh, March 2nd, 1844.

Dear Sir,—I fend you, as I promifed, the following from Lord Elphinftone's charter cheft, that I examined feveral years ago:—

Letter dated Edinburgh, 28 July, 1644, from W. Guild to Lord Elphinftone, where he alludes "to the fyve belles in the college fteeple of Aberdeen, founded by that worthie cadent of your hous to the eternal honor therof." and his Bifhop William Elphinftone, in reference alfo to the fact of the fteeple being ruined by a tempeft, &c.

Grant by King James III., June 25th, 1477, "Speciale et dilecto clerico noftro magiftro Willielmo Elphinftone Rectori de Kirk-michael in artibus magiftro, et in Decretis" giving him full power and licence to difpone at any time upon his lands, tenements, and goods, &c.,—"non obftante baftardia fua in qua genitus eft," &c., legitimating him "per omnia ficut de legitimo thoro effet pro-creatus." It alfo, in energetic terms, enables him to hold clerical preferment, from which he would have been barred by his baftardy. This Mr. William Elphinftone is clearly the Bifhop of Aberdeen, who was originally Rector of Kirkmichael.—See Keith's "Bifhops," p. 68 (firft edition). He ftarted in public life at home, according to Keith, in 1471.

There is alfo in the Elphinftone charter cheft a deed by James V., dated 28th of November, 1516, reciting that "Dominus Willielmus Elphinftone Canonicus Ecclefie cathedralis Aberdonenfis ac pre-bendarius de Clatt is propinquior agnatus, id eft confanguineus, ex parte patris Alexandro filio et heredi quondam Alexandri domini Elphinfton, et quod exceffit ætatem viginti quinque annorum," &c.,

and therefore conferring him in the office of tutor to the young
Lord Alexander. This William Elphinftone is, of course, not the
Bifhop, but of a higher and purer lineage. He, however, may
have been patronized by the Bifhop, whofe origin feemed very
obfcure.—I remain, yours truly,

JOHN RIDDELL.

No. II.

ELPHINSTON WRITS IN CUMBERNAULD HOUSE.—Notes taken by
JOHN RIDDELL, Esq., Advocate (1829).

Grant by King James III., 25 June, 1477, in favour of "fpeciale
et delecto clerico Magiftro Willelmo Elphinfton rectore de Kirk-
michel, in Artibus Magiftro et in Decretis," giving him licenfe to
difpone at any time upon his lands, tenements, &c. " Non
obftante baftardia fua in qua genitus eft," and legitimating him
" per omnia ficut de legitimo thoro effet procreatus" (rather in
ftrong and energetic terms).

No. III.

Subfequent to the date of the above letter the valuable work by
Father Auguftinus Theiner has been publifhed under the title
" Vetera Monumenta Hibernorum et Scotorum Hiftoriam, illus-
trantia, 1216-1547. Romæ, Typis Vaticanis, 1864," folio. In this
volume, among the " Epiftolæ Alexandri," P. VI., a letter, No. 894,
is addreffed to Bifhop Elphinfton, " Super fuo præfectione, tranf-
latione, ac defectu Natalium." In this letter of difpenfation the
" Defectu" is more than once mentioned, for inftance:—

DCCCXCIV, page 508.—" Alexander Epifcopus, etc., Venera-
bili fratri Willelmi Epifcopus Aberdonenfi falutem," etc., after
relating that Pope Sextus IV. (1471-1484) had preferred Elphin-

ſton to the See of Roſs, "teque illi prefecit in Epiſcopum et
paſtorum ac per alias tecum, ut non obſtante defectu natalium;"
and in his tranſlation to Aberdeen, no mention having been made
of this defect, in order to relieve him from any further trouble
or the riſk of ſuſpenſion, he, the Pope, "motu proprio, mero
liberalitate," had granted him a full and free diſpenſation: "non
obſtantibus defectu et aliis premiſſis, etc. Datum Rome, apud
Sanctum Petrum. Anno 1494, pridie Idus Decembris, Pontificatus
noſtri, Anno tertio."

No. IV.

REGISTRUM GLASGUENSE.

Vol. II.

Exſcripta ex Martyrologio Metropolis Glaſguenſis.

16 Panmure Place,
Edinburgh, 24th October, 1876.

Dear Sir,—I fpent four days at Aberdeen laft week, and made fearch regarding Mr. Alexander Gardyn, according to the note which I had from you. The refult is, I fear, not very fatiffactory:—

Searched Burgh Safines from 1609 to 1635: No entry.
Searched Council and Guild Regifter: Found—

> 15 May, 1629.—Decernes Alexander Gardyne, fometime of Banchorie, to pay to Thomas Gordon, merchant, £60 for hemp and iron bought from the latter.
>
> 30 Auguft, 1631.—*Inter alias:*—"Magifter Alexander Gardyne" admitted burgefs and Guild Brother.

I hope to fee you early next week, and to hand over the Elphin ftone MS.—I am, dear Sir, yours truly,

WALTER MACLEOD.

ABERDEEN BURGH SASINES.

Vol. xvi.

8 Aug., 1576.—Safine to Elizabeth Keyth, fpoufe of George Gardyn of Banchorie.

Ibid.

5 April, 1577. A young man, John Gardyn, fon of the brother german, and heir of the late William Gardyn, butcher, burgefs of Aberdeen, gets fafine of a tenement in Aberdeen.

Vol. xxx.

24 April, 1607.—Safine to "an honorable man," Alexander Gardin of Banchorie, son and heir to the late Arthur Gardin of Banchorie, of a tenement in Aberdeen.

[In March, 1603, it appears from a safine to the said Arthur Gardyn of Banchorie, and Janet Forbes his fpoufe, that he had a brother german, Patrick Gardin, who is a witnefs.]

Vol. xxxi.

10 July, 1610.—Safine to Alexander Gardin in Glaflerberrie, brother german and heir of the late William Gardin, fkinner, burgefs of the faid burgh of Aberdeen.

Vol. xxxii.

9 March, 1611.—Safine to Alex^r Gardin in Glaflerberrie, and Jean Trowp, daughter of Alexander Trowp in Murthill, his future fpoufe, in terms of marriage contract of fame date, of a tenement in Aberdeen.

THE

Lyf, doings and Deathe
of
the Right Reverend and
worthy prelat

Williame Elphinstom
Be the divyne providence
the 23 Bishop of Aberdone
Wha after 30 Yeeres goner
nament of this Sea. the
83 of his age departed in
Edinbrughe the Yeir of
Chryst 1514

Excerpted and translated out
of the Lyue of the Bishops
of Aberdone. Writtin in Latine
by the learned and famous
chronographer Maister
Hector Boas. first
principall of the K:
College thair.
be A.
Garden.

Aberdone. the Yeer
1619

THE

LYF, DOINGS, AND DEATHE

OF

The Right Reuerend and Worthy Prelat,

WILLIAM ELPHINSTOUN,

Be the Divyne Prouidence the 23 BISHOP OF ABERDENE,
wha efter 30 yeeres gouernament of this Sea,
the 83 of his age, departed in Edinbrughe,
the yeir of Chryſt 1514.

Excerpted and Tranſlated out of the Lyues of the Biſhops
of Aberdene, Wretin in Latine by the learned and famous
Chronographer, MAISTER HECTOR BOES, firſt
Principall of the K. College thair,
be AL. GARDEN.

ABERDENE, THE YEER
1619.

T O

The Richt Ancient be Defcent, and no lefs Old in
Virtues then Aged in Yeires, the Generofe
and Richt Nobill Lord, ALEXANDER,
LORD ELPHINSTONE AND KILDRIMMIE,
ane of his Maiefties honorabill
Priuie Counfell:

AND TO

The no lefs Ennobled by Virtue then ancientlie Noble,
the Rycht Honorable ALEXANDER, LORD OF
KILDRVMMIE, and one of the Lords of his
Maiefties honorable Priuie Counfall
and Seffioun:

MY LORDES,

THE occafioun of your Lordfhips prefent repair to
thir partes being the Vifitatioun of our famous and
publick Schooles, pioullie firft founded, refpectiuelie
perfected, and prouidentlie prouydet, be ane Reuerend
and Relligious Prelat, defcendet from your Lordfhips
honorable Hous, and of your Lordfhips name, hes
moued me more willinglie nor worthelie to fingle out
from among the zealous and weell difpofed Prelats,
Bifhops of Aberdone, the Lyf, Doings, and the Deathe
of this moft venerable and Relligious WILLIAM
ELPHINSTOUNE, be the prouidence Diuine the
23 BISHOP OF ABIRDENE, whiche with all deutifull
and humble reuerence, I prefent, as moft competent to

your Lordſhips for the diſcent and pœdegree of the departed Prelat, and moſt conuenient for the furtherance
of the preſent purpoſe, to ſpurre up, allreddy poaſting,
your Lordſhip's good will to the more narrowlie tend-
ring the labefacted frame and the affaires tharof, bothe,
be the tract of tyme, on the way running to ruine, gif
not with ſpeed and prudentlie preuented.   So praying
to the Almightie to fecoond this, and all your Lordſhip's honorable attempts with a fortunat ſucceſſe, I reſt
whollie, in what I am able to ſerve your Lordſhips,

ALL: GARDEN.

TO THE READER.

GIF withe reguard yow read,
   As beſt becommethe Clerks,
Yow's find this Compend peniſht withe
   A Prelat's worthie warks.
Sincearelie ſyn him ſelf
   Set and reſolued folie
A perfyt paterne for to proue,
   Of Paſtors humble and holie.

A. G.

William Elphinstone
23. Bishope of Aberdone.

When Bishop Blacater
    In palestine deceased
Transported was to Glasco's seat
    and protomyst their place
The Channons, Clerks, and all,
    all wonderfulls prone
prays't for pastor postulats
    ane William Elphinstone.
(But vaunting be it said)
    Into that tyme and age
A man of all, Most spiritfull
    Most-sanctified & sage.
Whairfor this worshipfull
    Indictiones divyne
To limne his Lyfe, does ask the aid
    of all the Triple Tryne
How shall I then, since I
    ame so infirme' sett forth
And wryt of this Great William all
    his virtues, works & worth
Unless my pen. wer pull'd
    from Delius sdrivat wing.
And with the Muses happie' hands
    Dypt in the Thespian spring.
That be their heavenlie helpe
    My braniestormed quill
Might fortion Numbers Nectar-lyk
    Elaborat distill.

                                    And

WILLIAM ELPHINSTOUN,
23 Bishop of Abirdene.

W HAN Bifhop Blacater
 (In Paleftine deceas'd)
Tranfported was to Glafco's Seat,
 And Protomyft thair plac'd,
The channons, clerks, and all,
 All wounderfullie proone,
Prayes, and for Paftor poftulats,
 Ane Williame Elphinftoune,
(But vaunting be it fayd)
 Into that tyme and age,   10
A man of all moft fpiritfull,
 Moft fanctifeed and fage.
Whairfor, this Worfhipfull
 Juditious Diuyne,
To limne his Lyf, dois afk the ayd
 Of all the triple Tryne.
Whow fall I, then, fince I
 Am fo infirme, fett foorthe
And wreat of this great Williame, all
 His virtues, works and woorthe? 20
Unlefs my pen were pull'd
 From Delius' facrat wing,
And, with the Mufes happie hands,
 Dipt in the Thefpian fpring;
That, be thair heauenlie help,
 My unaccouftom'd quill,
Mycht Golden numbers, nectar-lyk,
 Elaborat, diftill,

And fyned quinteffence.
 My lynes and labours than, 30
Conforme unto fome meafure too
 The Merits of the Man:
Who as his Nature good
 In th' adolefcing age,
His futur Grace and greatnefs bothe,
 Did promeis and prefage;
So in his Lyf weell led,
 Moft worthy Neftors yeers,
Muchemore nor could expeéted be,
 Performed was, appears. 40
Now, this great worthy, wyfe,
 And vigilant Diuine,
In Glafco Burrow he was borne:
 His pedegree and lyne
From ELPHINSTOUNE, a houfe
 Old, opulent, and trew,
And yit a famous famelie
 Legittimat he drew.
At Glafco firft he got,
 (Whair all fueet Science fownds) 50
In that thryfe Inclyt Academe,
 His Elements and Grounds.
There to be borne, to breathe,
 Did God and Nature give,
And there his louing Lord did learne
 Him laudablie to liue;
Thair did he fuck his Dame,
 Thair on the Mufes milk
His fragrant frefhe ingyne was fed
 And foftred firft, be whilk 60
The Tyare he attain'd,
 And that highe honour had

Will: [Elph.]
Inclinatioune

To haue his Name immortaliz'd,
　And all whair ſpars'd and ſpred:
There it reported is
　And taken for a trewthe,
He throghe his Nurſe's negligence,
　The ſourt yeer of his youthe,
On tyme a myſſing was,
　And ſearched for, was found,　　　70
Withe more appearing zeall nor yeers,
　Low proſtrat on the ground,
In the Cathedrall Churche,
　Into ane inner Yle,
Whair on the Virgin's counterſit
　His eyes war fixt the whyll,
So firmelie and ſo faſt,
　That doubtleſs diſcontent,
His litle mynding to remoue,
　H' expreſſéd be complaint,　　　80
Whiche ſeem'd to ſome a ſigne
　A preſage and a Note,
That he ſould proue, as came to paſs,
　Religious and devote.
Than he into his Sext
　Or ſevnt yeer at the maiſt,
To ground him in his Grammer, withe
　A pedagoge was plac't,
Whoſe pr' excellent ingyne
　Did ſo ſurpaſs his peers,　　　90
That it his prudence pre-expreſt
　In his perfeċtar yeeres.
His Wit, acute and quick,
　With Judgement joynd to theſe,
Yit being bot a Boy, ſo did
　The Archeprelat's ſpirits pleaſe,

That eache night once he hade
 Him haunted to rehearfe
A fentence of fome learned Sage,
 Or fome flected verfe.   100
Heir willing I wald pafs
 Unpennd his vifioun,
Since mony in thir days will deeme
 It doltrie and derifioun:
His Vifioun. Yit fince its plainlie penn'd
 Be our Chronographer,
I fhaw the fame, and thairof fhall
 The faithe to him referre.
It feem'd to him he fate
 On's baire and bended knees, 110
At th' Altar of the Mother-Maid,
 Whome he fuppons he fees.
Amidds his quyet reft
 Ae waking he was wount
T' uphold and heis his hands, his hart
 So to the Mayd did mount.
Then with fadde fownding fighes,
 Great groanings and agaft,
Into thir words he afks hir aid,
 Or lyk to thir, at laft: 120
" Moft facrat of thy Sex!
 " Chofe parent of thy Prence!
" Support me, that I flyd not in
 " No filthy fowll offence;
" Affift me in my fhort
 " And heer fmall tarcing tyme,
" That willinglie my weaknefs do
 " Commit no curfed cryme;
" Bot that moir holelie,
 " Each moment I may mend, 130

" And calmelie paſs my pilgrimage,
  " And pairt with peace in end."
To theſe deſyr'd demands,
  Benigne and Lovinglie,
Th' Immaculat ſole Mother-Mayd
  Appear'd thus to replye :—
" To Vertue wed thy Will ;
  " And when, as certanlie
" Thow ſall, that Prelacie poſſeſſe
  " Whiche is prepar'd for thee,   140
" Conſult Chriſts Churche hir weell,
  " And hir with care decore,
" And him the Sauiour of thy ſaull,
  " Devoitlie do adore."
His Teacher all this tyme
  The ſtarting ſtripling ſeis,
And marking this, amazed muche,
  His earneſt exerceis,—
He walks him, and he craves
  Th' occaſioun and the cauſe   150
Of his ſleep, paſſionat complents,
  Thoughts, agonces, and thraws.
The happie youth, who knew
  No nought bot to obay,
Moſt docill and moſt deutifull
  Unto his Doctours ay,
Yit with his dream, a dred,
  Made ſtupefeit, he fears
To ſhaw what he ſuppos'd he ſaw.
  Baſhfull, a whyll forbears,   160
And modeſt, mutelie ſtayes,
  Attracting breathe betueene ;
And then the whoill he ſignefeis
  What, ſleeping, he had ſene.

B

His Maister maiſt humane,
  Judicious and diſcreet,
Did preſentl' apprehend theſe his
  Perplexiteis of ſpreit;
And thairfor cheeflie cheeris,
  And him forbids to be   170
Ou'r carefull yit or curious
  To fix felicitie,
Or to confyd into
  Night viſiounes or dreams,
Since they of hum'rous brains be bot
  Superfluous extreams;
And, or we wit, they grow,
  So they agane ar gone;
Herfor truſt not into ſuch toyes,
  Nor panſe thow thair upoun.   180
Yit tacitlie him ſelf
  On th' apparitioun panſes,
And at the iſhew fine and end
  Oft he conceats, and ſkanſes,
Confiddring long, at laſt
  Quieſcing dois conclood,
Into this Williame lurking lay
  Things hidde, ſubleim, and good.
Thairefter he him ſelf
  Was marked much to be   190
More filent, ſad, ſtill grave, and gevin
  To taciturnitie.
So this Man-ſprighted Boy,
  His primeŭe paſſed thus;
In's age above his equalls all,
  To learne laborious.
And yit it was not paſt
  All way equivalent

To his ingene, adjudgd ſo quick,
  So ſharpe, and excellent.
His primage ſo expyr'd,
  Into his twentie yeer
He paſt, all Honor hatching, highe
  Philoſophie to hear,
Whairin ſuche increſs hee
  Great growthe and profit got,
As nane profeſſing with him wes
  Whome he excelled not.
Swa confirmat become
  Into philoſophie,
Into his fyve and twentie yeer
  His courſe conclooded hee;
And manumiſſed then,
  Withe laude the Laurell wraethe,
And at that tyme his preiſthood there,
  He got togidder baithe.
Bot, for a tyme reſtrain'd,
  He from his ſtudeis ſtay'd
For'ℭt be's affairs familiar,
  Aſyd his Learning lay'd.
Whiche withe incredible
  Dexteritie he dreſt,
That in gouerning of the ſame
  Suche prudence he expreſt,
Altho it ſeem'd he ſould
  Be procreat and borne,
Alon be letters for to live
  And literats t' adorne;
Yit in weel ord'ringe his
  Domeſticatt adois,
In freinds he did ſoir-knawledge of
  His future faℭts infuiſe.

Bot vilipending foone
  That forme of lyf prophane,
His fpirit modeftlie afpyrs
  To mak of glorie gain:
And leaving it, him felf
  Sequeftrats, and he draws
Therefrom, and all his paines employes
  To the Pontificque Laues.

His Studeis to
he Laues.

In that farere famous Scoole
  In Glafco, he gave care,
And heard the Jurifts, judg'd the beft,
  That red or teached thair.
Whair he fome yeers remain'd,
  Then paft for to procure,
And juftlie efter called was
  "The Pleader of the Poore."
So upright he did prove,
  But Auarice or Greed,
That noght for gold, bot for good will,
  He was fuppon'd to pleed.
A fae to wrong he was,
  A fautor to the right,
To mony laulefs Lauers now
  A guyding lampade light.
So exerceis'd fome whyll;
  Yit if at freinds defyr,
Or one his awne unknawne refpects,
  He on that trade did tyr;
Iff on of thefe hes bene,
  Or bothe the caufes war
I find it noght, bot fuir it is,
  He did forbear the Barre
And Glafco Borrou bothe,
  To live into the land

240

250

260

Whair he aſſum'd the ſacrat charge
  Of Michaell Churche in hand:
And four yeers ſullie ſurthe
  He ſerved thair, and that 270
But ony intermiſſioun maid,
  The man did miniſtrat.
At no tyme ydill ſund,
  Nor ſlewthfull ſene to ſit;
His priuat
Exerceis.
No day ore-drawe whairin he wrought
  Nor vertuous work in it;
He ather that did wreit
  Whiche he thought good to teache.
Or priuat did premeditat,
  Or publick pray or preache: 280
Into his charge diſcharge,
  Strick, painſull and preeceis,
And maid the ſame his nightlie and
  Diurnall exerceis.
Of naughtines his lyſ
  (Weel knawne it was denud,)
And as a Chriſtian became,
  It godlie was and good.
For ordinar he us'd
  Firſt to incall, than read, 290
Then pray, ſyn read, ſucceſſiue ſo
  Eache uther did ſuccead.
Bot O! he that was borne
  A greater ſtate t'obtain,
Long could not in that priuat place
  Continew and remain;
Bot back to Glaſco brought
  Be Laurence Elphinſtoune,
His Uncle on the father ſyd,
  And tutor, left alone, 300

Who eggerlie did urge,
    And cheeflie did him chyd,
That did content his tyme fo withe
    So fmall affays, fould flyd,
And that his ritche engene,
    Be all belev'd the beft,
He fould permit and fuffer, bot
    Reguard to rouft or reft,
Whiche God to him had gevne
    (As fkilfulleft did fkan,)   310
For to illuftrat, and decore
    His Cuntree, King, and Clan:
Quod he, " Wald thow, (to whome
    " Thy fates dois fauour fo,—
" Leave this thy Cuntree and thy Kin
    " T' augment thy Graces)—go
" In uncouthe forrane landis,
    " And thair withe Virtue varnifhe,
" And more and more thy Mynd yit withe
    " Far goodlier guifts regarnifhe?   320
" Perpotees cheerifhe help,
    " Increfs and mak muche more,
" Thy grounds and guifts alreddy great
    " With ftranger gottin ftore: ·
" For, be affur'd, gif that
    " Excel'flie to afcend
" And mount a Magne, or fteppe to State,
    " Thow purpofe or pretend—
" Or wald to Honor or
    " To Dignitie aryfe,   330
" Thow muft be Labors Palace pafs,
    " Whairin it lockéd lyis.
" And, furthermore, t' inriche
    " And give your learning light,

" Yow muſt in places peregrine
  "Seek out, and ſearche be ſight.
" And what fall coumpted be
  " Condigne to bear your charge,
" I promeiſe to ſuppeditat
  " And furniſhe furthe at large."   340
Whiche pearcing ſpeaches, ſprung
  From Faithe, and Laurence' love,
Moſt mightelie did William's mynd
  Stirr, ſtimulat and move:
So quicklie he reſolues,
  But tareing or ſtay,
Or neidfull neceſſars, that might
  Or hinder or delay,—

His Voiage He preſentlie depairts;
for France.   And coaſting, caſts his courſe   350
For France, the Muſes' manſioun than,
  And Learnings noble nourſe;
And ſyn to Paris paſt,
  As ancient Athens, whan
Shoe floriſht moſt in ſaculteis,
  So was this thought of than.
Whair he ſuch travells took,
  That thoſe conferr'd with theſe
His former paſſed pains, yow wold
  Judge idleneſs and eaſe.   360
In hearing th' Oratours'
  Or Juriſts' teaching, ay
He exerciſed was: and thus
  He did divyd the day;
And ordinar at night,
  What he had hard or wreat,
That ſole and ſecreat with him ſelf
  He haunted to repeat.

His pain paft all beleefe,
  His patience did exprefs,
Moft fpairing too of fleep, and for
  His fair, none liv'd on lefs.
So that it was fuppon'd
  Difficult to decerne,
Gif hee be lucubratiouns more,
  Or be day light, did learne.
His lyf, his literature,
  Indeed fo great and grave
With prudence, and his promptitud
  Soone Parcis did perceave.
Whiche whan thair eyes had fene
  What they of him did hear,
They could not bot amazed muche
  The matchelefs man admeir.
When Golden Virtue is
  Obfcured moft, the more—
For fuche hir natrall is—fhee will
  Grow, florifhe, wax and ftore.
His learning brought to light,
  His name renownd and knawne,
Requefted be the Canonifts,
  And much defyr'd, is drawne
In publiėt to prefent,
  And enter in the Lifts,
To give his proof in prefence of
  Thair graduat Canonifts.
Whair, as his modeftie,
  Great eloquence and fkill,
All thefe his hearers' harts and ears
  With wounder frefhe did fill,
That ravifhd with his witt,
  Rare gravitie and grace,

They then promovde and plac't him in
  The cheef Primarian place,—
Firft Lector of the Laues—
  A glorie never gevin
Nought to ane Inlands man, unlefs
  Bothe excellent, and evin
Of moft accomplifh'd partes,
  And of approued fpreit.   410
Licentiat in the Ciuill Law,
  And Profeffor pereit.
Withe fuche fedulitie,
  Allacritie and care,
He fyve yeers out, or fix (with fome,)
  Still teaching tarcid thair.
Whair bothe fuche faithe, and fuche
  Sinceritie, he fhew,
That all mens' eyes to him allone
  H' attracted and he drew.   420
Thefe fex yeers all outrun,
  Deferuing worthelie,
He got the Laurell of the Laues,
  And Doctor's Dignitie.
Then up to Orleance,
  Withe Doctors refident
Thair to conferre deem'd crudeit,
  Thryfe Laureat Williame went;
In whofe focietie
  A certan fpace he fpent,   430
Whair with a dictione delegat,
  Pure, apt, and eloquent,
All Theorems of Law,
  Hidde miftick and obfcure,
But ony pains, he did explane
  Be his large literature.
C

So withe incredible
  And admiratioun muche,
They did behold and faw that his
  Sagacitie was fuche.   440
Whair throw he rightlie raife,
  And came in fuche account,
That his renowne and name abone
  His marrows muche did mount.
Whill that the firft of France
  So did his guifts regaird,
That his advyfe they oft tymes us'd
  In Parl'ment efter-ward.

His fame for
his Erudi-
tionne.

Thus as his fame throw France,
  And all whair, famous flew,   450
So, honour'd be the beft, good will
  To him and freindfhip grew,
Withe thefe that did upoun
  The fage great fenate fit,
Bot withe De Gana moft, a man
  Of ryppe and reddie wit,
Whofe Wifdome efter-ward
  And Virtues did aduance,
And caus'd him Chancelar chofin be
  Of all the Realme of France.   460
Whiche freindfhippe ftill infring'd,
  Continew'd 'tuixt thame tway,
In forme and force fraternall lyk,
  Unto thair deeing day.
Whill his perfectiouns thus
  (That propre his did claime
Laud from each lippe,) had famous France
  Oreflowed with his fame,
Tuo Lufters one yeer, left
  That he had there foiorn'd,   470

His Returne
to Scotland.

He, much admeird and more renown'd,
  Intreated, home return'd.
And unto Glafco firſt
  Great Doctor Williame dois—
The natrall nurce of the none age,
  And of his morning Mufe—
Go, to the Prelat thair,
  A wyfe and worthy man
Of letters, and of literats
  A choife Excultor than;   480
Whome, courtefs, kyndlie he
  Did tender, and intreat
Withe correfpondence to his worthe.
  And to his awne eftate.
Whair to giue publick proof,
  And mak it clearlie knawne,
What learning from the fonts of France
  H' exhaufted had and drawne,
Of the Pontifique Laues
  Some problems he propon'd,   490
Which bothe percit and promplie he
  Refolued and expound,
And with fuche flowing phrafe,
  Fit, formall and profound,
Diſſolued doubte, and mifticks maid
  Significant and found,
That all the Clergic thair
  Admiringly amaz'd,
The proto-Prelat, prefent too,
  His pregnancie he praifd.   500
Whairfor fince thus they fie
  Him graced with fuche guifts,
They mynd (for all things aids that God
  Aduances and uplifts,)

And deulie dois determine
  With the advyfe of all,
To creat him thair Commiffare
  Judge or Officiall,
A dignit and degree,
  Commodious and large,   510
Gevine bot to fuche as could the fame
  Condignelie weel difcharge.
Bot fo withe equitie
  The ballance thair he buir,
In office faithfull fund, and ay
  Knawne incorrup, and pure:
A cenfurer feuere
  Of wrongs injurious,
And to all lewd litigians
  With reafoun rigorous: 520
This adage ufing oft
  And iterating ftill,—
" The Judge injures the juft that dois
  Unpunifht fpare the ill."
So laudablie he layd,
  With Reafon's reule aright,
The ground oft all his efter great-
  nefs, magnitude and might.
O! bot fo large a light,
  This litle meafure mean   530
Could noght inclus'd ecclipféd keep,
  Unthyning and unfeene,
Bot that it muft difperfe
  So ritche and radiant rayes,
Throw all the corners off this Yle
  Be many wounderous wayes.
That Court too clean and curt,
  For fuch a mynd unmeat,

The circuit of that Citie walls
  Too ſpair for ſuch a ſpreit.   540
For why? to come to Court
  The Counſell they him craue,
To giue withe thame, in things of weght,
  His good advyſe and graue.
Whair to aduance him more,
  Whilſt with the King he bade
At Court, he was of Andr'apole Judge
  And Officiall maid.
And efter that noght long,
  Yit his eſtate t' extoll,   550
Amongs the Kings cheef Counſalours
  This Reuerend they inroll;

He is maid a Counſalour.

Whairin him ſelf he us'd,
  And counſall gaue ſo good,
As withe the weel and honor of
  His Highneſs State ay ſtood.
Thus was his praiſes ſpred,
  And ore this regioune ran,
His gloree and his greatneſs thus,
  Here bothe to grow begane.   560
But now the Weirds inveits,
  And Williame will aduance
Withe fortouns yit more fair, and mak
  Him Orator to France!

Bp. Williame ſent Orator to France.

Withe th' Earle of Buchan, then
  The Juſtice Generall,
And that thryſe worthy worſhipfull
  The Biſhop of Dunkell,
Direct from Janes the Thrid
  Unto King Ludouicke   570
Th' Elevint, t' appaiſe ſuſpitiouns ſprung,
  Now kindled new and quick,

And lyk to bread bothe breks,
  Great difcords and debaits,
Betuixt thefe long Confed'rat tuo
  Stronge floorifhing Eftates,
A peruerfe poyfned platt
  Of Wraethe and wyld Enuy:
That gif thefe Kings fould juft and jarre,
  They then might gain thairby;   580
The whiche nought onlie hee
  A tyme reftrain'd and ftench't,

Bot withe this pleafant pitthie fpeache
  He quayld it clean and quench't:
" Illuftrious Prince of France!
  " Moft Chriftian King! (quod hee,)
" Wald God that Natur, Art, or Ufe
  " Voutchaifed had on me.
" Suche pow'rfull plent' of fpeache,
  " Suche welthe of words and wit,   590
" As in fome parts fould aptly proue
  " Convenient and fit,
" T' accord, to obuiat,
  " To correfpond and be
" Equivalent unto your Grace,
  " Your greatnefs and degree:
" Bot O! fo in my birthe
  " Siniftrous war my fignes
" That haplefs I inhibeit am
  " Since all the Thefpian fprings!   600
" So thus it comes, great King!
  " No fyllabe worthy can,
" By worthles me, all unexpart,
  " Weel be propond, O than!
" Admeir not, Sacrat Sir,
  " Tho' in your prefence plac't

" Amongs your Palatins and Peers,
 " Heir pallid, me almaiſt
" Amaz'd and moued mutche
 " To harrang yow behold,   610
" Whair Orators moſt exquiſeit
 " Skarce weel aduenture wold.
" Aduenture wold! who wold
 " In preſence of a Prince
" Renown'd, proclam'd victorious
 " In armes and eloquence?
" Heirſore, braue Prince! without
 " Diſpleaſur, paſs I pray,
" When weghtleſs words, unworthy thee,
 " My weakneſs fall bewray.   620
" Since no, nought raſhlie, nor,
 " As may be ſayd be ſome
" Upoun ſkild confidence, unto
 " Thy Court, O King, I come.
" No, no, bot be command,
 " Straght mandat, will and charge,
" Of my dred, deir and Souraigne Lord:
 " I come aboard my bairge
" To do his Highnes heſts,
 " Moſt gratious of all other,   630
" Wha does reguard and highlie hold,
 " Sir, yow his Royall brother!
" Whairfor, I rather to
 " Thy clemencie will cleaue,
" And anchor on theſe fauours firme
 " Your Highnes wount to haue,
" That I more boldlie bold
 " May ſomewhat ſay, thought ſmall,
" Yit trewlie poynting to a Peace
 " Publick perpetuall,   640

" Than to neglect, retard,
 " Poftpone, refuife, withftand,
" Aganis all dewtie, (God forbid!)
 " My facrat King's command,
" Then to accommodat
 " Refpects important moue.
" Our fpeaches firft, braue Prince! to peace,
 " To amitie and loue;
" The proper pedeftals,
 " Th' approv'de fupporting fpyrs, 650

" The nerue-ftronge ftable ftay of States,
 " The pillar of Empyrs,
" The fruitfull daughter fair
 " Of th' eu're liuing Lord;
" The glorie of the good,
 " Th' abater of the bloody fuord,
" The light and lyf of Lawes,
 " Trew Juftice, firme Defence;
" The patron of all policie
 " And pleafure of the Prence, 660
" Withe and whoes onlic ayd
 " Still ftands Eftates, and Regnes
" In quyet calme, but cros of cares:
 " Dukes, Empriours, and Kings,
" Publict nor priuat States,
 " Whow mightie muche or mean,
" Sans or but this State ftabling peace,
 " Unftreffed can fufteene;
" Nor to our felf, nor too
 " Our Countree, King or blood; 670
" But thefe we profitable proue,
 " Be gratious or good:
" Suche the opiniouns war
 " Of Nat'ralifts of old,

" And Wretars wyfeſt and diuyne
  " This for a Maxime hold,—
" That concord, loue, and peace,
  " Farre paffing earthlie eyne,
" Ar fuirelie facrat of thame felfs,
  " Uraniah and Diuine: 680
" To whiche effeⅽt th' arche foe,
  " To faⅽtious Catelene,
" Whofe melleit mouthe, and flowent phrafe,
  " So much admeired hes bene,
" Exclamis and cryis: 'O thay
  " 'Who fo audacious bold,
" 'Dares fo difrump the publick peace,
  " 'Pull from the Worlde wold
" 'The Golden Eye of Heauen,
  " 'The fpeciall nurce of things,   690
" 'That on the maffie Mother Earthe
  " 'All forming Nature brings!'
" Since noght a greater grace
  " Nor happines from Heauen,
" For confort of all creatures
  " Was, is, nor fall be gevin;
" And nought, Viⅽtorious Prince!
  " Is that more pleafant proues,
" Nor when tuo Monarches and thair men
  " Arⅽtlie Colleagued loues!   700
" And the Stragirian Sage
  " Protefts, tho' Kings poffes
" All other goods but freinds; this all—
  " Then nought is nothing les.
" What welthy wordlings, wife
  " Potentats, Princes, and
" What Fortoun's fau'rits, but thair freinds,
  " Suir in eftate can ftand?
                    D

" Pompe, peace, profperitie,
  " And what vain welthe, auails   710
" To Countreis, Kings, and Common welths,
  " Whan freinds and freindfhip fails?
" And whow, but freindfhip, may
  " Moft wyflie uneneru'd,
" Great Princip'liteis and pours
  " Be Princes be preferu'd?
" Whow muche more man abound,
  " Swell, and in fubftance fwim,
" So muche more oft ar moft mifhapps
  " Hard at the hand to him.   720
" In ev'rie greateft greef,
  " Whiche mortals marrethe moft,
" And in thair cheef calamiteis
  " Whair with tha' ar crufh'd and croft,
" Thair onlie left releef,
  " Refuge and confort ay,
" (Saif in the Lord thair God)
  " Into thair louing freinds they lay.
" Bot to comprend and coutche,
  " Yea in few words confyne,   730
" Bothe mony maters large and good,—
  " So concord is divyne :
" That heir throughe things thought mean,
  " Yit multipl' and augment,
" And but the fame, ritche Royall Crouns
  " Decay, ar torne and rent!
" Some brutifhe creaturs too,
  " Wha vaunting Reafon's ufe,
" That nature be th' Omnipotent,
  " Dois creat and produce;   740
" Wold we perceaue, they do
  " Prognofticat and preache,

" And whow men ought to liue, thair liues
  " Exemplifie and teache :
" Bot cheeflic theſe, that be
  " Experience we find,
" The oxin, horſe, and ſheepe, whiche ar
  " Moſt tractable; be kynd
" They kyndlie concord keep,
  " And lyk conburgers be,   750
" Without all foirthought, foſtred frawd,
  " Hait or hoſtilitie.
" Bot th' other ſavage ſort
  " To rapine prone and raiſ,
" Thair cruell natrall kynd ſtill dois
  " Thair kendled cholors chaiſe,
" That eache with other it
  " Holdis, jangling ſtill at jarre,
" And makes thame moue to mortall men
  " A brutiſhe bloody warre :   760
" And tho in uſe to us
  " They ſeldome be and rare,
" And verie few confum'd be withe
  " Th' inclemenc' of the air,
" Yit thir intractable,
  " Into thair numbers neuer
" To multitudes amount, bot ane
  " Alwayes almoſt ar euer.
" Againe th' innoxius kynd,
  " Depopulat thoughe thay   770
" By butchers be, and ſubject too
  " To wrack of weather ay,---
" Yit co-obſeruing loue,
  " They do ſtill more and more
" To hudge and numbers numberles
  " Proſper, incres and ſtoar.

" O fit fyn documents!
    " And leffons worthe to learne,
" And to be taught to all eftates,
    " Whow freindfhip dois concerne!   780
" And is right requifeit,
    " Yea neceffarlie brings
" Into this lyf to all a help
    " And increment of things.
" Bot from digreffing thus,
    " To mak a ftay, and ftand
" Aback, for to returne vnto
    " That whilk we haue in hand,—
" Th' illuftr'ous James, the Thrid
    " Of that renowned name,   790
" Our four'ane Lord, alone that bears
    " Unthral'd his diademe,
" Be us his Orators,
    " (Altho unworthy wee)
" Excellent and moft Chriftian King,
    " Salutes thy Majeftie!
" And with that reuerence
    " Moft dew, condigne and meet
" To thy degree, moft pow'rfull Prince!
    " Moft glaidlie dois the greet: 800
" Defyring nothing more
    " To him befall nor chance,
" Nor knaw your Highnes to haue helthe,
    " And florifhing be France!
" And cheeflie cheef in this
    " His Highnes hopes repofe,
" And with your Grace, for all good lucks,
    " He joyntlie dois rejois.
" His Grace's Grandfyr-great,
    " By thair braue mercits maid   810

" Thy France thair freind confederat,
  " Whiche but all bracks abaid,
" From Charles furnamd the Great,
  " And King Achaius' dayes—
" Sir, to your happie regne, that now
  " The Gallick fcepter fwayes—
" A louing league, a band,
  " And faft confedracie,
" Obferu'd and treulie intertain'd
  " With all integritie: 520
" And noght with wreat and wax,
  " Or Buls allon, hes bene
" This faithfull fœdracie conferm'd,
  " Bot fealed it was fenc,
" Oft with th' effunded blood
  " Of men moft choife, and cheef
" Of bothe the natiouns, feghtan'd for
  " Thair mutuall releef.
" This doolefull tryell taught
  " At th' expugnatioun long   530
" Of th' Englifhe Anwick Caftell, bothe
  " Be Art and Natur ftrong,
" Whair mony famous Frenfche
  " Throw Englifhe force did fall,
" And war in ftrait, yea at the poynt
  " For to haue perifh'd all,
" Gif that couragious Count,
  " The Douglas dred, had nought
' Withe fpeed approacht, and with him thair
  " His bands triumphant brocht.   540
" Whow mony worthy Scots
  " Of the Patrician ftate,
" I purpofe not thefe too, too old
  " Examples paft repeat.—

" At Wernoll, Crefcie, Blange,
　" In the defence of France,
" With martiall lawd, haue loaft thair lyues,
　" Be fhot, be fuord, and lance.
" Look, Ludouick, heirfore—
　" What cordiall loue we bear　　　　　　850
" To thee and thyn, of Englifhe force
　" But all regaird and feare;
" To perrels but refpect
　" We pas, and faill the fea,
" And venters lyfes our worthieft wares
　" To feght for thyn and thee.
" Suche is our reuerence,
　" Integritie, and trothe,
" That we haue borne, and alwyfe beare
　" To that fuorne facrat oathe,　　　　　　860
" That cuntree, goods and freinds,
　" Our childring, wyfes, and als
" Our lyfes fall lofe, or we be fund
　" Fidifragie and fals!
" Breack not than, facrat Syre!
　" The long unbleamifht band,
" That with fa mony Chriftian Kings
　" Unviolat hes ftand;
" And in that freindlie forme,
　" In force and in effect,　　　　　　　870
　Sa mony ages hes befoir
　" But bleamifhe bene, and breck.
" Which League, my fouraigne Lord,
　" His too too carefull cares,
" Whow he wald haue it fure obferu'd,
　" Deciphers and declairs;
" Altho fome fpreits impure
　" Oft impiouflie haue preft,

" Withe ſiniſter ſuggeſtiouns,
  " To gall it, and diſgrac't,   380
" And withe thair buſſie brains
  " Yit dois aſſay and ſeik
" To ſhak it to your ſhame: Syre, withe
  " Your patience, I ſpeak,—
' For gif in France default,
  " The League conſerud ſo long,
" A rupture fall, receaue, or breache,
  " A violence or wronge,—
" Moſt louing Ludouick!
  " This ſhall imputed be   390
" Unto thy gratious, too, too cre-
  " dulous credulitie:
" Since that the Scotiſhe King,
  " Our ſacrat ſouraigne Lord,
" Moſt conſtant curiouſlie dois keep
  " This conſacrat accord;
" His Highnes ſets befoir
  " His rev'rent Royall eye,
" His Grace's grand foirbears good,
  " Of matcheles memorie;   400
" And thairunto adjoyns
  " His Highnes' honor, that
" By might nor mundan means can be
  " Nor wrong'd nor violat.
" His nat'rall loue lykuyſe
  " Is lyk a circling chayne,
" His freindſhippe with the Realme of France,
  " Moſt ſtronglie to mantain:
" To beare record of this,
  " And manifeſt it mair,   410
" For France his highe ſollicitude
  " And his kynd countrees caire.

" That reuerend diuyne,
  " The Biſhop of Dunkell,
" And that right famous inclyt Erle,
  " Great Uncle to himſell,
" Withe this perexcellent grauc Ju-
  " riſt, whome we call
" (The vulgar vocable to uſe,)
  " Our Juſtice Generall,   920
" And me my ſelf, I grant
  " Unworthe, unapt, indigne,
" To undergo ſo great a charge,
  " Unto ſo great a King!
" Unto your Celſitude,
  " His Highnes heir hes fend,
" All maters marr'd, and manag'd wrong,
  " For to remeed and mend;
" And ſiclyk to your Self,
  " To ſhaw and ſignifie,   930
" And for to certiorat and make
  " This ſacrat Senat ſie,
" That gif reports hes paſt
  " Whiche may the peace ſupplant,
" Or gif ought hes bene ſayd unto
  " Th' old freindſhippe diſſonant,
" Or in his name if too
  " Your Royall hands be broght
" Some ſecret ſuits, or ſuche lyk things,
  " But warrand all ar wrought.   940
" And heirfor, Sir, for to
  " Decypher ſuche, as als
" To prouc thair miſreports to be
  " Bot fables faingz'd and fals,
" Unto theſe reuerend,
  " Great noble men, and ſage,

" Committed is his Highnes mynd
 " And matters to manage:
" The long confedrat League,
 " Gif harmed ony whair, 950
" Or labefacted they it find,
 " Thai haue powar to repair;
" And gif it ſo ſhall need,
 " Yit new conditions thay
" Sir, with your Graces's gevin conſent,
 " Adde at thair pleaſour may:
" And to promitt ſupport,
 " Commiſſioun and command,
" We haue aganis your preſent foes
 " That now infeſt your land: 960
" And ſpeciallie this, more
 " For to avert your harmes,
" To ſhaw our Prince, in perſon ſall
 " Now preſentlie tack armes:
" Suche is to you his loue,
 " Suche his weell meaning mynd,
" And to affect your France, ſo is
 " He cairſullie inclyn'd,
" That nothing he can coumpt
 " Convenient, good, nor grate, 970
" Whiche is not for thy publick weell
 " Thy Kingdome, Croune, and State,
" But whoſe proſperitie,
 " Great Segnyour, ſuir thy ſell,
" His Highnes' diſcontents and greivs
 " No terren tounge can tell!
" Your Gracefs bothe ar glaid,
 " (And I beleve dois gloire)
" Than in your mutuall amitie,
 " In nothing mortall moir. 980

E

" Victorious Prince! ar thou
 " Noght th' onlie earthelie King
" Inaugur'd with that facrat oyle,
 " That heav'nlie holy thing?
" And unto whome allone
 " Is graunted from abouc,
" By th' only tuitche, the wyld cheek rheume
 " To remeed, and remoue?
" Ar thou noght th' onlie Prince
 " By guift divyne that wears,   990
" And in thy badge, the beautifull
 " And braue, braue Lillie, bears?
" Whiche thy forbears bold
 " Haue prouidentlie fpaird,
" And to the Lyon left to be
 " His garland and his guaird;
" To giue ane euidence
 " Unto the World's end
" That Scotland France, France Scotland, fall
 " Protect, mantain, defend.   1000
" Ar thefe not arguments
 " Then, valeid, firme, and ftrong,
" For to mantene this amitie
 " Your Maiefteis among?
" Moft Royall King! then wee,
 " We pray, requeft, implore
" Your Grace, to keep us faithfull freinds
 " As France hes fund befoir;
" T' obferue this old contract,
 " Kythe, louing, conftant, kynd,   1010
" And withe a paritie in loue
 " Sir, meit our Maifter's mynd;—
" A chyld yit for his yeeres,
 " Bot into wifdome old,

" He dantoun'd hes his montane men—
  " Men fearlefs, fearce and bold ;
" And calmelie queyeted,
  " Yea he hes fatled fo
" His Realme, that thair no rumor is,
  " Nor fear of ony foe.   1020
" Since that he finds this tyme
  " Heir troublefome, to be
" Fit whairin he may bothe availl
  " And forder France and thee.
" Whairfor be loathe that once
  " It fould be fay'd or fene,
" That thow fould breck that band, at whois
  " Begininge bleft hes bene
" Incall'd th' Eternall treuthe,
  " God th' euer liuing Lord,   1030
" To punifhe the perjur'd in that
  " Commodious accord,
" Eftablifhed fo oft,
  " Conferm'd, affuird and feal'd.
" With bothe the Nations' nobleft blood,
  " For others quarrels fkeald.
" Then cherifhe, loue, efteme
  " Us louing, faithfull, and
" That 'tuix the People and Princefs, peace
  " May ftill and ftable ftand ;   1040
" Whairbe in profp'rous peace
  " Thow juftlie fall rejofe,
" Defend, keip, and conferue thy Crowne
  " But fear of all thy foes.
" But heir to put a poynt,
  " Sir, you fall know from thefe,
" All wyfe, renown'd and noble Lords,
  " When yee appoynt and pleafe,

" The forder will and pleafure of
  " Our Prince, whiche is commit   1050
" Unto thair judgements great and graue,
  " Skill, prudencie, and wit."
  Now hauing harrangd with
    Ane admirable grace,
  Withe the applaufe of Prince and Peers,
    The Prelat held his peace;
  Whofe words weell wealled and
    Convenientlie couch'd,
  The maters marche, the purpofe fp'rits,
    Inter other fo touch'd,   1060
  That amber-lyk to him
    They link't King Lues' loue,
  In maner fuche as could noght be
    Maid efter to remoue.
  So rofe the Gallick Roy,
    And louinglie imbraces
  Th' Imbaffadours, as there they ftood
    In thair appoynted places.
  Then, luifing Ludouick,
    Moft earneftlie defyres,   1070
  And efter bothe his Highnes' helthe
    And countree's ftate requyres:
  Wharof fuffic'entlie
    Affured and refolvde,
  He greatlie did congratulat,
    The Senate fyn diffolv'de;
  And th' Orators then, lyk
    A moft magnifick Lord,
  He feafted with all dainteis that
    His Francia could afford: 1080
  Expenfs he fpaired not,
    Nor gold he ought regairds.

Bot with maiſt princelie ritche propyns,
  Thame honors and rewards.
The day ſucceeding that,
  The Celtick Senat dois
Yeeld to our Legats' wholl demands
  And nothing did refuiſe
That to our Sou'rane Lord
  Or to his countree can,   1090
Or unto others weill availl
  Bot glaidl' all granted than—
Then with kynd countenance,
  Thoſe men of mekle mark,
From France took leaue, and out of Deep
  For Britain they imbark;
Whair ſaiflie ſet a ſhoar,
  Thair Sou'rane they ſalut.
Thus the Imbaſſad braue,
  Deulie diſpatcht and ſped,   1100
The Prince his grace and great good will
  Unto the Biſhop bred;
Whiche to mak clearlie knawne,
  He him preſents and chuſes
Unto the Biſhoprick of Roſs,—
  Whiche ſairlie he refuiſes:
Proteſting that was noght
  The place for him prepaird,
Whairin he ſould be conſecrat
  And call'd too he declair'd: 1110
And when his freinds inquyr'd,
  Whow hapned it that he
Wald not accept bot had refuis'd
  So ample a Prelacie?
" Thair is no ſeat prepaird
  " For us," quod he, " bot whair

He refuiſes the
B: of Roſs.

" The Holy Mayd Deiparent is
  " Approu'd Protectres thair"
Unto his former dreame
    Alluding, as appears,   1120
Or unto that he seem'd to fie
    Into his younger yceres.
Bot mark from thence he is
    More counted and refpected,
And on the Counfell worthelie
    Is chofen and elected;
So that the ftate affaires
    Of greateft importance
Ar cheeflie done be his advyfe,
    His wit and ordinance;   1130
And when be the effects
    That from his wifdome flows,
He came in credeit with his King,
    And more, more greater grows.
Then as a godlie man
    Wald noght betray his truft,
Bot graiv'l' exhorts his Prince to leaue
    Hie avarice and luft,
Tuo plagues moft peftilent
    And more nor deadlie thinges,   1140
To be predominant and regne
    In Potentats and Kinges;
And for to ftoppe and ftay
    The furie, and repres
Thefe robbers' rage, that daylie did
    His countree ftates diftres:
For certanlie bothe great
    And greuous wrongs be thofe
Oppreffiouns, fprung unto the Crowne
    And the Republick rofe.   1150

And ſiclyk he adhorts
  And labors muche to moue
His Highnes to adheare t' intreat,
  To cheariſhe and to loue
His chaiſt and fruitfull Queene,
  The Lady Margret, borne
And ſprung from princes' blood, & whome
  Great graces did adorne.
He ſorder to his Prince
  Intearlie dois intreat   1160
To uſe his great men's grave advyſe
  In ſteering his eſtate,
And to protect his poore
  From wrongs and injurie,
And he him ſelf to liue his lyf,
  More wholl and holelie.
Laſt, he beſowght he ſould
  Be clement ever more,
Becaus that qualitie a king
  Dois verie muche decoire.   1170
Thir exhortatiouns oft,
  Weell withe the Prince preuail'd,
For nather they in good effects
  Nor in thair fruits they fail'd;
He better liu'd, and was
  Religious more from thence,
And ever went to worſhip God
  With greater reuerence.
And all tymes efter that,
  To pray the Lord he lears,   1180
Bothe for his awne and Countree's ſtate,
  With trembling and with tears.
And to the indigent,
  The Churche, and Church-men all,

As it became his qualitie,
  Was muche more liberall.
About this tyme it chanc't,
  Into this cuntree come
A Bifhop or Imbaffadour
  Send from the Pope of Rome,   1190
With priuileges great,
  And muche immunitie,
In fauors of our Sov'rane Lord
  And his Nobilitie.
This Prelat, lo! the Prince,
  As it becomes great Kings,
He honors highlie, and rewards
  With mony Royall things;
And did about him felf
  This ftranger ftill retein,   1200
Delighting muche to hear him fpeek
  Of purpofe peregrine.
But once it chanĉt thair met
  His Highnes in the way,
As he unto Leftarik went
  Upoun a holie day—
A Noble-man, condemn'd
  And deftinat to die
For blood and flaughter, who, whow fone
  The Sovrane he did fie,   1210
Downe at his feet he falls
  Befoir him on his face,
Then lifts his chayned hands, with tears,
  And humblie calls for grace;
Befeeking him he wold
  Remember that renown'd—
That Royall vertew, clemencie,
  That mony Kings hes crown'd;

And whairbe oft the wretche
  Convick a hoip hes had,   1220
Yea at the poynt to fuffer too
  Has bene releu'd and fred:
Then, "Gratious Prince!" quod he,
  " Proue pitifull and fpair,
" (Since that my cryme come bot be chance,
  " And was involuntare,)
" Left that I be withe thofe
  " For foir confulted crymes,
" By fhamefull deathe be maid a ftane
  " Unto the efter tymes."   1230
The Prince, to pitie prone,
  Dois to the Legat look,
And from the damned man's demand
  A fit occafioun took,
To mak the Roman bold
  To be a fupplicant,
The author, mean, and th' inftrument
  To moue his Grace to grant
Lyf, lands, and libertie,
  And to the pris'ner peace,   1240
Yit did the Romeift rigorous,
  Stay fpeacheles all the fpace,
As inexorable.
  He dumme and mute remain'd,
Untill his Grace agane thus urg'd,
  And t' anfuer him conftrain'd;
" What is" quod he "to us
  " Thy counfell in this cace?"
The other, ruidlie, then reply'd,—
  " Let Juftice haue hir place."   1250
The myld and clement King,
  To Williame then converts,

F

And fayes, " Is this the clemencie
  " Of the Italian harts?
" Is this the pitie plac't
  " And bred into thair breafts,
" Of that renown'd and reu'rend rowt
  " Rome's Prelats and hir preifts?
" Thow often otherwyfe,
  " Ufe mony meanes to move   1260
" Us to inclyne to clemencie,
  " And pitifull to proue."
The graue and godlie man
  At that refponfe he fpights,
And on the ground for werie greef
  He fixed long his lights:
And hates th' immanitie
  And fcarcefnes that he fand,
Into that cruell Clergie man
  Come from the Latine land: 1270
Bot yit, unmyndfull noght,
  Kyths now the Chriftian King,
What glorie great this clemencie
  Dois unto Princes bring:
And th' other's fentence fharp,
  As tyrranous detefts,
And be his mercie to the man
  His myldnes manifefts:
For there the doome of deathe,
  And fentence he refcinds,   1280
And from the burding of his bands
  The Baron he unbinds.
Then with a gallant grace,
  The guiltie man difcharg'd,
And law free for that fact from thence
  To libertie inlairg'd:

Togidder ſhawing thair,
   That Princes great ſould be,
With meaſour meek and merciſull,
   And cled with clemencie;   1290
And that it is injuſt
   And alway impious,
For to perſuade and counſell Kings
   For to be rigorous.
Now daylie more and more
   His Grace' good lyking grew,
And princelie ſauors be effects
   To Biſhop Williame ſhew:
For when important things,
   Be cace in queſtioun came,   1300
He was alon elect, imploy'd
   And tain t' entreat the ſame,
Be reaſoun of his great
   Dexterit' of ingyne,
His muche admeired modeſtie
   With fair and faſhions ſyn.
About this tyme was ſawen
   The ſeminar and ſeeds
Of ane moſt wrackfull futur warre,
   Be ſome unhappie heads,   1310
Betuix King James the Thrid
   And th' Ingliſhe nightbour King:
Bot th' object is to ſtoppe the ſtreame
   Of this tempeſtuous ſpring.
Our worthy Williame wyſe,
   By ſearche the fitteſt found,
To be the healtheſum Cataplaſme
   To that appearing wound.

He is ſend to England.

This laſt he took on him,
   And to King Eduard went,   1320

Where with a harrang grauelie thair,
  Exceeding eloquent,
His Princes will he expon'd
  Dilucidlie and large,
And fo with Wifdome wyfelie wrought
  And execut his charge,
That bothe the Princes' harts,
  Difjoyned be difdain,
Be his Legation he alon
  Knits and uneits againe;   1330
So, as appear'd, they bothe
  Nought onlie War difarm'd,
Bot that thair was perpetuall peace
  Eftablifh'd and conferm'd,
Gif noght that wicked Warre,
  And that inteftine ill,

Had not begunne, that all thir bounds
  With factious force did fill,
Betuixt our Sou'rane Lord
  And the Albanian Duke,   1340
Whofe part (refpecting not the peace)
  The Englifhe Eduard took.
Altho a fugitiue—
  With money and with men,
He him affifted and fuppleed
  Aganis his brother then.
Whairfor not efter long,
  Betuixt thir Natiouns fprang,
And was proclaim'd a wofull warre,
  Sharpe, perellous and lang.   1350
Our moft couragious King
  Did nocht fo muche mifdeeme
The Englifhe armes, as fear'd his awne,
  Siniftrouflie that feeme

For to be freinds, and more
   To fauor and affect
The Duke's defignes than his, thair Prince,
   His part, for to refpect:
Bot in this change of things,
   And variable event,   1360
Whiche wrackfull warre this tyme betuixt

His 2d Voyage to England.

   Thefe Princes did prefent;
Our Prelat Williame, withe
   The States' confent, is fend
The fecond tyme, to put to warrs
   And to thefe ills ane end,
Unto the Englifhe King;
   With whome the peace he platts,
And queyet of the kingdomes bothe,—
   So now negotiats,   1370
That bothe a gen'rall peace
   He confumats and ends,
And with the King agrees the Duke,
   And maks thame fullie freinds.
Whairfore both th' Englifhe King
   Him royallie rewarded,
And all his guifts and graces great
   Moft gratiouflie regarded;
And for his paffed pains,
   Great mereits and deferts,   1380
Whan backe from his Legatioun laft
   And voyage he reverts,

He is prefented to the Bifhop: of Abirdone and Chancellarie of Scot:

His Sov'raigne Lord King James
   Gave him moft willinglie,
Be prefentatioun, Abirdone
   Hir fpacious Prelacie.
And fhortlie efter that
   His facts fuche fauor fand,

That he was maid call'd and declair'd
   Lord Chancelar of the Land.   1390
Soone efter this begane
   To brak out and to burft,
Ane execrable, wrongfull warre,
   And quarrell moft accurft,
Betuixt the Syre and Sone,
   The Thrid and Feird King James,
That, throughe fome corrupt Counfalours,
   Stood bothe upoun extreams:
Whiche querrell to compone,
   And contravers t' accord,   1400
And mak the Sonne fubmit him felf
   To his parentall Lord,—
Unceffantlie he feeks,
   And ufeth all his witt,
And what might pleafe the parteis bothe,
   To do, dois noght omitt:
Bot when he hes practiz'd,
   And all did enterpryfe
That could become a graue, a good,
   A virtous man and wyfe,—   1410
And nothing yit preuaild;
   He then did fermel' adhear
Unto the parent Prince his part,
   To th' ending of the warre.
Bot when this wrackfull warre
   With bade fucceffe did ceafe,
He came heir home to Abirdone,
   And prefentlie did preas
For to correct the Churche,
   And all things to repair,   1420
Neglected the preceeding yeeres,
   And growne irregular:

He taks
ordor with
Churche
effairs.

The facrat feruicefs
  He did appoynt, and wold
They fould be fung and celebrat
  With organs, as of old
The fathers in the Churche
  They ever wount to ufe,
And as we knaw the Catholiks
  Into thir dayes yit does.   1430
Whairfor to this effect,
  A veric modeft man,
Ane Johne Molyfoune, he appoynts,
  A learn'd Mufician,
To haue the charge, to be
  Cheef Chanter in the Chore,
That Mufick in his Churche might be
  Als frequent as befoir.
The knaledge and incres,
  Into this Boreall part,   440
Of Mufick, juftlie it belongs
  To this Molyfoun's art;
For nane into thefe dayes
  Was thairin cunning knawne,
Bot fuche as from his doctrine dulce
  Thair documents hed drawne.
Now mony other warks
  That worthie war of prais,
The Prelatt platts to interpryfe,
  And his accounts he lays   1450
For to accompleifhe heir,
  Bot is conftrain'd to ftay,
And to deferre his good defignes
  Unto ane other day;
For he was, with ane charge,
  Call'd to the Court to come,

For to be great Counſalour
  To James the Fourt, to whome
H'is reconcild, and is,
  With great reguard & grace,   1460
R eſtabliſhed and repoſſeſt
  Unto his prior place;
And with no les reſpect,
  Or in effect with more,
This Prince the Prelat held nor him
  His father had befoir.
Bot mark, ſome reſts remain'd,
  And coals of theſe diſcords
That had confum'd the King, his cheef
  Nobilitie, and Lords;   1470
Whiche gif they war not quyt
  Extinguiſhd and put out
Withe ciuill broyls, they wald re-burne,
  Northe Britan bounds, no dout.
All theſe aduenting ills,
  And that appearing peſt,
Our Prelat with exceeding pains
  Politiklie repreſt:
And whan he had remou'd
  Diſtractions and debate,   1480
Hidde hate, diſtruſt, and jelofees,
  Mongs members of Eſtate,
He counſald then the King,
  (That had no forrane foe,
Nor no domeſtick ane at hame)
  Then to begin and goe
Advyſedlie to wey,
  Yea tuichinglie to feell,
And treat of things that profeit ports
  Unto the publick weell;   1490

And to imploy his pains
   To what may honour bring,
Advancement, glorie, and renowne,
   Unto his Royall Regne.
Firſt then his Grace begins,
   And dois ordane all whair
His Kingdome throghe, neglected long,
   A Gen'rall Juſtice Air.
To puniſhe and repres
   All villaneis and vyce,   1500
Without a partiall reſpect
   Of powar or of pryce.
At laſt when publick peace
   In all parts ſpred hir palms,
And all the factions, feirce beſoir,
   Now queyeted and calme,—
It is decree'd, and paſt
   With generall conſent
Bothe of the Prince and the Eſtates,
   Into a Parl'ament,   1510
To furniſhe furthe and ſend,
   Some rare renowned man,
Unto the Roman Empriour
   Great Maximilian,—
To move a mariage,
   Betuixt our prudent Prence
And Cæſar's daughter Margaret,
   Hir Grace's excellence.
For th' adoleſcing King,
   Flamm'd with affection's ſyres,   1520
To wyne in marr'age with that mayd
   He ſecreatlie deſyres;
Beleeving ſuirlie that,
   Be that conjunctioun bred,

G

His great and royall glorie fould
  Be more difpers'd and fpred.
Then fit they to confult,
  To Cefar whome to fend,
And all into ane voce they vote
  Our Elphinftoune in end: 1530
Wha to Augufta goes,
  And thair but queftioun had.
Of all his limited demands,
  And of his purpofe fped,
Gif not th' Imperiall Mayd,
  Upoun fome great pretence
Had be hir parents bene efpous'd
  Unto the Spanifhe Prence.
Yit leaft it fould appear
  That he had doone no good,   1540
Since he could not the mariage
  As was decreed conclood,
A long depending plea
  With wifdome wyfelie he,
'Tuixt the Coloniens and ours
  This grave man did agree;
For he his perfon fo
  Tharin imployd and paynd,
That tharof no, no noght fo muche
  As ony mark remain'd.   1550
This tyme ane Eduard came
  From Flanders with ane oaft,
(Dead Englifhe Eduard's fone fuppos'd)
  Upoun the Scotifhe coaft,
And from the King afk't ayd
  Whairbe he better might,
Gif not be fair and freindlie formes,
  Be force then or be fight

Regain his Kingdomes Crowne,
  His livings and his lands,
Iniuſtlie then injoyd, out of
  Th' Uſurper Henrie's hands.
Th' egregious King, King James,
  Upoun requeſt he yeeldis
To give and furniſhe him with force,
  And feat thame to the feeldis.
But lo! whow foone King James
  Th' exyled Eduard dois
Grant a fupport, behold, alfoone
  King Henrie did refuis
For to repair all wrongs,
  To render and reſtoir
All fpoyld and taken goods, as was
  Agree'd on before,
Whiche was the cheefeſt caufe
  That ſhortlie warrs enfcuit,
Whiche maid bothe kings and countrie too
  Long tyme regrait and rew it.
Th' ufurping Henrie then,
  Whow foone herof he heires,
And finds thefe forces wynd in on,
  Now nought in vain, he fears:
Whairfore, he fend to fea
  A fextie faills of warre,
And fourtie more he furnifht furthe,
  That all thair bagage bear
Withe a directioun ſtrait,
  And abfolute command,
To ufe the means that might moleſt
  Us bothe be fea and land;
Divyning thairby right,
  And fure fupponing fo,

1560

1570

1580

1590

The preparatiouns to impead,
  That fould in England go.
This quippage and fea-force
  From England heir fend northe,
They fhew thame felf about the Mey,
  And entred firft the Forthe;
Whairas it did, and got
  Exceeding hurt and fkaithe,   1600
Whiche maid this warre a wrackfull work
  And banefull to thame baithe;
Whill bothe the parteis thoght
  Expedient to prove
Gif be good arbiters they might
  Thefe mifereis remove,
And plat a perfect peace,
  And former wrongs repair,
Doone on the Scotifhe Marches heir,
  Or on the Englifhe thair: 1610
It is agreed that fome
  For England's part thair fhall
Deputed be, and for our Prence
  Propon'd as principall,
Our Bifhop Williame was,
  With other men of fpreit;
Who, be appoyntment paft befoir
  Did all in Melros meit;
Whair efter fermon fet,
  They enter and intreats,   1620
And with thair contrar arguments
  Thair buffines debeats:
All with thair reafons ftrong,
  From out thair wifdomes wrung,
Thair aduerfars' opinions
  They publicklie impugne:

Whair throughe the difference
　It almoft did appeare,
They thence without appoyntment bothe
　Sould difcontent reteir,　　　　　　　　　　1630
Gif they had not had hope
　In Bifhop Williame's wit,
Whiche now they all do look upoun
　And onlie leans to it,—
Protefting plainlie he
　Had prudence to compone,
And caufe the contraverting Kings
　Become be concord one.
Bot when they him behold
　With fuche a goodlie grace　　　　　　　　1640
Protefting thair and praying thame
　To be difpos'd to peace,—
There pert'nacie they put
　And wilfulnes away,
And the perfecting of the peace
　On him alone they lay:
Whiche when he had perform'd,
　Impoffible to thame,
Whair be bothe kingdomes got great good,
　And he a noble name,—　　　　　　　　　1650

His prudent
advyfe to his
Prince.

He prudentlie propons
　And did perfuade his Prence,
To bring his Highlandis and the Yles
　Under obedience.
For all the Clans and Macks
　Were out of ordour ay,
Gif not the powar of the Prence
　Thair ftryfes inteftine ftay.
Withe exortatiouns than,
　Bothe oft and earneftlie,　　　　　　　　1660

The Prince his fubjects all inceits
    To civill policie.
His Highnes will preceed,
    And by example fhaw,
The obligatioun he and thay
    Unto the countrie aw:
Three palaces he builds,
    Prepolifh'd work and rare,
In Falkland, Stirling, Edinbrughe,
    All bellifant and fair: 1670
All riche and royall rowmes,
    And admirable moft
For ftatelic ftanding, ftructure, ftrengthe,
    For carpentric and coft;
All whiche he plenifhed
    With Princelic pleafant things,
All fit and correfpondent to
    The qualitie of Kings.
Then mony men of mark,
    As he thair Prence befoire,   1680
With ftrong and ftatelic holdis began
    Thair countrie to decore:
His Grace this ciuill courfe
    Infifted in begun,
And layd his coumpts the Race of Rule
    And Reafon he wald run:
And firft he did fecure
    From violence and wrong,
His poore and popular, from thofe
    More powerfull and ftrong: 1690
His great and Nobles, nixt,
    In concord he contains,
Withe lib'rall loue, or than thereto
    Be force of law conftrains.

Sua be his clemencie,
  Lib'ralitie or fear,
His people peceablie and all
  Moft profperous appear:
Wharof the cheefeft praife
  It properlie pertenis,   1700
And juftlie fuld be attribute
  Unto our Prelat's painis;
Wha whill a priuat man,
  And publick, he did live,
The labours of his lyf unto
  The commound good did give:
For he perform'd the peace,
  Th' aggrements and accords,
Betuixt the King and High-land Clanns,
  The Laicks and the Lords.   1710
No perrell on the land,
  Nor danger on the fea,
No, noght his bodei's helthe, no nor
  His age reguardethe he!
This proper his appeard,
  And his peculiar,
Withe more induftrie his devyfe
  He did exceed and war:
And yit his providence,
  His paffing pains furpaft;   720
And what he did, it feem'd beft done
  Wharin he labour'd laft.
Whair throughe his credeit great
  He with the King increft,

His credeit increft more and more.

And efter his imployments oft
  Moft plainlie hes expreft:
For when his Highnes had
  Heirwith his awne t' intreat,

Or for to knit contracts with Kings,
   Or ony forrane ftate,   1730
Or gif be' occafioun of
   Agreements new, his Grace
Withe cities, touns, or provinces,
   Was to appoynt a peace,—
To Williame worfhipfull,
   Thefe works of worthe and weght,
To be accomplifht and perform'd,
   War all committed ftraght:
And what befoir the King
   In confultation came,   1740
He was cheef counfallour that did
   Sight and confult the fame.
Whairbe unto the prince,
   The people, and ev'rie peere,
The accomplis't prelat Williame was
   Undoubtedlie moft deere.
Officious, light, or vane,
   Nor fimulat, this love
Did in the Prince, or in his peeres,
   Unto the preachour prove   1750
For fo his woundrous wit,
   And mony precious parts
Attractiue war, and drow to him
   Unfengzedlie thair harts:
This kynd, this conftant loue,
   And permanent good will,
We feldome fic is conquefhed
   Or trewl' attain'd untill,
And being got conferu'd,
   But graces excellent   1760
Into the partie purchafer
   Exceeding eminent!

As in our Williame was
  In all affembleis fhawne,
So oft and too too noturlie
  To mony countries knawne.
Bot when he his paffed pains,
  The Prelat dois efpy
His Prince at peace in ev'rie part,
  He then prepairs to applye   1770
His lyf and labours left,
  T' illuftrat and adorne
His natiue fole,—this Kingdome whair
  He was begotten and borne.
He heirfor in the Northe,
  Whair 'twas to live his lucke,
Concluds a Regall Accademe
  And College to conftruct;
Since fome into the Sowthe,
  And in the Weft fome had,   1780
Be inftituting publick fcooles
  Thair countries honored.
For, lo! fome worfhipfull
  And men of mightie zeall,
Upoun moft fpeciall refpects
  Unto the publict weell,
And more nor commond loue
  Unto the librall artes,
Bothe in moft proper, competent,
  And moft commodious partes.   1790
Had founded abefoir,
  For all the faculteis
And forts of Sciences then taught
  Four Uniuerfiteis;
Wharof in Glafco ane,
  One Williame Durrifdere

He did erect, and inftitut
  That tyme Arche-Bifhope thair,
And in Sanct Andra-poll,
  A worthy man Wardlaw,   1800
His love and lyking in his lyf
  To Sciences did fhaw;
For thair he firft did found
  A commound College, whence
Excellent, great and mony Clerks,
  Hes bene produced fince;
And daylie yit we fie
  Bothe learned men and wyfe,
Fit for the Churche and Commound weell

M:
  Inftructed thair aryfe;   1810
R: H:
And thairfor muche renown'd,
  Bot rather famous farre
and
For th' eloquent and profound men
M:
  That thair Profeffors ar;
F: F:
Some borne with us, taught too
  In Germanie and France,
And for thair cuning called thair,
  The commound weell t' aduance.
Thairefter to inlarge
  Wardlau his worthy wark,   1820
A reu'rend Primat Kennedie,
  Thair in his tyme a Clark,
Wha for his learning great,
  Did of all others then
Deferve and mercit moft of all
  The Mufes and thair men,—
Did build Sanct Saluator's,
  But ayd, upoun his awne,
For beutie of the building braue
  To mony Kingdoms knawne;   1830

And thair unto annext
  Bothe lands and livings large,
For all that thairin burden buire
  Or exerceis'd a charge.
The thrid, a Prior thair,
  John Hebburne, efterwards
Did found and inftitut that now
  Is namd Sanct Leonard's.
Bot hola! foft my Mufe!
  What means and thinks thow thus   1840
To pafs our awne, and pen thofe things
  Impertinent to us?
R'affume thy fubject firft,
  And reconvert thy ftyll
Unto the Prelat Elphinftoune,
  Left of this former whyll:
Thefe forfaid virtuous works
  Of weell difpofed fpreits,
Our Williame, weell inclynd, unto
  Lyk worthy works inveits: 1850
For as he had decreed
  A Regall Scoole t' erect,
His former refolutioun now
  He followes to effect:
And firft fundatiouns frams
  For all the members meit,
That was for fuche ane interpryfe
  Reputed requifeit:
Then Doctors he dois chuife,
  To reule and to Regent,   1860
As Chancelar, Rector, Dean and Pri-
  mar, or a Prefident.
He Hector Boæs was,—
  A weell deferving man

Of all his countrie since; in Pa-
    rish a Profeffor than:
For eloquentlie he
    Our Cronicles contryues;
And firft did wreit and congregat
    Thir worthy Prelats' lyues.   1870
Of Williame's worthynes,
    In France, from fame inform'd,
Bot with propynes and promifes,
    Propyned and perform'd,
Alluird, he hither came.
    This philofophe approu'de,
And learnedlie the lib'rall Arts
    And Mufes all promov'de.
Thus come and fatled heir,
    Our worthy wyfe divyne,   1880
And all his Channons, chofen Clerks,
    Lamps that in learning fhyne,
With gratious looks, as beft
    Men bothe fo good and graue
Became, moft lovinglie they him
    Accept of and receave.
He to his ftudeis than,
    And to his tafk he takis him.
And ane his fellow-ftudent Hay
    His fellow Maifter maks him,—   1890
A learnd judicious yowthe
    That neuer his paines hes fpair'd,
T' informe, inftruct, and tymelie teache,
    As efter th' end declair'd:
For be ther neuer fpair'd paines,
    Eache in thair fev'rall places,
So mony learn'd, in litle tyme,
    Withe fo great guifts and graces,

M. W. H.

Into this common Scoole
  Was Laur'at, and inlarg'd,   1000
That bothe in Churche and Commound weell
  No deuties mean diſcharg'd;
Whoſe catolog to call,
  To coumpt, or to declair
All thair promotions or thair place,
  I do of purpoſe ſpair,
Since Heɛtor has to there
  Great gloreis and renowne,
Thame ſev'rallie, in his awne book,
  Deſcrybed and ſet doun.   1010
And gif all thoſe that ſince
  That famous hous brought forthe,
Heir I ſall name that paſt be proof
  For wit of woundrous worthe,
For faculteis profound,
  And mony pretious parts,
Skill, cunning and intelligence,
  Exaɛt in all the Artes,—
I think my curt compend
  Sould lend a larger ſhow,   1020
And rather than unto a mean
  To monſtrous greatnes grow;
For no Vniuerſitie,
  Since this ereɛtioun, may
Brag of the bringing better up,
  Nor ſhe did to this day,
Of more, yea mony may,
  Bot for the publiɛt uſe,
Whiche will preſume praiſe worthy more
  It ever did produce: 1030
Bot as the former, ſo
  This nameles number, I

I pas, and to my purpofe will
  Agane my pen applye.
This prudent Prelat now
  Beyond compair content,
And muche delighted with the learnd
  And Clergeis increment;
That his defigne moft fure
  And ftabill moft might ftand,   1940
He purpofes and all prepairs,
  Prepaird, puts to his hand;
And in a proper place,
  He meafures out and mooldes.
A manour, for the Mufes meit,
  And inftantlie he buildis
A ftatelie ftructure thair,
  A fabrick firme and faire,
Whiche hes a tempill tabulat
  Of polifht ftones and fquair;   1950
With tables, celrings, feats,
  Lights of difcolord glas,
All inftruments for fervice us'd,
  Of gold, of filuer, brafs;
Hingers with filuer fet,
  Noght few with gold ingroft,
For veluet veftments vulgar was
  All reft, non left, now loft;
Yea thowfand things that than
  The Churche did haunt to haue,   1900
More nor ar heir, guifts of great worthe,
His Guifts.   The gratious Guill'ame gaue,—
As cenfers, phials, lamps,
  Of gold and filuer all,
With croffes, coups, and candlefticks.
  Large, hollow, trim and tall;

A ſtraght ſtronge ſteiple too,
   A pleaſant princelie frame;
Beautiſeit with bells, within, without.
   Deckt with a diademe,   *1070*
This his new College Churche,
   But ſpairing of expence,
He furniſht thus, as he had hed
   The powar of a Prence.
With pearle and pretious ſtones,
   A ritche wrought Cypres cheſt,
Wharin the Reliques of the Sanĉts,
   With great reſpeĉt war plac't.
Bot gif what he did give,
   I ſould declair and count.   *1080*
His guifts, ſo great togidder groſt.
   To multitudis ſould mount.
Bot to proceed,—he dois
   For this highe Churche ordaine
Aught Chaplanes, and ſevin ſinging boyes.
   Thair choriſts to remain.
Then all this wark almoſt,
   And Churche to keep more ſover.
Withe no ſmall coſt and cunning, he
   With cakes of lead caus'd cover   *1090*
And that from theſe his paines
   Sould forder flow more fruit,
Inſtitutioun of 4. Doĉtors. Profeſſours four, four Doĉtors more,
   Than he did inſtitute.
Amongs theſe four, the firſt
   He ordains the Divyne,
The Canoniſt, the Ciuiliſt,
   And ane for Phiſick ſyne:
Then he prouiſioun maks
   For ev'rie one of theſe,   *1100*

And enters to erect and rear
  Four duellings for thair eafe;
Bot noght perfected all,
  Nor furnifht in his dayes,
For he, prevented lo! be deathe,
  This work unended ftayes.
Licentiats Laureat ten,
  Or Bach'lars ordinar,
To hear the Doctours, and t' inftruct
  All others ordanit ar: 2010
Of thefe the firft and cheef
  Was the Subprincipall,
Who next the Primar hes the place
  In governing of all:
Then fourtene yowthes he founds,
  And thefe the Burfars be,
That fould imploy thame in and ply
  Thame to philofophye,
And laft, he inftituts,
  For to inftruct the young,   2020
Ane learned in humanitie
  Into the Latine towng;
Whiche rowme, when Hector wreit their Lyves,
  Ane Waufius held,
Moft eloquent, in labours great,
  And learning that excel'd.
The members founded all,
  Fit for this famous frame,
From th' Ecclefiaftick lands h' acquirs
  Rents competent to thame.   2030
And yit this worthy never,
  Than with fuche cairs as crais'd
Or fpent his foot, his hand, or mynd,
  To eafe or reft him rais'd;

Bot lyk Briarius hudge,
   Thought t' haue a hundrethe hands,
He doethe ſtill, or wretethe ſtill,
   Deuyſethe, or commands.
Unto his countries weell,
   Or Churche, his travells tends;   2040
And evre his interpryſes aym'd
   At good and godlie ends.
His Churche, then Cathedrall,
   He to adorne converts,

Reparatioun of his Cathed.

And gave it mony coſtlie capps,
   Gold wrought with antique arts:
Than to the Prelats' uſe,
   Proper, perpetuall,
He gave, and caus'd tuo Myters mak,
   With gold ſtitche browdered all;   2050
And to a Thrid, of old
   Moſt ritche and thair beſoir,
Compois'd of gold, inchac't with ſtones,
   He added mony more.
That four ſquair turret fair,
   Or the great ſteiple than,
Whiche Biſhop Lichton, long beſoire,
   To raiſe and builde begane—
Compleitlie he perfytes;
   And all the Churche with lead,   2060
A work great yit to veiw, now tirr'd,
   He theaked or his dead;
And thairinto three bells,
   Tuell thowſand weght, he plac't,
To ſerve for ſacrat uſe, pull'd doun,
   Demoliſh'd and defac't.
In hand heirefter he
   No litle a turne he taks,

I

And to rebuild his Churche's Chore,
  No mean prep'ratioun maks;   2070
For, all that for fo great
  And fair a frame was fitt,
Or he wold put a hand thairto,
  He all provyded it.
That martiall mightie King—
  The Bruce—myne Author fayes,
(The Bifhop Cheyne, exyl'd) this Chore,
  Erected in his dayes;
Bot feing it futed noght
  Proport'nallie the Seat,   2080
He purpofed to haue it maid
  Agreablie as great;
Bot loathe the old t' undoo,
  And to pull't doun, whill he
Bot ony intermiffioun might
  The new re-edifie,—
That worthy interpryfe,
  It onlie was begun,
Bot throughe his other great adois,
  And deathe, was never doone.   2090
And yit a wark als great,
  And neceffar muche more
Unto his awne, his countries good,
  And bothe thair greater gloir,
Annon tharefter he
  Refolv'd, and firft intends,
That evrie age and eye that views,
  Ameirs yit and commends:
This was the Brige ou'r Dea,
  Which ev're man may mark,   2100
Ane neidfull, moft expenfiue, great,
  A good and gallant wark;

Knit clofs with quadrat ftones,
   Free all, incis'd and fhorne:
Of thefe the pend, with arches fevene,
   Supported is and borne:
Sharp poynted butreffes
   Be bothe, that braks & byds
The powar of the winter fpeats,
   And ftrengthe of fimmer tyds: 2115
Above it's beutifeit
   With ports and prickets four,
And all alongs it rayled is,
   And battaild to look over.
A great and goodlie work,
   Whiche, whow long 't ftands & ftayes,
It ay fall mater miniftrat
   Unto the Author's praife.
Yit this muche mark, this Brigge
   Remembred heir, was bot   2120
Be him intended, in his tyme
   Begun, and finifht not.
Now whill this working was
   In part, his exerceis
Was to find furthe, and fcharplie fearfe
   Out our antiquiteis;
Cheeft' in the Hebreid Ifles,
   Whair fome tyme bureid lay
Our Kings deceas'd, and keeped was
   Our Monuments, they fay: 2130
All whiche, whilk he could find,
   Bothe be him felf, and fearche,
He wreat thame in a volume all,
   And fome fuppons in Verfe.
Bot by thefe ciuil works,
   And thefe religious deeds,

His love unto and caire of kin,
  All common fort exceeds.
To mony of his name,
  Almoft and kinfmen all,   2140
He did poffeffiouns give, or char-
  ges ecclefiafticall:
To mony too befyd,
  Whofe gifts and treuthe he try'd,
In his particular adois
  H' inricht'd and dignify'd:
Oft tymes exhorting thame,
  This worthy Divyne dois,
That they thair fortoun and thair welthe
  Weell war and wyfelie ufe;   2150
Remembring whence they raife,
  And that it once might fall,
When he war hence thair fortoun change,
  And changes crofs thame fall;
And they conftraind and fore't
  To feill and fuffer than;
That once fkars cairles they wold look
  Too in ane other man.
This fingularlie rare,
  Brought furthe and borne, but dout,   2160
The Kirk and Commound weell t' aduance,
  His cuntree wholl throughe out,

For preaching Minor Freers
  And Carmaleits, in means
He bothe fupports, and what to build
  Thair palaces perteins.
Thir war the works almaift
  This worthy wrought, whiche never
Sould be oblit'rat, nor cancelled,
  Bot be recorded ever.   2170

In acting yit thefe all,
  And doing ftill but reft,
Yea almoft with infincit caires
  O'rewhelmed and oppreft,
Yit neuer a myte the more
  Did he avert his mynd,
Or from his book or exerceis
  Into his charge declyn'd;
Bot bothe in yowthe, and when
  His leafure ferv'd, in age,   180
He ty'd him to thefe tuo, and ftill
  Him felf did there t'ingage.
His Studeis.   Bot in the Scriptures cheef,
  He greateft pleafure had;
The Doctors oft, and Sages too,
  With great regaird he redde
And what was meiteft fund,
  And to good lyf conduc't
Thairin he did delight him moft,
  And that his Lecture chuis't.   190
And when to eafe him, whylles
  He from his reading refted,
His Medita-
tiouns.   He meditatethe with him felf,
  Difputed and contefted;
Recalling to his mynd
  What deuteis him became,
Whow unto God, and whow to man,
  He had difcharg'd the fame.
And that refrefhing tyme,
  Oft he confumit and fpent   200
In off'ring up his priuat pray'r
  To the Omnipotent.
Thus was he folitare,
  Alon this was his eafe,

Thus whill he refts from his effaires,
  H' is buffied in thefe.
In converfatioun fueet
  Nought ftubborne nor auftear,
Bot as the Company requyr'd
  He plyable did appear: 2210
At meat moft mirrie ay,
  Yit fober tho folatious,
And unto all and evric ftate
  Welcome and gratious.
In his hous holding large,
  Lord lyk, magnificent,
No thing unprofitablie yit
  Nor prodigalie fpent.
Flat'ring fcurrilitie,
  Fooles, fengyeit, and prophane,   2220
His difpofitioun naturall
  Did hate, difpyfe, difdaine;
Bot modeft merriment,
  Sport pleafant then and now,
At turnes and fitting tyme, he bothe
  Did lyk of and allow:
For nothing to the wyfe
  Can come awrye nor wrong,
For they do earneft ufe with fports
  And mirthe to mix among.   2230
So highe was his engyne,
  So quick his naturall,
And fuche viuacitie of fpreit,
  Was he indew'd withall,
That nothing laicking feem'd
  That needs concerne, or can
Be fitting for ane priuat, or
  A publick placed man.

His Behaveo

The quickne
his Wit and
Ingen:

Vrban and tuniſhe turns,
  Or for the land's effairs,   2240
Or what foeu'r befyd, his wit

**His Learning
& Eloquence.**

  Him fit for all declairs.
Nane liv'd then in this land
  More learned in the Laues,
Nor nane nor he more eloquent
  Hir age nor cuntree knaws;
For the beſt Orators,
  Moſt facund & difert,
Into his dictiouns delicat
  He equal'd in thair art.   2250
And nev're a man unto
  His countries quyet more,
Or to her well, nor he did do
  Hes ever done befoir.

**His Conſtitu-
tioun of Body.**

His body feem'd of braſs,
  Of flint, or marble hard,
That kythed nev're with paines oppreſt,
  Nor withe its motiouns mar'd:
For in his countr' affairs,
  And in the Churche's things,   2260
Still freſhe, he fuir as he had flowne
  With the fleet falcon's wings.

**His magnitud
of Mynd.**

His ſpreit invincible,
  And could not be oppreſt
With accidents that could occurre,
  Or mortall men moleſt.
Into inevitable
  Age, and decreped yeares,
Difcouraged nor broken nought,
  Skarfe brufed he appears.   2270
When he was outlie paſt
  Wholl aughtie yeires and three,

And moſt part tharof ſpent in Crowne
  And Church oeconomie,
In maters great and graue,
  As when in fourtie ane,
To reaſoun, councell, and decree,
  As ſoleid than he's ſeene:
For ſtill his memorie,
  His judgement's ſharp and found.   2280
And neuer dulled to his deathe
  In his effaires was found.
His age had with it helthe,
  Contentment, pleaſure, joy,
And did not, as age uſes oſt,
  Moleſt him nor annoy:
Bot, muche in few to fang,
  It nev're his maners chang'd,
Nor from his wounted formes & uſe
  Him in a poynt eſtrang'd.   2290
About this tyme the Pope,
  That Secund Julius,
Heir ſend from Rome to James the Fourt,
  A noble Nuncius:
Congratulating muche,
  Of Chriſtian Kings, that he,
Bothe from externe, and warrs at home,
  In peace alone was free:
Thairſor, to gratefie
  And honour him, he hathe   2300
Proclamed him Protector, or
  Defendar, of the Faithe:
And lykwayes hes propyn'd
  Him with a purple hat,
And with a ſword, with guards of gold,
  And ſheathe déaureat,

This tyme the Frenſhe, with force,
   In Italie purſew'd
Some townes, and ſome be parley got,
   And ſome be ſeedge ſubdew'd;   2310
And grytumlie theſe Galls,
   Whair euer they went in armes,
Th' Italian Peers and People too
   Did damnifie and harmes:
Whairfore they do aduyſe
   Whow to auert this warre,
Whiche ſcarcelie did afflick, & thame
   So much moleſt and marre:
And haifing quickl' aduys'd,
   So they reſolved ſtraight,   2320
For to ſoliſt the Engliſhe King,
   Hendr' of his name the Aught,
A quick, ſharp, flor'ſhing Prince,
   In's rage of yowthe, and whiche,
That lyk't as ony livand lov'de,
   Renowne and gloir' als muche.
To him they ſend t' inceit
   Him to tak armes in hand,
For to protect the Churche, that than
   In no ſmall ſtrait did ſtand;   2330
Who ſhortelie efter, ſoone
   S' inflamm'd and ſet on fyre.
Denunced warre, defy'd the Frenche,
   Evin as they did deſyre.
Whairfor, to counter matche,
   And coole King Henrie's heat,
The King of France to James the Fourt,
   His cheef confed'rat, wreat;
Exhorting him, that he
   Wold, as his College, ryſe   2340

K

Warrs in
Italy.

In armes to hinder Henrie's hopes,
    T' impead his interpryfe.
For weell King Lues knew,
    If once King James arrofe,

He fuld not fearel infefted be
    With force of Englifhe foes.
The Frenfhe King's courfe declar'd,
    The King and Counfell fit,

I aduyfe what fall be done be thame,
    And for the Frenfhe moft fit.   2350
Some thought that freindlie art
    They th' Inglifhe fould colift,

To leave th' invafioun of the Frenche
    And from the attempt defift:
And gif it war denyit
    That reafonable requeit,

Than iuftlie might they do denunce,
    And give thame warrs in haift.
Our prudent Prelat vit,
    And mony thought alfo.   2360

Bot cheeflie he it perlous was
    To time fo ftrong a foe:
The wracks and woes of warre,
    Th' incommod, hurt and harmes,

Try'd oft of favours infolent,
    And of the armed fwarmes,
Suld mak us flaw to temp,—
    Yea evin altho for freinds,—

A Prince and People of the pure,
    Warrs hes fo wofull ends,   2370
A Prince in pryme of yowthe
    Haut hardie and in helthe,

Right refolut, moft ritche and flow-
    ing in his Father's welthe:

When as a murmur great was maid,
    And mony raife in rage,   2410
Tho' they had neuer feene
    Mar's count'nance fueet nor fowre,
And muche reproache and fpightfull fpeache
    Did gainft the Prelat powre;
Yea mightelie malign'd
    This Worthy mony wayes,
Upbraiding him as dotting than
    Into his latter dayes;
As he both foolifhlie
    And fantinglie had fpokin   2420
Aganis the common good, to haue
    The band with France be brokin.
Thus followd was the will
    Of youthe and numbers moft,
And th' aged wyfe advyfe of few,
    Not credited bot croft.
A herauld than, poft haift,
    Reid warre for to proclame,
In England they did fend, into
    The King and Countrie's name.   2430
Whiche vi'lent warre to bothe,
    What efter wraks and woes
It did, the Author's Cornicle,
    Than wretand vivelie, fhoes.
Bot leaft I ftay too long
    Relating this, I will
My proper tafk, my Prelat's Lyf,
    Againe returne untill:
Wha whowfoone he hes hard
    This warr's fo bade fucceffe,   2440
For verie greef, he grew almoft
    Bothe fpeache and fpiritleffe,

And evin contracted then
  That seiknes, most assuir'd,
That vext him ever, and left him never,
  Bot to his deathe induird.
Neu'r was he seene to lache,
  Nor trews with greef to tacke,
Nor thence so muche as seene to smyll,
  Nor any mirthe to mak.   2450
Short and soone efter this,
  The whoill estates, that they
Upoun the Govern'ment might meit,
  At Perthe appoynts a day:
Whair met, they act, intreat,
  And handils many things,
And our divyne, Arche Bishop of
  Sanctandrois, all designes.

His modestie
in refuifing the
Arche. Bish.

Whiche ample Primacie
  He plainlic hes refuis'd,   2460
And sayd he had als muche and more
  As he could get weill us'd;
Altho expresl' appeard,
  Whill as this Prelat spir'd,
The worthy works that he had wrought
  War of all men admeir'd.
So withe the Bishoprick
  Content that he had heir,
The Counsall and Conventioun up,
  Unto 't he did reteir,   2470
To spend what yit was spaird
  Of his short race to run,
In's Churche's charge, and building of
  His Chore, and Brigge begun:
For he defyred muche,
  In peace and pietie,

Into his Abirdone at hame,
  To end his dayes and die.
O! bot the defteneis
  Wold noght he fuld conclood   2480
His works intended and devys'd,
  So neceffarlie good!
For quicklie he's recall'd
  For fatling fome difcords,
That fince his coming from the Court
  Was mov'd among the Lords;
Whairthrow, what doing was,
  Now neidis a tyme muft ftay,—
And fome tharof to his returne
  Some fall, and ever lay.   2490
This tyme to be difeas'd
  And feiklie he began,

His difeafe   Thairfor his freinds requefts and dois
  Diffuaide his going than,
" Bot all for nought;" (fayd he)
  " You preas t' impead me now;
" For I am not borne to my felf,
  " Bot to my countrie too,
" And muche more to hir good,
  " My freinds for certan knaw,   2500
" And commod, I, nor to my awne,
  " Or to my helthe I awe."
So feik, Southe fordward fettis,
  Bot wors wax't on the way:
Unto Dumfermeling he divertes,
  And thair's conftrain'd to ftay.
Whair whill fome dayes bed faft,
  And fever afflicted he,

His Tefta-   His gold, his goods, all what he had,
ment   He leaves in legacie,   2510

To confumat his Brigge
  And College works, that yit
Were not outred; and to fome freinds
  The reft bequethethe it.
In gold, ten thoufand punds
  He had, in purfe and pofe,
Befyd his plate and tapeftrie,
  Things exquifeit and choife.
His freinds t' awayt on him,
  Thair frequentlie reforted,   2520
And for his cafe to Edinbrughe
  The Prelat they tranfported,
The fext day efter, thair
  Incrediblie increft
His fevers force, yet buir he't fair,
  And paffing pain fuppreft.
The Doctors then are call'd,
  And exerceife thair art;
Yet fruitles, hopeles of his lyf,
  Into difpair depart.   2530
Bot not the lefs of this
  His fever fyring ftill,
And thairwith weakned as he was.
  To Churche yit walk he will:
And thair as when he wount,
  And was bothe whoill and ftrong,
He piouflie did pray and preache.
  Moft learnedlie and long.
And fyne the Sacrament,
  He afked and did crave;   2540
Than hartlie, humble, and proftrat, he
  Thair did the fame receave.
Hence then they had him home,
  Unto his houfe again,

Whair with sum freinds he supt that night,
  And still suppreft his pain:
And as he sat by use,
  He silent was and sadde,
Whiche evrie ane appr'ends to be
  A signe presaging bade.   2550
Then gois he to his bed,
  Bot gets no reft nor fleep;
And yit a slum'ring simulats,
  And quyet him dois keep.
In prayer priuatlie;
  And loathe his servands sould,
Withe too much waking weareid be,
  Gif other wyfe he could;
Bot neir the day he finds
  The rotle and rheume to ryfe,   2560
And bold'ne his breaft, and heirfor he,
  Law as he could, he cryes:
His fervandis, at his call,
  And kinfmen comes, and fie
That then he waxed weak, and wold
  Ere long expyre and die.
Then him th' exhort to be
  In faithe and courage ftrong,
For he wald breeflie better be,
  And get releef ere long: 2570
And fome, of tend'rar hearts,
  Stood by him then; bot thay
Did burft for baill, and weep for woe,
  To fie his deeing day.
Thefe hearing, he, his eyes,
  Than dim and deeing, clears,—
And gif that was there conforts that
  From thame h' expected, fpears:

" I did conceate," fayd he,
 " Farre other wyfe of you, 2580
" Nor to be fo difconfolat
 " And thus dejected now:
" I will foliccit be
 " For wordlie things no more,
" For foone I fall haue heavenlie helthe,
 " Reft and eternall gloir;
" And fhortlie be exim'd
 " From fleflic groans and greef,—
" For th' hour is hard at hand, I hope.

His exortatioun to his
Freinds &
Seruands.

 " Whiche brings me my releef. 2590
" Whairfor, I pray yow all,
 " That each of yow and other,
" Opitulat as Chriftians kynd,
 " And as becomes a brother:
" My felf, God knaws, I liv'de
 " a Chriftian, and I,
" Lawd, praife, and gloir to God therefor,
 " This day the fame fall die."
Then, whair he fould b' interr'd,
 Thair afked fome of thefe: 2600
To whome he meeklie anfuer maks,—

His laft
Speaches.

 " Evne whow and whair ye pleas.
" For long fince I my fowll
 " Vow'd, and to God I gave;
" And this my flefhe, diffolv'd thairfor,
 " The earthe muft hold and have."
Now, yit once more again.
 Tho deing, they demand,
Gif then his abfent other freinds
 Withe ought he wold command? 2610
" No, nothing, now," fayd he.
 " Command thame with I will,
    I.

" Bot prayes and wiſhes to thame weell,
    " Grace and good fortoun ſtill:
" For unto greater good,
    " From grace to gloir I go."
And, conſtantlie incalling Chryſt,
    Sueetlie deceaſed ſo.
The honour of his age!
    And to his cuntree borne,   2620
A ſplendour, ornament, and grace
    Ordain'd the Churche t' adorne!
For theſe precedents ſhaws,
    What credeit and renowne
His wiſdome wan unto the Churche,
    His Countrie, Clan, and Crowne.
Yea from his actiouns all,
    Sprang fruitfull, fair effects;
For in the Clergie, muche corrupt,
    He ſkilfullie corrects.   2630
Exenterated then,
    His body they imbalme
With ſpyce perfum'd, & Cretan wynes,
    The raireſt in this Realme.
And withe more pitifull
    Nor princelie pomp, the fame,
From Edinbrughe to Abirdone
    With mony mourners came:
Then with exceſſive greef,
    Yit with all honour, thay   2640
Into his College it befoir
    The cheefeſt altar lay;
Benethe a monument
    Of no mean coſt nor charge,
Of Helian ſtones, thrie for the baſe,
    Abone ane long and large:

Whiche, with six pedaſtalls,
   Upholden was, and borne:
Whair lay his ſtatue tall of brafs,
   Caſt, carved, cut or ſhorne: 2650
Withe facrilegious hands
   Direpted now and reſt,
And nothing bot the pondrous ſtones,
   That wold not lift, is left.
This happie Prelat, his
   Departour was 't appears,
In th' aughtie three yeer of his age;
   When fullie threttie yeeres,
Belov'de and honor'd ev're,
   Heere he had Biſhope bene;   2660
Whiche from the bliſſed birthe fell ſyſ—
   ten hundreth and fourtene.
This tyme things markable
   And mervalous, they tell,—
As monſtrous births, and others more,
   Moſt fairlie full furthe fell:
Thanes from the houſes wholl,
   Breack or unforꝗt did fall:
And ſiclyk, at his buriall borne,
   Brak his ſtaff paſtorall.   2670
A voce unknawne was heard,
   That vivelie feem'd to ſay—
" The Myter with the Williame ſould
   " Be buried this day."
Theſe mervalous things and ſtrange,
   Both ſeene and cenfurd than,
To be the ſignes prefaging deathe
   Of this maiſt matchles man!
Thus what our Williame was,
   I haue deducit and drawne;   2680

The yeer of his age & deathe.

Prodigious things at his deathe.

When priuat, and when publick too,
  Succinctlie I haue ſhawne.
And that muche, breeflie more,
  I muſt of faithe confeſſe,
Nor did demereit and deſerue
  His wit and worthines.
Yit ſince that fame from facts,
  As from a fontane flows,—
And from men's deeds, done in thair dayis,
  Thair praiſe and glorie grows;   2690
Than, from theſe, juſtlie muſt
  B' extollit and commendit,
Our worthy Williame wyſe, that weell
  Began and better endes.
For 's great and good deſerts,
  Weell dois demereit now,
A book of braſs, and tooles of ſteel
  Thairin t' ingrave thame too.
For wha throw witt ſo weell
  And towardlie did treat,   2700
So mony tymes, ſo mony turnes,
  So weghtie and ſo great!
Wha in politick changes
  So prompt, and prudent prov'd?
And wha the Churche and Churche effairs
  Advanc't more and promov'd?

His Com-
mendatiouns.

Wha in his lyſ ſo wholl
  In maners ſo modeſt!
Wha in his calling cairfull more,
  Or gryter paines expreſt!   2710
To Vanitie and Vyce
  Wha was a greater foe!
And wha to Virtue ſuche a freind
  And it advancit ſo!

Who lawl' and humble more,
  And who the proud prophane
Did les accompanie, refpect.
  Support, or intertain!
In handling Holie thinges
  O, wha was fo devoit!
And pitifull unto the poore
  That he out paffed not!
And what age erft, or fince,
  Hes ev'r, or did produce,
A wit alwayes fo worthy for
  Eache good and godlie ufe!
No nane, or few, was fund
  That in his dayes did fall
That could compare with his good partes,
  Or equall thame at all:
And heirfore he The Heavens
  Moft happie now inherits,
In pleafure and in peace prepaird
  For beft and bliffed Spirits!

FINIS.